Rebekah's Journey
An Historical Novel

Rebekah's Journey

An Historical Novel

by

Ann Bell

Katy Crossing Press

REBEKAH'S JOURNEY: AN HISTORICAL NOVEL
Published by Katy Crossing Press
300 Katy Crossing
Georgetown, TX 78626
http://www.katycrossingpress.com
annamaebell@yahoo.com

ISBN: 1-4537-3942-4
EAN: 13-978-1453-739-426

Library of Congress Control Number: 2010912016

Cataloging-in-Publication Data provided by publisher.

Bell, Ann.
   Rebekah's journey : an historical novel / by Ann Bell.
   407 p. ; 22 cm.
   ISBN 1-4537-3942-4 (pbk.)
   EAN   13-978-1453-739-426

Summary: Fourteen-year-old Rebekah Bradford is forced to
sign an indentured servant contract to leave her home in
London and work for a Philadelphia Quaker family.

1. Quakers–Fiction. 2. Family life – Pennsylvania–Fiction.
3. Philadelphia (PA) –History–18th century -Fiction. I. Title.

813'.6–dc22   2010912016

In my years of research, reading the works of Margaret Hope Bacon has been extremely helpful and inspiring.

18th Century Quaker Background

The 18th Century Quakers (Religious Society of Friends) dressed simply and, as a mark of respect, addressed each other by their full names – "John Reynolds", not just "John."

Quakers used thou, thy, and thee in addressing a person "plain language," as they called it, as a means of expressing a belief in the equality of all people. This attitude towards equality was also demonstrated by their refusal to practice "hat honor" (Quakers refused to take their hats off or bow to anyone regardless of title or rank), and also refused to address anyone with honorific titles such as "Sir," "Madam," "Your Honor," or "Your Majesty."

They called the months "First Month," "Second Month," "Third Month", instead of "January," February," etc., which they regarded as Pagan names and they numbered the days of the week beginning with First Day (Sunday).

The Quakers opposition to oath taking caused many problems throughout their history and they were frequently imprisoned because of their refusal to swear loyalty oaths.

"And he said unto me, 'My grace is sufficient for thee; for my strength is made perfect in weakness' …" II Corinthians 12:9 KJV

One

London, Eighth Month 1715

Joseph Bradford trudged homeward on a crowded street on the outskirts of London, the holes in his gloves exposing his calloused hands. A broad-brimmed Quaker hat tipped to one side of his head. Slumped shoulders belied his years.

With so much filth around, no wonder my beloved Mary is ill. He kicked a pile of decaying garbage aside. *She deserves much more than this. It's not fair. Rebekah is the brightest fourteen-year-old in her class. She shouldn't have to quit school to take care of her mother and brothers. She's losing her childhood through no fault of her own.* He looked down at his stiff, chaffed hands. *If only I could make enough shoes to hire a maid, she could go back to school.* He shook his head and tried to wring away the ache in his neck. *I doubt that will ever happen.* He gripped his rumbling stomach. *The seaman last week was my first customer in two months.*

[1]

Ann Bell

Joseph opened the door of his small house and his two sons, ages five and seven, rushed to his side. The dark circles beneath their eyes accentuated their hungry faces.

"Father, what didst thou bring us for supper?" They said in unison.

Joseph stooped and pulled his sons against his breast. Tears welled in his eyes. He watched his daughter add water to the pot at the hearth. "Rebekah, what is for supper?"

Rebekah looked up and smiled sadly. "We only have two potatoes and three carrots left. I've chopped them thin and made soup, but it is not nearly enough for us."

Joseph hugged his daughter. "I love thee," he said. "Things will be better tomorrow. A ship's officer is picking up a pair of sea boots before evening. When he pays me, I'll go to the market and buy food as well as medicine for thy mother."

Joseph's eyes drifted to his wife's thin frame huddled under a tattered blanket in a bed in the corner. He knelt beside her and took her hand. "Good evening, Mary. How art thou today?"

A faint smile spread across the sick woman's face. "Hello, Joseph. I'm glad thou art home," she whispered. "I'm tired and have been coughing a great deal, but the children have been very helpful today."

"I'll get some food for thee. That will give thee strength." Joseph took a wooden bowl and spoon from the shelf, filled the bowl with weak soup, and carried it to his wife's bedside. He leaned down and kissed her on the forehead. He lifted a spoonful of soup to her lips. "God willing, soon I'll sell a pair of shoes and can buy groceries and medicine. If Rebekah helps me in the shop tomorrow, I will be able to finish the sea boots earlier."

After feeding his wife and the children finished their meager meal, Joseph Bradford took the Holy Bible from a shelf and joined his children at the timeworn kitchen table. As was their custom, the Bradford family ended their day with devotions and prayer. Tonight Joseph's prayers were even more desperate. He prayed for his family, health, peace, and understanding from the community toward his Quaker friends. His bowed head fell lower on his chest as he humbled himself before God in thanksgiving, ever mindful that his family had a mighty God to lean upon.

When Joseph Bradford looked up, he was moved by the awe and sweet innocence on his children's faces as they looked up at him. If only they could have an easier life than he had had. "I know these are difficult times, but it will not always be this way," he promised.

[3]

He took both his sons' hands in his. "Thou must always remember to trust in God, treasure family, and work hard. Being able to read is the key to making thy dreams come true. Whatever the cost, thou all must learn to read."

"We promise, father."

Joseph turned to his daughter across the table. "Rebekah, promise me thou wilt help thy brothers' dreams come true and teach them to read. Thou hast already surpassed what thy mother and I have been able to attain. I'm certain that someday thou wilt be blessed for all thy hard work."

~~~~~

His Majesty's Ship *Grafton*, out of London and bound for Barbados, encountered heavy seas and strong winds for three days. The ship suffered severe structural damage, and five crew members were washed overboard and drowned. The rest of the crew was demoralized and frightened, forcing the *Grafton* to return to London for repairs. When the ship docked, more than half the remaining crew left the ship and disappeared into the narrow streets of the city.

Confusion and frustrations engulfed the ship's officers. "Lieutenant Briggs, we have to be back at sea before the winter storms begin," Captain Clive Burroughs shouted. "The Royal Navy will not tolerate this kind of disloyalty. Those deserters must be caught and hanged. In the meantime, form the remaining marines into a press gang who will force twenty-five strong men into service. Go to the pubs, the shops, anywhere you can find able-bodied men, preferably experienced seamen. We have every legal right to impress men into the Royal Navy, whether they want to or not."

"Yes, Sir." Lieutenant Briggs gave his commander a sharp salute, pleased with his new assignment. Of all the officers on the ship, he knew how to make men obey.

Within an hour, the press gang was organized. The sun was lowering into the western horizon when the press gang from the *Grafton* entered the outskirts of London. Most Londoners were sitting down to their supper, and the streets were deserted.

"I want to go to the pubs before it gets too late," Lieutenant Briggs shouted to his marine sergeant. "Finding twenty-five men is going to take time, so let's press the first men we see, whether they have had sea experience or not. They'll learn once they're on board."

The press gang continued down the dark streets with only a faint glow from the moon. "I agree," the marine sergeant said, smiling to himself. "I want to get this over as soon as possible so I can do some drinking myself."

A candle flickered in a window at the end of the block. As the press gang approached, they saw a cobbler bent over his bench hammering on a pair of boots. His muscular arms and shoulders evoked power and strength.

Lieutenant Briggs opened the door and entered the cobbler's shop. "He's perfect," he said to no one in particular.

"May I help thee?" Joseph Bradford asked as he rose from his cobbler's bench. He handed Rebekah the finished sea boots.

"You are hereby pressed into the Royal Navy. Fall in," Lieutenant Briggs commanded.

"I cannot join His Majesty's Navy. I am a Quaker."

Rebekah set the boots on the customer counter and ran to her father's side.

"You were not asked to state your religious preference. You were ordered to fall in."

"But my wife is gravely ill with consumption. We need the money from these shoes I've made to pay the apothecary to treat her." He drew Rebekah even close to himself.

"Are you disobeying my command?"

Joseph set his jaw. "I must obey the God of peace."

[6]

"Do you know the penalty for disobeying a lawful order?" Lieutenant Briggs shouted.

Joseph's muscles tightened, his eyes glazed. "My faith propels me to obey the God of Heaven and earth rather than man."

Turning to the marine sergeant, Lieutenant Briggs commanded, "Bring him along. We'll punish him later for his disobedience to a lawful order."

The sergeant nodded to two burly marines who grabbed the cobbler by the arms while a third marine yanked Rebekah away from her father and held her with her feet dangling in mid-air.

Joseph twisted his arms free from their grasp, flung them from him, and ran toward the back door. He flung open the door and raced into the alley. He knew the marines were interested in him and wouldn't harm Rebekah. He had to survive to protect his family.

The marine holding Rebekah tossed her aside like an empty gunnysack and joined the chase. She scrambled to her feet and dashed after them.

"Halt in the name of the king!" Lieutenant Briggs shouted.

Joseph ignored the command and increased his pace. A dog barked in the distance. His heart pounded. As he ran, he focused on the turn in the alleyway a few yards before him.

Suddenly a shot rang out. Joseph slumped to the ground, blood streaming from the back of his head.

"Father!" Rebekah ran screaming to his side. "Don't die."

Joseph reached for his daughter's hand, his eyes searching her young face. "Promise. Dreams. Love God."

Joseph Bradley closed his eyes and Rebekah pressed his hand against her tear-stained face. "I promise, Father." She knew he had passed from this life into God's hands, but she spoke as though the portals of heaven stood open to hear her vow. "I will not let thee down. We will stay together and I will teach the boys to read God's word."

~~~~~

The sun shone through the slats of the simple one-room dwelling. The flames in the fireplace burnt low as the chill of early spring permeated the Bradford family home. Rebekah looked at the large pile of wood near the hearth as the pot of meat and vegetable soup was beginning to bubble over the fire. The heating soup splashed against the rim, threatening to boil over. She watched the tiny spikes of soup leap in the middle of the kettle. That was what the time since father's death seemed like to her, everything searing hot and leaping this way and that, almost out of control.

As neighbors attended to her father's body, she had had the presence of mind to go back to the shop to secure it against other intruders. To her horror, the sea boots were not on the customer counter, nor her father's workbench. She turned aside everything, looking high and low. When at last she stood trembling in the middle of the room, tears blurred her vision. Through the prism of teardrops, she saw an envelope leaning against the moneybox her father kept on the shelf below the customer counter. Locking the box away was laughable. Her father joked that leaving it out might cause someone to put something in it.

She wiped her eyes and walked to the counter. The writing on the front simply said Cobbler.

I'm the cobbler now. This was mine to open. Holding it steady to make an even tear across one end, she held her breath and slowly peeled away the edge.

Coins, many coins filled the envelope. The note was short—Cobbler, the boots are worthy of the hire. I'm adding a bonus for having them ready early. Consider the extra a commission for another pair when I return to port next year.

Ann Bell

Rebekah sat down and dumped the coins in her lap. There was enough money to pay for the boot leather for the new commission, fill the wood box, and buy meat and vegetables, candle wax, medicine, and a heavier blanket for her mother. Her father's funeral expenses were more than she expected, but with careful management, she would have enough to keep her family from starving for three months. She locked the shop and hurried away to begin her life as the family provider.

~~~~~

Rebekah tucked the new wool blanket tighter around her sick mother lying on her rope bed in the corner of the room. "But mother, I cannot leave thee," she protested. "I promised Father I would take care of thee. I can keep the shop open. He taught me to make shoes and boots."

She looked at the Quaker gentleman standing at the head of her mother's bed, beseeching him with her eyes to understand and support her claim. He had a kindly face, but today that wasn't comfort enough.

Mary Bradford lifted her frail hand and intertwined her fingers with those of her daughter. "Rebekah, please understand. This is the only way our family can survive. Thou art not strong enough to work the leather, to soften it, and stretch it on the pegs. Thou art not tall enough to use the rendering vats safely. This is the only way."

[10]

Rebekah's eyes filled with tears. She lifted her mother's hands to her lips and kissed them. "Who will care for thee? Who will teach the boys to read?" Her lips trembled, the image of cradling her father's head in her lap when he took his final breath flashed before her. "I promised father I would teach them. I cannot go back on my promise."

Mary Bradford sank deeper into her pillow. Her fragile hand relaxed within her daughter's firm grasp. "God will surely find a way for thee to keep thy promise to Father." She hesitated and took a deep sigh. "John Reynolds promises to leave enough money for my care and the care of thy brothers if thou wilt agree to work for him for five years."

Mary's eyes moistened. "Rebekah, I know it's difficult, but remaining in London will only hold poverty and hopelessness for thee. Being in Philadelphia among Quakers will protect thee from carnal talkers and worldly influence."

Rebekah looked away to avoid seeing the pain in her mother's eyes. She sat still observing their humble home as if for both the first and last time. If she had to leave, she wanted to remember every detail. She had spent many hours leaning over the brick fireplace trying to stretch the meager food other Quakers had gifted her family. The straw mats where she and her brothers slept were stacked neatly in the corner. Wooden bowls and plates carefully lined the shelf her father had hung beside the hearth. A table with two crudely carved benches sat in the center of the room. A straight, high-back chair was under the small window. If she tried hard enough, she could still see her father resting in the chair after a long day working in his cobbler shop.

Rebekah wiped a tear from her eye and lifted her gaze to John Reynolds. "I don't think I'll ever be able to leave my family," she said softly. "I'm all they have left."

Compassion and firmness intensified on his face. "Rebekah, I know this is a difficult time for thy family. However, thou must trust God to meet all thy needs. Perhaps when thy brothers are older they may be able to come to America to join thee."

Rebekah was silent, numb with fear and trepidation. *For mother's sake, I must be strong. I know they are right.*

Clearing his throat Friend Reynolds said. "The High Street Quaker Meeting will care for thy family. London is too unsafe for Quakers today, especially young women."

Hearing those words, Rebekah buried her face in her hands and began sobbing uncontrollably. "Father... my beloved father. Why did they have to kill him? He was a man of peace and love. It is not fair."

Mary Bradford's weak voice trembled. "Thy father died because he treasured God and his family more than life itself," she whispered. "As you said, he remained true to his faith of love and peace by refusing to be pressed into the King's Navy. We must follow his example and be brave."

The shadows lengthened while Rebekah's sobs grew further and further apart. Finally, she dried her tears on the sleeve of her dingy gray dress and forced a smile. "I'll be brave and do whatever thou ask of me, Mother," she said weakly.

The edges of Mary Bradford's lips curled with approval while her breathing continued to be shallow and labored. Her voice became even fainter and Rebekah leaned closer in order to hear her. "Friend Reynolds will take good care of thee."

Noting Rebekah's agreement, John Reynolds took a piece of paper from his pocket and reached into his knapsack for a quill pen and ink. He handed the paper to her.

The paper shook as Rebekah read the document.

> "I want everyone to understand my terms. I am agreeing to arrange a home and care for Mary Bradford with Friend Smith's family and a home for her two sons with Friend Miller's family in exchange for the

> household services of Rebekah
> Bradford. I will provide her fare to
> American plus room and board in my
> home in Philadelphia. Rebekah
> Bradford promises her services to the
> Reynolds family for five years."

I'll not be free until I am over nineteen, she considered. *That's a lifetime away.* She hesitantly handed the paper to her mother.

"Rebekah, I'm proud thou art able to read the agreement," Mary Bradford whispered.

Rebekah looked down, tears gathered in the corner of her eyes. *How will I survive without my family? Learning to read had been easy for me. But what will it be like for my brothers without me being there to help?*

John Reynolds carefully dipped the quill in ink and handed it to the ailing woman.

Mary Bradford took a deep breath and made her shaky mark at the bottom of the paper. She held out the pen to her daughter. "To help thee remember the importance of this commitment, Rebekah, write thy name beside mine. We will be bound together forever."

Rebekah obeyed and carefully wrote her name beside her mother's shaky mark. She handed the agreement back to Friend Reynolds without a word.

"Thou wilt not regret this decision, Rebekah. Thou must be strong in the time of great weakness. In America thou wilt always have enough food to eat and clean water to drink in a city of peace and love. I want thou to have the same advantages my own children have had."

Rebekah's eyes brightened. "Is America as beautiful as they say?"

A distant, longing gaze appeared in John Reynolds's eyes. "It is hard to explain the beauty and peace of Philadelphia. William Penn established a haven for Quakers from all over the world. There is no persecution and we are left alone to practice our beliefs in faith. We all work together in harmony."

Rebekah watched him return the inkpot and quill to his bag. He straightened his back and tucked the bag under his arm.

"Since all is agreed, I will return for thee a week from Second Day when we board the ship *Good Hope*," he promised. "Good day. May God bless this family." With those words, he slipped through the roughly carved plank door and disappeared into the growing dusk.

Rebekah stood motionless and finally slumped into the high-back chair beside the bed. She gazed at her mother whose eyes had closed in a well-deserved

Ann Bell

rest. The silence in the simple room enveloped her while the shadows lengthened. She, too, closed her eyes. *What will happen to me? Will I ever see my mother and brothers again?*

Suddenly a child's high-pitched voice brought her back to reality. "Rebekah! Rebekah! Come quickly. Thy brother is hurt."

Rebekah ran out the front door of their tiny dwelling into the litter-strewn street and blinked against the setting sun. The neighbors were already gathering around a small brown lump on the side of the muddy street. Samuel, her five-year-old brother, was sitting on the ground patting the lump and crying.

Realizing the lump was her seven-year-old brother, Rebekah screamed, "Joseph!" and raced toward his limp body. "Samuel, what happened to Joseph?"

"A horse and carriage ran over him," Samuel sobbed. "Is … is he going to die? I don't want him to die like father."

Rebekah knelt beside her injured brother and took his hand. To her relief she could see a slight rising and falling of his chest under his muddy shirt. "Joseph, can thou hear me?"

A painful silence followed. Rebekah held her breath while she watched the blood oozing through his right shirt sleeve and his tattered breeches. The grey

[16]

coloring of her brother's face reminded her of the look on her father's face after he had been shot. *Please God, save my brother. He's so young and innocent. He doesn't deserve this.*

Joseph's eyes fluttered and slowly opened. "Rebekah, my leg hurts," he moaned. "I want to go home, but I can't move."

Fear seized Rebekah's heart. *What do I do? He's bleeding too much. I cannot carry him.*

She looked around her for help and was relieved to see the face of a neighbor woman who had frequently brought food to their home. Martha Miller knelt beside Joseph. Rebekah watched as Martha gingerly ran her fingers over the boy's right arm and leg. Joseph moaned loudly when her fingers touched his lower right leg.

"Joseph, please remain still. Thy right leg could be broken," Martha Miller said and turned to her son standing wide-eyed above them. "Richard, run to the shed and get the garden cart and three short slats of wood we use to start the fire in the fireplace. Then go to the kitchen and get at least two towels. Hurry."

"Yes, Mother. I'll be right back."

Rebekah watched Richard turn and race across the street to the small shed behind their house. Within

Ann Bell

seconds, he reappeared in the doorway pushing a crudely hewn cart with a rusty wheel.

Meanwhile, Samuel snuggled closer to her and buried his head on her chest. She wrapped her right arm around her sobbing youngest brother while she continued holding Joseph's left hand. She took a deep breath and bit her lip to keep from crying.

Martha patted Rebekah on the shoulder. "Do not fret. God will heal thy brother. I will help thee care for him."

Rebekah sighed. "I think God has forgotten my family," she said softly. "I will not be able to care for him? Second Day next week I must leave for America and may never see them again."

Martha shook her head. The compassion in her eyes comforted Rebekah. "I'm sorry for all the tragedies that have befallen thy family," she said. "Rest assured there are brighter days ahead for thee."

"I wish I could believe that," Rebekah mumbled under her breath.

Ignoring Rebekah's comment, Martha continued, "Thou can be thankful John Reynolds arranged for thy brothers to stay with us while Rachel Smith cares for thy mother. We'll do our best to see that their needs are met and the boys grow into strong, well-mannered Quaker men."

[18]

"I thank God they will be in good hands," Rebeka said. "After my five years of work for the Reynolds is over, I'm going to come back to London. I have to help my family."

The crowd of curious neighbors and onlookers had increased when Richard returned with the requested items.

Martha Miller took the small boards from the cart and laid one on each side and one under Joseph's right leg. She tore each towel into four strips and pulled off the tattered breeches from Joseph's injured leg. Gently she wiped the blood from his shin and wrapped a tight bandage around his leg. "Rebekah, wouldst thou hold the splints in place while I tie them to his leg?"

Joseph let out another moan when Rebekah let go of his hand. She motioned for Samuel to take his brother's hand.

"Don't cry, brother," cooed Samuel. "I'll take care of thee."

Rebekah smiled and patted Joseph's shoulder. "These kind people will help move thee to thy mat by the fireplace in our house."

Martha affixed the splints to the broken leg. "I have an extra bed in my house. It will be easier to care for Joseph there," she said and turned to her son.

"Richard, help me lift him into the cart. It's critical we keep his leg straight."

He pulled the cart closer to the injured boy. Carefully, they lifted Joseph. They positioned him at an angle, so his entire body fit into the cart. Color began to reappear in his face as the lines of pain subsided. Richard lifted the handles of the cart and pushed it down the crooked street toward the Miller's front door while Rebekah and Samuel walked on the right side holding hands. Martha flanked the left side.

Bells tolled in the distance. The sound of horses' hooves on cobblestones blended with far-away voices. The darkness of the London evening enveloped them, while the neighbors silently withdrew into their own homes. Rebekah gazed into the blackness and considered reality. *From this day forward, my life will never be the same. I will not be here to comfort my brothers when they are hurt or to listen to their fears and joys. I will not be able to keep my promise to my father.*

~~~~~

When Rebekah awoke the next morning, she pulled on her gray dress and tied her white bonnet under her chin. She took a small log from the wood box, placed it on the smoldering embers in the fireplace, and stoked the fire.

"Rebekah," a feeble voice from the corner said. "How is Joseph? I wish I could get up and care for him."

Rebekah hurried to her mother's bedside, took her hand, and sat on the edge of the bed. "He was in a lot of pain last night, but Martha Miller made a special tea that seemed to help. He was asleep when I came home. Samuel would not leave his side, so I took his mat across the street so he could sleep beside Joseph's bed. I am almost ready to visit him. I'll be back in a few minutes and tell thee how he is this morning."

Mary Bradford convulsed with a series of coughs. Her frail body shook. "Tell Joseph I love him," she whispered. "Tell him I'll be praying for him."

"Mother, we all treasure thy prayers. They give us the strength to carry on," Rebekah said as she gently moved a lock of hair away from her mother's eyes.

Raindrops blew into the house through the slats in the wall. Rebekah looked around for something to stuff between the slats. She took the threadbare pillowcase from her own limp bag of feathers and tore it into strips. Thankful for a sturdy chair to climb on, she was able to keep the mist from showering down upon her mother.

"My precious daughter, do not fret. It will be a good environment for thy brothers with the Millers," Mary said as she stroked Rebekah's hand. "The

Ann Bell

Millers need help in their tailor shop and the boys can learn a trade."

"But what about them learning to read?" Rebekah protested. "I promised father I would teach them."

Mary shook her head. "The boys won't be able to attend school for a while, but I'm confident God will find a way for them to receive an education."

"But, Mother, they have to go to school. I cannot break that promise."

A faint, reassuring smile spread across Mary Bradford's face. "Rebekah, trust in God. The Inner Light will guide thee. In spite of all that has happened, He has always been faithful. Now stop fretting and go see how Joseph is doing this morning."

The next day, a sharp rapping sounded on the Bradford's door. Rebekah put down the knife she was using to slice potatoes and hurried to the door. Cautiously she opened it a crack and peered out.

"Rebekah Bradford?" a short, elderly Quaker man greeted.

"Yes. May I help thee?"

"I am the Society Overseer of the High Street Quaker meeting. I need to talk to thee and thy mother," the man said. "May I come in?"

Rebekah turned to her mother and watched a look of confusion spread across her face. Finally, her mother nodded her head in approval.

Rebekah hesitantly opened the door and motioned him to enter. "Do come in."

The visitor stepped confidently into the dark home and surveyed the humble furnishing. "Greetings, my name is George Fell. I am the Society Overseer of the High Street Quaker Meeting," he said as Rebekah stepped back shyly.

"To explain the reason for my visit," he continued, trying to make her feel more comfortable, "John Reynolds approached me about thy journey to Philadelphia. I have spoken to the women's meeting and several of thy neighbors. Before thou leave for America, I would like to present thee with a certificate stating Rebekah Bradford in 'walk and conversation' has been orderly and acts in accordance with the dictates of the Truth. This document will confirm thou are in good standing with the local Quaker meeting. When thou arrive in Philadelphia, please present this to the local meetinghouse for consideration." He reached into his pocket and handed the document to Rebekah.

Mary Bradford smiled. "I'm extremely grateful for thy forethought," she said. "I'm certain Rebekah doesn't fully understand the importance of such a certificate for her Quaker journey. As she grows in her understanding of the faith she'll cherish its value."

The Overseer handed the document to Rebekah. "Place this in a waterproof bag and keep it close to thee; it may be one of the most important papers thou wilt ever possess. Now I must take my leave. I wish thee well in thy travels." With those words, George Fell walked solemnly from the house.

After the stranger was gone, Rebekah turned to her mother. "I don't understand. Why is this piece of paper so important? I shouldn't have to prove to anyone what I believe."

Mary Bradford sighed and with slow measured breathes she said, "Just trust him, my daughter. If thou ever confront an unexpected crisis thou can always depend on a Quaker to help thee. Thou must always cherish thy Quaker heritage and faith. Helping each other during adversity is our greatest strength."

During the next two days, anticipation and sadness co-mingled in Rebekah's mind. She moved her brothers' few pieces of clothing across the street to the Millers' home. She washed all her garments, examined them for tears, and packed her meager possessions into a single bag. *Will my threadbare dresses hold together until I get to America,* she wondered.

Many of her friends from the meetinghouse came to say goodbye. Each of them told her how lucky she was to escape the harshness and persecution of London and immigrate to America. All of them said they wished they could find a sponsor and go with her.

Their words of encouragement and "The Inner Light will guide you" comments increased Rebekah's pain of leaving her family. *No one understands what it's like to say goodbye forever unless one actually has to do it herself. I feel the same as when I knelt over my dying father and said goodbye to him.*

On the day of her departure, Rebekah forced herself to get out of bed, dress, and prepare food for her mother and brothers for the last time. Feeding her mother, she studied every feature on her face and tried to remember the days when her cheeks were full of color and her eyes sparkled with laughter. When the time came to leave, Rebekah kissed her mother and brothers goodbye, and bravely followed the Philadelphia Quaker out the door and down the street. She was afraid to look back for fear she would not be able to move forward.

Ann Bell

Rebekah tried to keep pace with John Reynolds as she walked the streets of London for the last time. As they approached the shoreline, dread washed over her aching heart much like the ocean sloshed against the shore. *As a small child, I often sat on the rocks along the same beach watching the ships sail and wondered who the travelers were, where they were going, and what the land over the sea was like. Now I'm the one who is leaving her homeland, possibly never to return.*

"Friend Reynolds, how long will it take to get to Philadelphia?" she asked.

"If the seas are calm, we could be there in ten weeks, but if the seas are rough, it could take as long as thirteen," he replied. "I hope we get there before the weather becomes too harsh."

The ship *Good Hope* loomed before them in the distance. Rebekah's uncertain future began to haunt her. What will life be like as an indentured servant in a strange land? Would they welcome her warmly? Would they treat her well or would she be treated as a slave?

As they neared the ship, Rebekah's curiosity drew her attention to John Reynolds. "How many children dost thou have? What will I be expected to do when we arrive in Philadelphia?"

The tall Quaker looked down at the fragile young girl beside him. A note of concern appeared in his eyes. "Sarah is about thy age. Mark is twelve. Adam is nine. Mary is seven. Lillian is five and Matthew is an infant," he said. "The work of caring for such a large family has become too great for Elizabeth. I'm certain thee will enjoy working with my wife. She is very kind and understanding."

As they approached the wharf, and it occurred to Rebekah that the ship didn't look nearly as large up close as it did when she was sitting on the rocks on a nearby bank. The deck was already crowded with passengers and freight. Her questions about Philadelphia seemed minor compared to the turmoil brewing inside her about life on the ship. *Where will I sleep? What will I eat? Will these strange men be kind to me? How do they know how to steer the ship to get across the ocean? Will I die before I get to America?*

Ann Bell

Two

Rebekah's knees trembled as she and John Reynolds approached the London wharf. In one hand, she carried her clothing in a linen bag and in the other, a basket of food. *The neighbors were kind to bring food to me before I left*, she thought, as she eyed the fresh baked bread, apples, eggs, and potatoes in the basket. *This will only last a few days. Will John Reynolds have enough food to last the entire trip? I heard travelers have to eat a lot of hard tack bread, which has a consistency almost like a rock. I hope there is enough fresh water to last the trip. They tell me many people starve to death while crossing the ocean.*

John Reynolds walked tall and erect beside her, pushing a cart loaded with personal supplies. She smiled when she saw a pile of blankets on the cart. *At least we shouldn't be cold at night. I have heard some people freeze to death without enough covers at night.* Suddenly her smile faded. *What if someone takes our blankets and we are left with nothing?*

Rebekah followed her employer up the gangplank. Stepping on board, she surveyed her surroundings with dread. It was already crowded with freight and passengers rushing back and forth carrying heavy bundles. Strange sounds and smells permeated the deck. There were several children her age she might talk with, but Rebekah wondered if they would want to talk with her?

"Excuse me, Rebekah," John Reynolds said as he parked his cart near the railing of the deck and nodded to a stack of wooden boxes nearby. "I need to talk with the ship's captain. Thou may sit on one of these boxes until I return."

Rebekah quietly obeyed. While she waited, she studied the faces of each passenger who walked up the gangplank and onto the deck of the ship with their bundles. Everyone seemed happy and excited about the voyage. *Why do I have so many doubts? Am I the only one who suspects possible dangers ahead? Am I the only one who is leaving their family behind?*

She waited nervously, watching her employer talking with the ship's captain and then crossing the deck to talk to a humbly dressed family that had just stepped onboard. A few moments later, John Reynolds returned to where she was sitting.

"Rebekah, the captain has made arrangements for thee to share a cabin with the Smith family. I'll be sharing a cabin with nine other men. I'll keep most of the supplies with me and will find thee when it's time to eat in order to share our food. We should have more than enough to last until we get to Philadelphia."

Rebekah shuddered. "I thank thee," she murmured while the ship's bell began to clang, signaling their departure. Tears rolled down her cheeks. She stood on the deck watching her homeland become more and more distant. The church spires, bridges, and tall buildings faded from view. *Will I ever see my family again? Will the Reynolds family treat me well in Philadelphia?*

As if he were reading her thoughts, John Reynolds put his hand on the girl's shoulder. "Don't be sad, Rebekah. Look to the future and trust thou wilt be happy in the new world. Philadelphia is a place where dreams can come true. Let's celebrate thy new and exciting future by sharing some sweet bread. We need to eat it while it is fresh. Later, I'll show thee where thou wilt be sleeping."

John Reynolds reached into a bag and took out a small loaf of bread. He tore off a piece and handed it to her. The two sat quietly enjoying the late afternoon breeze watching the sailors working on the masts. Within minutes, a short, plainly dressed man and woman approached them.

"Edward Smith," John Reynolds called as he rose to his feet. "Dost thou have a moment?"

[31]

Ann Bell

The stranger smiled. "Of course. I have nowhere to go for the next few weeks."

The men laughed. John Reynolds motioned at the girl beside him. "This is my employee, Rebekah Bradford. I thank thee for letting her share the cabin with thy family. Wouldst thou permit us to take Rebekah to thy quarters and help her put away her possessions?"

Edward Smith nodded and motioned to the woman beside him. "This is my wife Abby Smith. We would be more than willing to share our cabin with Rebekah," he said as he reached for Rebekah's bag. "Let me carry her things to our cabin. It is very small, but it will be adequate for our needs. Please follow us."

John Reynolds took two blankets from his cart and motioned for Rebekah to accompany them into the passenger's quarters. She followed Abby Smith down a shaky ladder into a dimly lit section of the ship and waited while Edward Smith pushed the cabin door open. It took a few moments for her eyes to adjust to the darkness. Two sleeping bunks lined the wall, while mats and blankets were piled in the corner. Boxes were stacked under and beside the bunks. They could scarcely move across the room without bumping into something.

Edward Smith knelt and rearranged boxes until there was a space big enough for another mat. "You may sleep in this corner next to my daughter, Priscilla, and keep your things beside you."

Surveying the tiny quarters Rebekah tried to look grateful. *I can't believe how nine people can possibly sleep in such a small space much less keep their extra supplies close to them.* She breathed a sigh of relief when the men didn't wait for her to express her approval.

After rearranging the sleeping space the foursome climbed the wobbly ladder. "If you will excuse me," Edward Smith said. "There is an older woman in the corner who needs help with her bundles. I will join you later."

Abby Smith nodded to her husband and turned to Rebekah. "Come and meet my daughter," she said. "I'm certain John Reynolds needs to take his things to his cabin before it gets dark."

Rebekah looked down. "I thank thee," she whispered. "It is very kind of thee to introduce us."

While John Reynolds filled his arms with his belongings that were still loaded in his handcart, Abby Smith led Rebekah to a girl sitting on a bench in the far corner of the deck staring at the setting sun. She knelt before her daughter. "Hello, Priscilla. You look sad."

"I'm missing my friends already," she said softly, "and I've only been onboard for a few hours."

Ann Bell

Abby Smith hugged her daughter and smiled. "I understand how you must feel. However, I have a cure for your loneliness."

The girl looked up cautiously. "What could that be? I'll never be able to see my friends again."

Abby Smith nodded toward Rebekah. "Priscilla, this is Rebekah Bradford. She will be sharing our cabin with us."

A faint smile spread across the girl's face as she surveyed the Quaker girl before her. "Hello."

"Hello," Rebekah replied shyly.

Abby Smith rose. "The two of you can get acquainted while I help the other children get acquainted with the ship. I'll meet you in our cabin at bedtime."

Priscilla slid to the edge of the bench and patted the seat beside her for Rebekah to join her. "Where are you from?"

"London, near the wharfs. Where art thou from?"

"Bristol. My family is going to Pennsylvania. Where are you going?"

"I'm going to Philadelphia," Rebekah answered.

Priscilla studied Rebekah's plain gray dress and white bonnet. "Are you a Quaker?"

"Yes. How didst thou know that?"

A mischievous twinkle appeared in Priscilla's eyes. "You dress like one and you talk like one," she said and then became serious. "I've never understood why Quakers always say 'thee' and 'thou' instead of just plain 'you'. It seems strange to me."

Rebekah hesitated. *I've never had anyone ask me such a bold question about my religion. How can I answer her without offending her?*

"My father told me how important it is to use plain language," she explained cautiously. "He said 'thee' or 'thou' are the words used for friends, children, servants, and enemies. When non-Quakers want to show respect, they use the word 'you.' Quakers believe everyone is equal and will not treat anyone better than another, not even the King. That's why they do not use the word you or remove their hats to show extra respect. Some Quakers have even gone to jail because they refused to remove their hat for the king."

Priscilla remained quiet for a few moments causing Rebekah to wonder if her explanation had offended her. She was relieved when Priscilla finally said, "That makes sense. My family belongs to the Anglican Church. I never understood Quaker ways before. I always thought it was strange Quakers

[35]

Ann Bell

never called the days of the week by the real name of Sunday, Monday, Tuesday, but used First Day, Second Day, Third Day."

"My father said many of the names of the days and months refer to pagan gods and it would be wrong to use the name of a pagan god." Rebekah hesitated. "Why are thou going to America?" she asked, trying to change the subject to hide her discomfort.

Priscilla smiled. "My father's an excellent farmer and he was able to obtain a large parcel of land several miles from Philadelphia near Germantown. They say the soil is extremely rich in America. She studied her new friend's sad face. "What does your father do?"

Rebekah looked down. Tears gathered in her eyes. "My father's dead," she said softly. "Quakers don't believe in bearing arms. One night, some sailors came and tried to press him into the Royal Navy. He refused to go, and so they shot him on the spot. I was with him when it happened. I'll never forget those moments for as long as I live."

The two girls sat in uncomfortable silence watching the sun disappear behind the horizon. Priscilla reached for Rebekah's hand. "I'm sorry," she finally said. "Is that why you are going to America? Are you trying to get away from the memories?"

Rebekah shook her head. "It's more complicated than that," she said with a sigh. "Mother is very sick and I wasn't able to take care of her and my two brothers, plus earn money to buy food."

Priscilla wrinkled her forehead. "So why are you on this ship?"

"A Quaker merchant from Philadelphia was visiting in London and heard about our situation. He needed help with his large family and offered a contract for me to return to America with him and work for his wife for five years. He also left a large amount of money to pay for my mother's and brothers' care. I had no other choice but to sign the contract. That was the only way I could help my family."

Priscilla's eyes widened. "How sad," she said. "It must be terribly frightening to be alone. I'll be your family until we get to Pennsylvania."

Rebekah smiled. This was the first time she had been able to relax with a friend her own age since she left school more than a year before to care for her mother. "I thank thee," she replied. "Thou are very kind." She surveyed Priscilla's strong chin and mature eyes, far beyond her years. *I wonder if she has known the pain burning within me. Does she know how it feels to lose the people she loves?*

The girls spent hours sitting in silence, lost in their own thoughts. Weatherworn crewmembers walked back and forth in front of them carrying wooden crates to the hold of the ship. The ship rocked gently as the waves beat against its sides. As the cool breeze blew unobstructed across the deck, they wrapped their shawls tighter around themselves.

If she didn't have a new friend beside her, Rebekah didn't know how she could bear watching her entire world fade from view. Their uncertain future bound them together as if lifelong friends.

After darkness enveloped them, a few candles on the deck provided enough light for the girls to find their way to their cabin. The other Smith children were already sleeping when they entered their small sleeping quarters. Six-month-old Joshua was lying on a bunk with his mother; three-year-old Martha's mat was on the floor next to her mother's bunk, followed by six-year-old Peter's, nine-year-old Deborah's and finally Priscilla's and Rebekah's empty mats. They stepped carefully across each one, and lowered themselves to their own mats.

Before lying down, Rebekah knelt and folded her hands. "Dear God," she whispered, "I thank thee for giving me these new friends. I thank thee for my food. Please take care of my mother and heal her body. Bless my brothers, and help them grow into fine, strong men. Please help us have a safe voyage to America. Amen."

Long after Rebekah closed her eyes, sleep continued to elude her. She could hear a woman in the next cabin coughing uncontrollably. Another began vomiting followed by painful moans. It seemed that few onboard actually slept, and those who did snored so loudly that they could be heard throughout the ship. She could hear the ship creak and the water lapping against the bow of the ship. Every sound seemed to be magnified. Priscilla's baby brother cried incessantly throughout the night. Nothing his mother did seemed to comfort him. She rocked him. She snuggled him close to her breast and sang lullabies to him, but to no avail. The baby whimpered most of the night. It was not until just before dawn Rebekah fell into a fitful sleep.

~~~~~

When the sun began to shine across the deck the next morning, the passengers gathered in small groups to prepare their breakfast. Edward Smith helped his children quietly roll their mats and stack them in the corner, leaving Rebekah sleeping in one corner and his wife on the opposite side of the cabin.

In spite of the bustling noise onboard the ship; Rebekah did not open her eyes for several hours. When she finally awoke, it took several moments before she remembered where she was and why she was there. Her stomach was whirling and her head ached. None of the faint shapes around her looked familiar.

Within minutes, the cabin door opened and a faint silhouette appeared. Priscilla knelt beside her.

"Good morning, Rebekah," she whispered. "You were not awake for breakfast, so I brought you a roll and tea. It will be a long time before we will eat again."

Rebekah tried to sit up, but her head continued to spin. She collapsed back onto her mat. "I thank thee for thy kindness," she murmured, "but my stomach is too upset. I don't know if I can eat anything now."

Priscilla put the mug to Rebekah's lips. "At least try and drink some tea. It will help calm your stomach."

Rebekah took a sip of the tea. The warm liquid strengthened her and she lifted her head and took several bites of the bun. Slowly she finished drinking the tea. The pain in her head ceased. Although she continued to feel seasick, Rebekah placed her hand on the wall, and slowly rose to her feet.

"Come with me to the deck," Priscilla encouraged. "The fresh air will be good for you."

As they left the cabin, the girls noticed Priscilla's mother lying in the dim light with her eyes wide open, trying to comfort little Joshua who lay limp in her arms.

"Wouldst thou let us take care of Joshua while thou get some rest?" Rebekah asked, ignoring her own discomfort.

"Thank you," Abby Smith replied wearily. "It would be a great help to me. Nothing seems to make him content. He hasn't eaten since yesterday. Maybe someone else will be able to calm him."

Priscilla stepped forward and took her baby brother from her mother's arms. "We'll do our best. Between the two of us maybe we can at least get him to drink a little water."

While Priscilla's mother slept, the girls took turns walking around the deck with Joshua, singing to him as they went. Every few minutes they stopped and tried to put a few drops of water on his tongue. Rebekah forgot her own seasickness as her concern for Joshua grew. "Priscilla, is he getting too hot?" she asked, as she sat on the bench beside Pricilla to rest.

Priscilla ran her hand over her baby brother's forehead. "He's burning with fever. We need to get help right away. Would you hold Joshua while I awaken mother?"

Tears streamed down Rebekah's face. She cuddled the sick baby next to her chest. His movements were becoming weaker and his breathing shallower. Joshua's coloring was becoming sallow like her father's face had been when she tried to comfort him after his fatal shot.

Ann Bell

Within minutes, both Edward Smith and his wife, Abby, appeared with a bowl of water and a cloth. Edward Smith reached for the baby. "Thank you for helping," he said. "We'll wash Joshua with cold water and see if that lowers his fever."

While the Smiths tried to cool their baby, Rebekah and Priscilla walked around the ship for the remainder of the day asking everyone they met to pray for baby Joshua. By nightfall, all the passengers onboard knew of the sick baby and the concern of the family. The evening meals were eaten in hushed tones. None of the noisy jubilation of the first night on the open sea was apparent. The perils of the sea could no longer be ignored. More and more passengers were experiencing seasickness, and now a baby was gravely ill.

That night Rebekah retired early to her mat in the corner of the Smith's cabin. Even though her stomach churned and her head pounded, she could not get her mind off the hot, limp body she had cuddled that afternoon. After hours of blankly staring into the darkness, she fell into an exhausted sleep completely unaware of the moaning, coughing, and snoring of the other passengers that permeated the ship.

When she awoke the next morning, the cabin was empty. She ran a comb through her long brown hair, tied her bonnet under her chin, and hurried to the deck. She spotted the Smith family standing near the railing talking with the ship's captain. Abby

Smith was crying while Priscilla was hugging her three-year-old sister; the other children clung to their father. Priscilla motioned for Rebekah to join them. By the looks on their faces, she realized what had happened.

Rebekah crept closer to her friend in order to listen to the conversation. "Mistress Smith, I'm sorry there is not an Anglican priest onboard to officiate a funeral," the captain was saying. "However, there is a prominent Quaker who might be willing to read from the Bible. His name is John Reynolds. I'm certain he could be of comfort to your family."

"Thank you, Sir," Edward Smith said solemnly. "I've met Master Reynolds and he appears to be a kind man. We would like to speak with him."

Rebekah watched as the captain walked the length of the ship looking for John Reynolds. When he found him, the two talked for a few minutes and the pair returned to the grieving family.

"I am sorry for thy loss. It is extremely difficult to lose a child. Is there anything I can do to help?" John Reynolds asked.

"We would like to have our son have a proper committal unto the sea, but there is not an Anglican priest available to do the service."

"I would be willing to conduct a funeral service for thy son. I want thou to understand Quakers do not believe in having a priest. We believe that everyone, male or female, has access to Christ through the Inner Light within. I will pray with thy family and seek His blessing before we commit thy son to his eternal resting place."

"We appreciate your concern," Edward Smith said. "I have been accustomed to turning to my priest in time of need but it is very comforting that in the middle of the ocean we can seek God directly without a priest."

News of baby Joshua's death spread rapidly among the passengers. Many sought out the Smiths to give them their condolences. Children clung closer to their parents with bewilderment, and adults talked in hushed tones.

As the sun settled into a red glow in the west, more were becoming ill. Passengers began to wonder who might be next. All who could walk gathered on the main deck of the ship *Good Hope*. The captain spoke a few words followed by John Reynolds talking about the promise of an afterlife, and that the sea would someday give up its dead. He read words of comfort from the Holy Bible. After he had finished speaking, everyone stood in silence when the tiny body of Joshua Smith was committed to God and the deep. The sun disappeared behind the horizon, and the stars and moon illuminated the deck. One by one, the passengers returned to their cabins. An eerie silence enveloped the ship.

~~~~

After the death of little Joshua, the days passed slowly for Rebekah. More and more people were ailing and several died. The stench of the slop buckets became unbearable at times. One night Rebekah was kept awake by the screams and moans of the woman in the next compartment. The woman's friend was trying frantically to deliver her baby, but after several hours, both the mother and baby died.

In spite of the suffering around her, gradually Rebekah accepted what she considered her lot in life. She adjusted to the swaying of the ship and the bland foods, but boredom became her worst enemy. She often joined Abby Smith on a bench watching intricate designs appear on a variety of pieces of cloth in her hands. Abby Smiths's fingers seemed to fly as she wove the colorful thread in and out of the fabric.

"Would you like to learn to embroider? It will help pass the time," Abby Smith asked one afternoon when Rebekah appeared unusually restless.

Rebekah hesitated. She had been fascinated with what her friend's mother had been doing. "In London I was not allowed to do fancy work," she said. "Father said that fancy work was a frivolous waste of time and Quakers need to spend time helping others."

Abby Smith smiled. "On this voyage we have too much time to waste. Just think of it this way: 'Idle hands are the devil's tools.'"

Rebekah thought for a moment. *Will fancy needlework be displeasing to God? Surely, God will understand if I only do it while I am on the ship.* She turned back to Abby Smith. "Yes, I would like to learn to do fancy needlework, but I would never be able to make things as beautiful as thou do."

Abby Smith smiled. "With a little practice you will be able to create a piece of beauty and enjoyment your father would be proud of. I'll help you learn a few stitches my mother taught me. It is very simple to do."

With that assurance, Rebekah joined Priscilla and her mother for many hours of intricate needlework. She even embroidered flowers on the tattered sack she used to carry her meager possessions. However, the words of her father were never far from her thoughts. She would never want to do anything to displease him.

Often Rebekah's thoughts drifted back to her home in London during happier times with her family. To overcome her depression, she would reach into her tattered sack for her most treasured possession. Early one morning when she was especially discouraged, she again reached into her bag. *I'm glad mother insisted I take the family Bible to Philadelphia.* She clutched it to her chest. *Until now, I had not realized how fortunate I was to be able to learn to read. My parents expected me to have the same opportunities the most prosperous of boys had.*

While Rebekah was reading from her Bible, Priscilla joined her on the bench. "Rebekah, you seem to enjoy reading. Would you teach me how to read?"

She looked up, trying to hide her shock. Priscilla seemed to have had all the advantages a girl her age could possibly have had, yet she had never been taught to read. She reached for her friend's hand. "I'm not as good a reader as I would like to be," she said, "but I will try to teach thee what I know."

Priscilla squeezed Rebekah's hand affectionately, and then released it. "Thank you. I'd accept any help I can receive." Priscilla sighed and shook her head. "I don't like the idea how many people think only boys need to be able to read. I want to be able to read myself."

Rebekah smiled. "That is why I'm glad I'm a Quaker," she replied. "We believe both sexes are equal. The only book I own is the Bible. Wouldst thou like to learn to read it?"

"Definitely. I've seen how much comfort reading the Bible gives you; that's why I want to learn to read it myself." Priscilla hesitated. Her face flushed. "I've never told this to anyone, but it frightens me

Ann Bell

when all we can see day after day is water. It's beginning to get cold and the seas are getting rougher. How many of us will end up like little Joshua?"

"I sometimes wonder that myself," Rebekah replied. "But my Bible says God protects His people and prepares a place in heaven for those who believe in Him."

Priscilla gazed across the open sea. "That is why I want to learn to read and learn more about God."

"Let's agree to read together every afternoon," Rebekah said. "By the time we get to Pennsylvania, thou should be able to read an entire chapter of the Bible without assistance."

"I wouldn't know where to begin," Priscilla said. "The marks on a page are confusing to me."

"Once you learn the basic principles, you'll be reading in no time," Rebekah assured her. "To learn to read, thou must first learn the alphabet and the sound each letter makes. John Reynolds gave me a graphite pencil that I keep hidden with my extra dress. If we could find a board to write on, I could teach you the alphabet."

Priscilla's eyes brightened. "I remember seeing a board from an old crate on the other side of the deck. Let's go get it."

The girls hurried to the other side of the deck, then to their sleeping area to locate the graphite pencil, and back to the corner of the deck where they could sit and lean against large wooden crates. They scarcely noticed the biting wind that was stirring white caps on the ocean around them.

As Rebekah slowly wrote each letter of the alphabet on the board with the graphite pencil, she had Priscilla repeat the letter and sound after her. After all twenty-six letters were on the board Rebekah said, "This may sound silly to thee, but I learned to read by combining letters into rhyming words. Let's substitute different letters before the word 'at'. Cat, hat, mat, rat, sat."

"That's amazing," Priscilla said. "You are so smart."

"I'm only passing on to thee, what was taught to me. When thou learn to read thou must teach someone else."

"I will, I promise," Priscilla exclaimed. "This is so exciting. It's not going to be as difficult as I thought."

When her first reading lesson was over, she did not waste any time spreading the news that she was learning to read. Rebekah watched from a distance as Priscilla's parents expressed their pride and encouraged her to keep working.

The next afternoon the other Smith children joined Rebekah and Priscilla. They, too, were eager to escape the boredom of the long voyage. By the end of the week, at least six other children were joining Rebekah and Priscilla for their reading class.

Never before had Rebekah enjoyed the exhilaration of watching the eyes of inquisitive children while they mastered another letter, word, and, last of all, a full sentence. Her most gratifying moments were when a student read their first verse from her family Bible. Everyone in her small class would cheer and applaud their accomplishments while Rebekah beamed with pride.

~~~~~

Edward Smith leaned across the railing and pointed into the surrounding vastness of the sea. "Look, girls. Do you see that?"

Rebekah and Priscilla peered over the deck railing in the direction he was pointing. "All I see is more water," Priscilla replied with disappointment. "What should I be seeing?"

"Look a little further to the right," her father persisted. "It's a twig."

The two friends exchanged puzzled glances. "So what does seeing a twig mean?" Rebekah asked. "That seems strange to me."

[50]

"It means that land is near," Edward Smith replied with a broad smile. "Soon we'll see larger and larger branches and later sea birds will appear. We'll be in America before Christmas."

One by one, a throng gathered on the deck of the ship *Good Hope*. After ten weeks, bland food, poor sanitary conditions, illness, and death had ravaged their morale and strength. Each passenger was hoping to see the first sign of land since they left the London harbor.

The next day, passengers again lined the railing, peering into the dark waters below for another sign of land. The cold Twelfth Month wind chilled their bones, but they continued to wait on the deck. When the sun set that evening, they returned to their cabins disappointed.

Edward Smith must have been imagining the twig," one said.

"Maybe he's just a liar," responded another.

"I'll never believe another word Edward Smith says again," still another said.

The next morning, fewer passengers braved the biting cold to stand near the railing watching for another symbol of hope. Again, they were disappointed. On Third Day, only six passengers gathered on the deck. Before long, they were rewarded for their perseverance. They cheered wildly when a large branch drifted within twenty meters of the ship. Their waning hope was restored. The following day floating branches became commonplace and sea gulls could be seen in the distance. Five days after the sighting of the first twig, land became visible along the horizon.

Rumors spread rapidly among the passengers of the ship *Good Hope* until the captain spread the official good news. "This is our last night on board. In the morning, we will be sailing up the Delaware River. We should be able to disembark midday in Philadelphia. However, once the ship drops anchor, we have to wait offshore for a doctor to check for contagious diseases before releasing passengers to go ashore."

That evening, songs echoed from the ship late into the night. Strength seemed to have returned to those whose eyes had become listless with boredom, hunger, and pain. In spite of the joy, a bittersweet mood settled over Rebekah as she lay beside her friend that night. "Priscilla, will I ever see thee again?"

"I hope so," Priscilla answered. "Whenever father goes to Philadelphia to get supplies I'll try to visit you. Since John Reynolds is a prominent merchant, it shouldn't be hard to locate you."

Tears rolled down Rebekah's cheeks. "I will pray for thee every night when I pray for my mother and brothers."

[52]

"And I will pray for you as well," Priscilla promised.

As the night passed, a wave of nausea spread over Rebekah and her body became hot and clammy. In spite of how she felt, she continued talking with Priscilla far into the night. Hopes and dreams poured from both of them. Priscilla described the family she would someday like to have, while Rebekah shared how much she someday wanted to become a schoolmistress.

When the first ray of sunlight hit the decks of the ship *Good Hope*, the passengers began packing their meager possessions. They stacked their bags on the deck eager to go ashore. Their nightmare would soon be over. While others hurried to organize their things, Rebekah rose slowly from her mat. Every fiber in her body ached. Slowly she dragged her bag of belongings to the deck to prepare to go ashore.

John Reynolds was waiting for Rebekah at the top of the ladder when she stepped onto the deck. When he saw her, he gasped. "Rebekah, art thou ill? Thy face is red and thou look too thin."

Rebekah hung her head. Her shoulders slumped. "I do not feel well at all. I just want to go onshore and lie down."

John Reynolds's chin dropped and his eyes widened. "Before a person can leave this ship, they

Ann Bell

must receive clearance from the doctor verifying they do not have a communicable disease. I hope thy illness is from the perils of a difficult voyage and not a disease that can be spread to others. If it is contagious, I do not know what we will do."

Three

Rebekah lay on the deck of the ship *Good Hope*. Her frail body shuddered beneath three tattered blankets. The blankets had been nearly new when the ship left London, but rubbing against rough planks and loose nails had taken its toll. She watched while one by one the other passengers were cleared to go ashore.

After waiting with his young employee for more than two hours, John Reynolds knelt beside her and felt her forehead. "Art thou feeling any better? The doctor should be getting to thee soon."

Tears streamed down Rebekah's cheeks. "I…I…I am so cold and miserable. I just want to get off this ship, but I don't think I'm strong enough to walk."

John Reynolds carefully laid another blanket over her. "Don't worry, Rebekah. I'll take care of thee. Thou can lie in the cart and I will push thee to my friend's house near the wharf. They will take care of thee until thou art strong enough to travel to my home."

She nodded, though she was not convinced she would ever be able to leave the ship. Through her tears, Rebekah watched a short, stocky, well-dressed man walk across the deck toward them. He knelt beside her. "I'm Doctor Browning. I need to examine thee before thee can go ashore."

"Please let me leave. I want to feel the earth under my feet again." Rebekah sobbed uncontrollably.

"Just relax. I have to make sure thou dost not have smallpox. It will just take me a few minutes," Doctor Browning said. "I need to check for a rash or scabs."

The doctor helped Rebekah sit up. She shivered in the cold as he removed the blanket and carefully checked her back and chest for scabs. He listened to her breathing.

Within minutes, Doctor Browning helped Rebekah lie flat again and recovered her with blankets. He rose and turned to John Reynolds. "This young woman doesn't have smallpox, but she's extremely ill from malnourishment. You may take her onshore, but make sure she gets plenty of food and rest or she may not survive the cold winter ahead."

~~~~

Snow gathered on the blankets covering Rebekah as John Reynolds pushed the cart down a narrow path toward the Logan home. "Richard Logan has a mercantile across town from mine," he said. "Our families have been good friends for many years. His wife, Naomi, has nursed many people in our Society back to health. They will have fresh food and water for thee. Thou will receive excellent care."

"I'll be grateful," Rebekah whispered. "It has been so long I've nearly forgotten what fresh food was like."

Rebekah could hear John breathing deeper and deeper as they trudged through the snow. Finally, he said, "I see their house now. We only have one more block to go." As slow as his steps were becoming, Rebekah was beginning to wonder if he was going to make it to the door. Even though she had lost a great deal of weight on board the ship, she still was a burden for him as he pushed both her and their remaining supplies.

John knocked at the door of the large frame house. Within moments, the door creaked open and a small face appeared in the gap and soon disappeared.

"Mama, we have visitors."

A stocky Quaker woman appeared in the doorway. "Friend Reynolds, how good to see thee. Come in. It's much too cold for anyone to be outside."

John Reynolds stooped, brushed the snow from the blankets, and helped Rebekah from the cart. "Naomi, I would like thee to meet Rebekah Bradford. I brought her back from London to help Elizabeth with the children."

Naomi smiled, opened the door wider, and motioned for the pair to enter. "Hello, Rebekah. Welcome to Philadelphia. Come in and rest. Thou look ill." She wrapped her arm around Rebekah to help support her weight as she walked.

"I don't feel well at all," Rebekah murmured.

"Thou wilt be better in no time. We'll care for thee until thou are well," Naomi Logan assured her as she pointed to her daughter. "This is my daughter, Ruth. My husband will be home from his store after dark."

"It's nice to meet thee," Rebekah said shyly. "I thank thee for taking us in from the cold."

"In Philadelphia we Quakers try to help each other." Naomi Logan led her across the room and helped her remove her threadbare coat. "Please lie on the cot by the fireplace while I heat some tea."

Rebekah collapsed onto the cot while Naomi Logan covered her with a fresh, clean quilt. The warmth of the hearth permeated her shivering, frail body. It had been months since she had felt warm. She readily accepted the hot cup of tea Ruth handed her. She clutched it tightly in her hands and savored the warmth of the tea as it trickled down her throat.

After seeing that Rebekah was comfortable, Naomi Logan turned her attention to John Reynolds, who was sitting at the plain wooden table in the center of the room. "John, I have missed seeing thee at the meetinghouse during thy voyage to London. Didst thou have a good trip?"

John cradled his head in his hands and sighed deeply. "It was extremely eventful, and very exhausting," he said. "Besides buying supplies for the mercantile, I spent a great deal of time with the Quaker community. While there, I met Rebekah and learned of the plight of her family. It was such a desperate situation that I decided to bring her to Philadelphia to live with my family. She and her mother agreed Rebekah would work for us to pay for her passage as well as the care of her brothers and mother in London. I only regret that I wasn't able to bring her brothers at the same time, but they were too young, and I was afraid they would not survive the trip."

"Maybe thou couldst bring them to Philadelphia when they are older. Both thou and Richard go to England occasionally to purchase merchandise. I'm

Ann Bell

certain Rebekah would like to have her family close to her."

"I'm giving that serious consideration." John Reynolds glanced out the window at the freshly falling snow. A drift was building next to the gate as the wind added the blowing snow with what was already on the ground. The shadows were beginning to lengthen. "I'm feeling rested now and am anxious to see my family. I should be on my way in order to get home before dark."

A scowl spread across Naomi Logan's face. "No one should venture forth in this storm. It's much too dangerous."

"I'll be careful," he said confidently. "I know several homeowners along the way where I can stop and warm myself, but Rebekah is too weak to travel. May I leave her with thee and return with a wagon when the storm is over?"

"I'll be glad to have Rebekah stay with us as long as necessary. However, thou must have some warm food before leaving. Thou wilt need all the strength possible to face the biting elements outside," Naomi Logan stated firmly.

The Quaker woman took a ladle from the side of the chimney and dipped it into the huge kettle hanging in the fireplace. She poured a thick stew into two earthen bowls and set one before John Reynolds and one across the table from him. She turned and helped Rebekah walk to the table.

"I hope thee enjoy thy food," Naomi said. "I'm glad I followed my impulse and made extra today."

"I thank thee for thy kindness. Thou hast often been sensitive about following the Inner Light," John Reynolds said. "Art thou and Ruth not going to eat?"

"I thank thee for thy concern, but we ate about an hour ago."

John Reynolds paused and said a short prayer before lifting his spoon. While he hurriedly ate his stew, Rebekah savored the warmth and taste of the meat and vegetables.

"I've never tasted such delicious food in my entire life," she said as she tried to eat slowly and watch her manners. However, she was unable to hide her hunger. The months of cold bland food had taken its toll on her.

Naomi Logan set a loaf of freshly baked bread before Rebekah and John Reynolds along with a small bowl of freshly churned butter. Rebekah reached for a slice. *If only my mother and my brothers could have such food. Life has become too harsh for the Quakers in London. I wish they all could move to Philadelphia with me.*

Rebekah watched John Reynolds finish eating, say good-bye to the Logans, and step into the crisp Twelfth Month weather. While she watched him leave, a wave of loneliness engulfed her. *The only person I know on the entire continent has left me among strangers.* Tears built in her eyes. *What will become of me? I cannot take care of myself. I feel so helpless and don't know what to do. If ever I need my mother and father, it's now.*

While Rebekah slowly finished eating her third bowl of stew, she watched Naomi fill a large kettle of water and hung it over the fire. She took a giant tub and set it beside the hearth along with a sliver of soap and a towel. When the water was hot, she poured it into the tub. Finally, Naomi lowered her hand into the water to make sure the temperature was right for bathing.

After eating a large meal, Rebekah's body gradually relaxed and her eyes became heavy. She propped her head in her hands and closed her eyes.

"Rebekah, before thou can go to sleep, thou wilt need a warm bath," Naomi said. "Thou must feel extremely dirty from the trip."

Rebekah forced her eyes open. "I do. I've never felt this unclean in my life, but I am so sleepy." Without thinking, she scratched her head and smiled at her reaction to feeling unclean.

"Feeling unclean is common for new arrivals," Naomi said. She wrapped her arm around Rebekah and walked her to the tub. "Many people have contracted lice while on board. This soap is guaranteed to remove all the grit and grime along with any lice or their eggs that might be hiding in thy hair."

"But I don't have clean clothes to put on after I bathe. Everything I own is filthy."

"That is no problem," Naomi Logan assured her. "I have a shift, dress, apron, and bonnet thou may have. Tomorrow we can wash the clothing thou brought from London, but my guess is thou wilt need to start with an entirely new wardrobe."

Rebekah hung her head. "Thou art very kind. I'll never be able to repay thee."

"All I ask is that when thou see others in need, thou wilt pass on any help thou can give."

Naomi Logan helped her slip out of her tattered clothing and step into the tub of warm water. Rebekah curled her legs against her chest, leaned back, and closed her eyes. All her pains and discomforts seemed to melt into the water. *This is pure luxury. I wish mother had a tub like this to use and the strength to get in and out of it.* She rubbed the soap over her soft skin, while Naomi Logan helped wash her hair.

While Rebekah rinsed herself, Naomi Logan disappeared into the bedchamber and reappeared with a stack of clothing. She handed Rebekah a towel. "After thou dry thyself, slip into the shift."
Rebekah nodded and smiled. "I thank thee." She said and finished rinsing the soap from her body. She gingerly stepped from the tub, and rubbed herself with the towel, basking in her newfound cleanliness. When she was dry, she reached for the shift and relished in the feel of the soft fabric as it slid over her slender frame. Every cell in her body cried for sleep.

Naomi Logan helped Rebekah to the cot beside the fireplace. "If thee become too cold just ask for another quilt."

Rebekah nodded and lay back onto the cot, too tired to speak.

Naomi Logan tucked the quilts around the exhausted girl's chin. "Have a good rest."

Within seconds, Rebekah was asleep and slept undisturbed throughout the night. She did not hear Richard Logan return home that evening and the conversation occurring around the kitchen table. It was not until she heard Naomi Logan and Ruth doing laundry in the metal tubs late the next morning that she awoke.

When Ruth saw Rebekah's eyes open, she said, "Good morning. Thou had a long sleep. How art thou feeling today?"

Rebekah smiled, stretched her arms overhead, and sat on the edge of the cot. "I feel much better this morning. I haven't slept this well since I left home three months ago."

Naomi Logan left the laundry tub and took a pan from near the hearth. "Come and eat some porridge." She motioned for Rebekah to take a place at the table. "We made extra this morning and yesterday was baking day so we have plenty of fresh bread."

~~~~

The remainder of the day, Naomi Logan insisted Rebekah rest on the cot by the fireplace while she and Ruth did the household chores. Part of the day, Rebekah closed her eyes and faked sleep to hide her tears. *I wonder how mother is. I hope someone is taking good care of her. I don't understand why everyone thought I wasn't old enough to take care of her myself. I wonder what the boys are doing. I probably will never be able to see them again.*

Dusk was settling over the city when Richard Logan entered his home. He greeted his family while Rebekah quietly watched from a distance. She found him much like John Reynolds – kind and gentle, yet aloof.

After Richard Logan greeted his family, he turned his attention to Rebekah who remained lying on the bed by the fireplace. "Welcome, Rebekah. It's good to have thee stay with us. Thou were asleep when I came home last night so I didn't get a chance to talk with thee. I'm anxious to learn the details of thy trip and the plight of the Quakers in London."

"It is good to meet thee," Rebekah said shyly as she joined the family around the kitchen table. "I've heard so many good things about thee."

For the rest of the evening, the Logan family listened with fascination while Rebekah described her ocean voyage, the night her father was murdered, the condition of her mother and brothers, and the state of her neighborhood and the people who attended the High Street Quaker Society.

For the next two days, Rebekah savored the love and hospitality of the Logan family. Richard Logan returned from work early on Third Day in order to finish household chores before it was too dark to work. While he was fixing a broken kitchen chair, there was a knock on the door. He laid his hammer aside and hurried to open the door. "Friend Reynolds, welcome," he shouted with excitement. "Come in and warm thyself."

John Reynolds stomped the snow from his boots and followed his friend to the straight back chairs at the table. "Richard, it's good to see thee again. I've been looking forward to this time together for months."

"I thank God thou had a safe and productive voyage to London. I am anxious to learn all about it. Rebekah shared some of the difficulties thou faced at sea."

John Reynolds smiled and nodded at Rebekah. "Hello, Rebekah. How art thou? Thou look much improved than when we left the ship."

Before she had time to answer, John Reynolds had turned back to his friend. "I want to thank thee for caring for Rebekah. I would have been back sooner, but many chores at home required my attention. I was pleased at how well my family managed in my absence, but I needed to tend to those things only I am strong enough to do. I hope Rebekah was not a problem for thy family."

"It was a pleasure having her," Richard Logan said with a smile. "She's a delightful child and extremely knowledgeable. She tells me she will be working for thee for five years."

Rebekah took a deep breath and watched John Reynolds. *Would he present her as a hired maid for his wife or an indentured servant? A maid doesn't sound bad, but to her an indentured servant meant being a slave for five years.*

What seemed like hours for Rebekah, John Reynolds finally answered. "Yes, we're looking forward to having her with us for five years. Her situation is most tragic. Life for young girls in London without someone to protect them can be filled with danger. Her brothers were too young for a perilous ocean voyage and had to live with other Friends in London. Rebekah didn't want to leave them, but there was no other way for her to have a life outside of the poverty of the London slums."

Richard Logan paused and rubbed his chin. "Her family needs to be reunited. Maybe I could help in some way. I plan to travel to London myself within the next two years. I could check on her family while I'm there. How old are the brothers?"

"The boys are five and seven. Everyone who knew them said they are delightful, compliant children."

"If my wife is willing, perhaps I could pay passage to bring them back to Philadelphia with me. They could serve as my apprentices until they're able to live on their own. We would treat them like the sons we were never able to have."

Rebekah noticed Richard Logan exchanged knowing glances with his wife and saw Naomi smile in agreement. Rebekah was scarcely able to conceal her excitement. "I would do anything if thou wouldst bring my brothers to America," she inserted bravely. "I miss them so much."

Richard Logan patted her shoulder. "I can make no promises," he said. "We'll have to see what God has planned for the future." He turned his attention back to his friend without further comment.

After an hour of lively conversation with the Logans, John Reynolds loaded the baggage into his wagon and helped Rebekah into the front seat. He handed her a quilt to wrap around herself, climbed into the seat beside her, and snapped the reins to signal the horses.

As they traveled the snow-covered city with wide tree-lined streets and new, well-kept buildings, Rebekah's eyes were wide with awe. There was such beauty in the simplicity of architecture, and the cleanliness of the city was far different from the disgusting garbage on the crowded London streets. She had seen snow in London, but never in such depth. She marveled at how the horses could walk through the drifts as if nothing were there.

The blocks turned quickly into miles as Rebekah continued surveying her new hometown. Upon arriving in front of the Reynolds' massive, two-storied wooden house an hour later, John Reynolds pulled the horses to a stop, jumped from the wagon, and tied them to the hitching post before helping her to the ground. Carrying her single bag, he led the way toward their large dwelling.

[69]

Elizabeth Reynolds met them at the front door. "Welcome, Rebekah. Please come in and rest; thou hast been through so much. I've been looking forward to meeting thee."

"I thank thee," Rebekah murmured as she entered the large living room/kitchen combination. Her eyes studied its tidiness. A long, plank table surrounded by eight chairs was in the center of the room, while a fire blazed in the hearth on the back wall.

"This is Matthew," Elizabeth Reynolds said, affectionately squeezing the infant in her arms. "Lillian, who is five, is the one sitting by the fire; Mary, the dark-haired girl in the corner, is seven; Adam is nine and Mark is twelve. Thou wilt enjoy Sarah since she is also fourteen."

One by one, the children joined their parents and Rebekah at the doorway.

Rebekah smiled at the children. "Hello."

"Hello, Rebekah," they said one by one.

"Sarah, would thee show Rebekah where she will sleep and where to keep her clothing, while I put Matthew down for his nap," Elizabeth Reynolds instructed. "I'm certain thou wilt want to get acquainted."

Sarah scowled and laid her knitting on the table beside her. "Follow me," she said dryly and led the way up the stairs. When they reached the top floor, she pointed to a door on the right. "The boys sleep on that side. The girls sleep here."

She pushed open a door to a dimly lit room on the left. Its furnishings included two double beds, a single bed, and a chest of drawers. "You can use the bottom drawer. The single bed is for thee," Sarah said. "Father thought it best thou have thy own bed instead of sharing mine. Thou wilt have more work to do and will come to bed much later than I."

Rebekah wrinkled her brow. *I wonder what that means. What is expected of an indentured servant? I hope I won't be treated like a slave.*

After Sarah left the bedchamber, Rebekah placed her few articles of clothing in the drawer. She was now a resident of Philadelphia; the place people called 'William Penn's holy experiment.' She placed her freshly laundered clothes and family Bible in the bottom drawer and folded the sack she had carried them. She had scarcely finished unpacked when she heard her name being called.

"Rebekah. Wouldst thou come and help me prepare supper."

"I will be right there." Rebekah hurried down the ladder and joined Elizabeth Reynolds in the cooking area. *I wonder if I'll be able to please Elizabeth*

Ann Bell

Reynolds. I have never used many of the utensils that line their hearth.

Elizabeth Reynolds handed Rebekah a knife. "Wilt thou peel the potatoes and cut them into squares for the stew while I get the bread?"

Rebekah nodded, took the knife, and did exactly what she was told. In minutes, she had perfectly squared pieces of six potatoes. "What wouldst thou have me do next?"

Elizabeth Reynolds smiled. "Thou did an excellent job preparing the potatoes. I can tell thou hast had a great deal of experience in a kitchen. Next, we'll need water brought in. Wouldst thou go to the well and get another bucket of water?" She turned to her eldest daughter who was engrossed in her needlework. "Sarah, wouldst thou show Rebekah where the well is and how it works? It can be a little difficult at times."

Rebekah took her shabby cloak from a hook beside the door while Sarah took her finely woven shawl from one nearby. When the girls were outside, away from where her parents could hear, Sarah said, "I'm glad this will now be thy job. The weather is getting much too severe and I'm subject to coughing attacks. Father says I must take care of myself so I don't become ill like I did last year."

Rebekah shuddered. *Now I know why the Reynolds wanted me to come – to do all of Sarah's chores. She is the most unkind Quaker I have ever met.*

After the girls had retrieved the water, Sarah led the way back to the house. Cold water slopped against Rebekah's thin legs as she carried the water bucket with both hands trying to keep pace with her. When they came to the kitchen, she could scarcely lift the bucket to set it on the worktable while Sarah returned to her needlework.

"I thank thee," Elizabeth Reynolds said. "We're almost ready to eat. Wouldst thou get the little ones?"

The children needed little reminding and raced to the table. After a few moments of calm while John Reynolds said the blessing, the meal was eaten with a great deal of laughter and gaiety among the younger ones. Sarah sat with downcast eyes, detached from the others. From the corner of the table,

Rebekah watched the interaction of the children with amazement and loneliness. *I wish I were laughing with my own parents and brothers around a table loaded with an abundance of good food. What did my family do to deserve such harsh treatment? I'd gladly trade this warmth and good food just to be with them now.*

When the meal was completed, Rebekah washed the dishes and placed them in the cupboard beside the sink. Afterward, she sat quietly in the background while the family gathered around the hearth where John Reynolds read from the Holy Bible. He read two chapters from the Gospel of John, and handed the Bible to Sarah who read the next two. When she finished, Mark and Adam each read a chapter, followed by Mary reciting her favorite Bible verse she had memorized.

"May I read, too?" five-year-old Lillian begged.

Everyone smiled. "Now that Rebekah is here, maybe she can teach thee to read," John Reynolds said. "She's a very good teacher. She gave reading lessons while she was on the ship, and several children learned to read on their way to America."

Rebekah felt her cheeks grow warm as everyone turned toward her with a puzzled look. "It helped make the time pass faster for me," she said meekly.

Lillian took Rebekah's hand and looked into her face with pleading eyes, the same eager anticipation Rebekah had seen on the faces of the children on the ship. "Please."

"Lillian, I'd be happy to give thee reading lessons every night after family devotions."

Elizabeth Reynolds took her youngest daughter's hand. "That is very kind of Rebekah to offer to help

[74]

thee, but right now we all must go to bed early since tomorrow is First Day. Come along and we'll show her what our nighttime routine is."

The next morning the entire Reynolds family arose early and put on fresh, clean clothes. While she was dressing, Rebekah watched Sarah combing her hair and adjusting her bonnet using her reflection in the bedchamber window. *How silly and vain. I wonder if Sarah wants to impress some boy at the meeting. Doesn't she know it's inner beauty that's important and not outer beauty?* She sighed and hurried down the stairs. There was too much work to be done before they left.

The Reynolds family ate a quick breakfast of bread and tea. Rebekah fed and dressed baby Matthew while Elizabeth Reynolds helped the younger girls get ready to go to meeting. When Mark and Adam were ready, John Reynolds took them to get the horses and wagon.

While Rebekah and Sarah waited on the porch of the house, Rebekah's eyes widened in terror. The blackest person she had ever seen was leading the team of horses from the barn. "Who is that? I've never seen anyone that color before. Is he dangerous?"

Sarah laughed. "You mean you have never seen an African?"

Ann Bell

Rebekah felt her cheeks grow warm; she focused her gaze on the plank on the porch, and shook her head. "No, everyone in my neighborhood in London had the same skin color. A few people did have red hair though."

Sarah's laughter turned to a sneer.

Hearing the girls' discussion and sensing Rebekah's discomfort, Elizabeth joined them on the porch carrying Michael. "Moses is from Africa. Many people in the colonies use Africans for slaves, but most Quakers don't believe in slavery. John hired Moses to tend to the animals and work the fields. He lives in a house behind the barn. He's free to come and go as he pleases."

Amidst her confusion, Rebekah breathed a sigh of relief. *If the Quakers in Philadelphia feel strongly against slavery, maybe I'll not be treated like a slave during the five years of being an indentured servant.* Her sense of relief was short lived as other harsh concerns mounted. *If the Reynolds would turn me away, will I have to become someone's slave in order to survive?*

Everyone climbed into the wagon and the children took blankets from a wooden box in the front of the wagon bed to wrap around themselves. John Reynolds snapped the rein and the horses started on a steady walk. The brisk wind nipped the children's faces, but the others seemed exhilarated by the crisp winter air. In spite of the added warmth, Rebekah shivered with cold.

During the bumpy ride to the meetinghouse, the younger children giggled among themselves while the older ones sat quietly, each absorbed in their own thoughts. When they reached the Market Street Meetinghouse, ten other wagons were already lined up under the trees. John Reynolds helped his family from the wagon. They nodded at their neighbors as they approached the building. Silently, he led his sons to one side of the room while Elizabeth took the girls to the opposite side.

The members of the Society sat in silence for ten minutes. At first, Rebekah appreciated the moments to rest, but it wasn't long before she found the benches unbearably uncomfortable. When boredom was about to overwhelm her, a man rose to his feet and read a passage from the Book of Acts. When he was finished, they again sat in silence until a woman stood to read from the Psalms. When that woman finished, an old woman stood and told how God had answered her prayers. Rebekah's thoughts went back to the meetings she had attended in London with her parents. It had been the highlight of their week. Her spirits lifted. It was good to be in a meeting with Friends once more.

Again, they sat in a long silence. Lillian began to wiggle and quietly whispered. Rebekah looked down and motioned for her to be silent. An image of her mother years ago holding her finger in front of her lips to signal her to be quiet, flashed before her. She smiled to herself thinking she was now playing the parent role even if it wasn't her own family.

Slowly one of the elders rose to his feet and walked to the front. "Friends," he announced in a loud booming voice. "I have great news to share with thee along with a request. Two traveling women missionaries will be coming to Philadelphia within the month. Their names are Charity Jones and Hope Jamison. We will be extremely fortunate to have them in our midst for they will bring a great deal of spiritual insight with them. However, we need someone to provide lodging and food for them while they're here. Does anyone feel a leading to invite them into their home?"

Rebekah surveyed the group. Nearly everyone's eyes remained fixed on the floor during an embarrassing silence. Finally, John Reynolds announced in a loud clear voice, "I feel the Inner Light is leading me to invite the missionaries into our home for as long as needed."

A sigh of relief seemed to echo through the room. Rebekah felt a slight nudge on her right and listened to Sarah's forbidden whisper. "We're already too crowded. I'm not going to give up my bed or spend extra time on baking days cooking for total strangers. I'm glad thou wilt be able to do the extra chores."

Four

Rebekah quickly settled into her new life in Philadelphia. She felt surrounded by kindness and respect. Yet, underneath it all, she sensed a formal distance from the other Quakers in her community. She compliantly went about her daily chores with constant insults from Sarah. She longed for the embrace of her mother and the loving words of her father. Whenever she would hear the adage of being a stranger in a strange land a lump would build in her throat. That was exactly how she felt.

Sarah's resentment of her presence became increasingly painful for Rebekah. She would lie awake at night struggling as to how to handle the situation. *If I'm not kind to her, she'll tell her parents and they could turn me out from their home. Where would I go? I could end up starving on the streets or being a slave in an abusive household. If only her parents understood what she has been doing to me.*

Rebekah realized Sarah was trying to compete with her for her parents' attention, but it was obvious Sarah was not strong enough to keep pace with the

Ann Bell

work she did. Rebekah worked constantly from dawn to dusk to try to earn the approval of her employers, but there was no way Sarah could compete. With every passing day, she had to stop and rest more often and for longer periods. As Sarah's energy level decreased, her resentment and cruelness toward Rebekah multiplied. Sarah's coughing became more frequent and intense as she struggled onward.

After two weeks of pushing herself beyond her endurance level, while carrying an armload of logs to the wood box beside the hearth, Sarah dropped the logs into the box and collapsed toward the burning flames. Within seconds, a lock of her blond hair began to smolder.

"Sarah, thy hair is on fire!" Rebekah screamed as she pulled her away from the fire, and swatted the burning hair. When the fire was out and Sarah was a safe distance from the fire, Rebekah knelt beside her. "Art thou all right? Let me help thee to the chair."

Sarah shrugged off the help and stumbled to her feet. "I'll be all right. I can take care of myself." Before she was completely upright, she again began to slump.

Rebekah put her arm around Sarah and helped support her weight. "Please go to bed and rest."

Sarah adamantly shook her head. "If thou can keep

working, so can I. I'll prove to father that thou are not any better than I am."

Ignoring the sharp words, Rebekah helped her shuffle to the nearby rocker. After Sarah sunk onto the chair, Rebekah put her hand on Sarah's forehead. "Thou art dreadfully hot. Please go to bed, before thou get worse."

Before she could answer, another coughing spasm racked Sarah's trim body. Rebekah watched in horror as Sarah collapsed from the chair to the floor. She tried to make her as comfortable as possible by placing a folded towel under her head and raced upstairs to gather enough bedding to make a sleeping pallet near the hearth.

Within minutes, the makeshift bed was complete. Rebekah carefully helped Sarah to the pallet and covered her with a quilt.

"How didst thou learn to make such a bed so quickly?" Sarah whispered, trying to mask her pain and weakness.

Memories overwhelmed Rebekah. The constant rocking of the ship. The stench of the lower deck. The long hours with nothing to do. "I learned all kinds of bed-making ideas on the ship *Good Hope*. I did not have much else to do during those long months," she answered as she hurried to the sink.

Rebekah took the ladle hanging over the counter, dipped it into the water pail, and poured the refreshing liquid into a wooden cup. She knelt beside her and lifted the cup of water to Sarah's lips. "Drink some water. It will help thee rest." She watched while Sarah slowly sipped its contents, set the cup aside, and fell back onto her pillow.

Rebekah returned to the counter, filled a large bowl with cool water, and found a fresh, clean washcloth. She ran her fingers across Sarah's face and placed the wet cloth on her forehead. *I wish Elizabeth Reynolds would hurry home from the neighbors. She would know what to do.* Rebekah again wiped Sarah's face with the cloth and rinsed it in the cool water. Folding it lengthwise, she placed it on Sarah's forehead once more.

Rebekah watched as Sarah closed her eyes and drifted into a feverish sleep. She remained constantly by her side, watching her chest laboriously rise and fall. Whenever Sarah's forehead warmed the cloth, she rinsed it in the cool water and returned it to the girl's forehead. She kept glancing out the window, hoping to see Sarah's mother returning from helping a neighbor.

Two hours passed before Rebekah saw her employer walking down the lane, and she ran to meet her. "Mistress Reynolds. . . Mistress Reynolds. Come quickly. Sarah collapsed. She's very feverish. I don't think she knows what is going on around her."

Elizabeth Reynolds didn't say a word, but began running toward the house. She spent the next few minutes examining her daughter before turning to Rebekah. "Thou did exactly the right thing for Sarah. She is extremely ill. All we can do now is to keep the cold cloths on her forehead, wait, and pray. When she awakens we can give her some warm tea."

When John Reynolds returned that evening, he was shocked to see his eldest daughter lying on a makeshift bed beside the fireplace, her face flushed with fever. He went immediately to her side, knelt beside her, and felt her forehead. He turned to his wife. "Elizabeth, what happened? I thought Sarah was getting stronger these last few weeks. From what I observed, she was able to keep pace with Rebekah."

Elizabeth shook her head. "I thought so, too, but when I returned from helping Widow Black this afternoon, Rebekah ran out to meet me and explained what had happened. For the last few weeks, Sarah has been trying to outdo Rebekah, but she wasn't strong enough. We'll have to make sure she doesn't exert herself any more."

The couple exchanged worried glances when Sarah leaned forward and broke into another coughing spasm. In a few moments, she again collapsed onto the pillow exhausted and drifted into a deep sleep.

Ann Bell

John frowned and turned to his wife. "With that cough we can't let her sleep in her cold upstairs bedchamber. Some mornings, the girls can see their breath when they get out of bed."

"She's not strong enough to make it up the stairs," Elizabeth added. "I know it will be crowded, but we'll have to move Sarah's bed downstairs close to the hearth. We can push the furniture together to make room for it."

John Reynolds nodded and motioned at Rebekah, Adam, and Mark. "Rebekah, wilt thou and the boys help me move the bed frame down the stairs?"

Without hesitating, they all dropped what they were doing and obeyed. One-by-one they climbed the narrow staircase. The sun reflected through the small window at the end of the room as they crowded around Sarah's bed. Rebekah stripped the remaining bedding from the mattress while John Reynolds and his sons lifted the mattress from the bed frame. They dismantled the frame and piece-by-piece they carried the bed down the stairs. John reassembled the bed in the space Elizabeth had cleared. As soon as he was finished, Rebekah remade it.

John Reynolds lifted his daughter onto the bed. "Thank you, Father," she whispered before breaking into another coughing fit.

"Please try to get some rest. We will take care of thee," John Reynolds comforted her.

While the others were busy moving the bed, Elizabeth and the younger girls had busied themselves preparing the evening meal. When all was complete, the family gathered around the kitchen table. What use to be a time of laughter and small talk, was now a time of grim silence. Sadness hung heavily over the entire household. The evening prayers lasted longer that night as every member of the family expressed their concern for Sarah and prayed for her healing.

Following the devotions, Elizabeth prepared a kettle of chicken broth for Sarah. When it was warm, she poured the broth into a bowl.

"May I feed her?" Rebekah begged. "I feel helpless seeing her lying there and not being able to do anything to help. She looks so pathetic and forlorn."

Elizabeth wiped sweat from her brow with the sleeve of her dress. "I'd appreciate that. There's so much that needs to be done and I'm exhausted."

Steam rose from the bowl while Rebekah walked silently to Sarah's bedside. "Sarah, Sarah. Wake up. Thou must have some nourishment."

Sarah roused, opened her eyes, and moaned. Rebekah lifted a spoonful of broth to the sick girl's lips. She cradled Sarah's head with her other hand

and watched her swallow the nourishing liquid. Slowly she lifted another spoonful to the sick girl's lips. Little by little, Sarah more readily accepted the food waiting at her lips. The warmth of the broth seemed to give her strength.

Sarah's eyes moved from family member to family member and back to her caregiver. "I thank thee, Rebekah," she mumbled, and laid back on her pillow, breaking into another fitful cough.

Hearing her daughter's repeated coughing, Elizabeth appeared from the bedchamber with a dark-colored bottle in her hand. "Rebekah, help me give Sarah a spoonful of this," she said softly as she unscrewed the lid. "It will help her cough."

Rebekah wrinkled her nose. "What is it?"

Elizabeth laughed. "It's a mixture of honey and whiskey. My grandmother gave it to my mother when she was sick and my mother use to give it to me. It helped Sarah last winter when she was sick, and I hope it will help her now. Thou wilt have to ignore the smell."

Rebekah helped lift Sarah's head while Elizabeth guided the spoonful of homemade tonic into her daughter's mouth. Rebekah wiped away the drops that fell on Sarah's chin with a damp cloth and offered her a sip of water. Sarah wrinkled her nose, took the water, and lay back onto her pillow. Within minutes, she was asleep.

Elizabeth Reynolds remained at her daughter's bedside until she was certain she was asleep. The lines deepened on her forehead as the minutes passed. When she was certain Sarah was asleep, she turned to Rebekah and her husband. "Her breathing still sounds too shallow. I think we should take turns staying up with her tonight."

Without hesitation, Rebekah said. "I can stay with her all night. Thou both need to rest. I've stayed up many nights with my mother. I'll awaken thee if there is a problem."

Elizabeth and John exchanged amazed glances. "I thank thee," Elizabeth replied. "I appreciate thy offer. If thou wilt stay up tonight, I'll not ask thee to do anything tomorrow so thou can sleep."

After everyone in the Reynolds household had retired, Rebekah sat alone in the darkness, lost in her own thoughts and imagination. The candles flickered throughout the night while she kept vigil at Sarah's bedside. She tried not to think of her home in London, but memories brought tears to her eyes. Even though all the Reynolds, except Sarah, had shown Rebekah their appreciation, she continued to feel as if she were merely a servant girl. *Will I ever feel a part of a family again?*

Every time Sarah awakened, Rebekah spooned more warm chicken broth into her mouth and rinsed her forehead with cool water. As the night wore on,

Rebekah began splashing cold water on her own face to help fight off sleep. It seemed as if dawn would never come.

When the first rays of sunlight shone through the east windows, Elizabeth Reynolds stumbled into the living room wearing her night clothing. A single braid cascaded down her back, making her appear more tired and worn than usual. She paused at the bed by the fireplace and gazed at her sleeping daughter. "How is she doing?"

"She doesn't seem as warm as she did last night," Rebekah said. "She awoke several times during the night and ate a little broth each time."

Elizabeth Reynolds smoothed the covers over her sleeping daughter before turning to Rebekah. "I thank thee for staying up all night with her. Thou look exhausted. As soon as I am dressed, I'll stay with her so thou can get some rest."

Rebekah thanked her and returned to her chair to await her employer's return. She had not realized how hungry she was becoming until Elizabeth emerged from her bedchamber. Rebekah hurriedly ate two pieces of bread, drank a glass of milk, and tiptoed up the wooden staircase so as not to disturb the other Reynolds children. Silently she removed her dress, slipped into her nightgown and collapsed onto her bed. Within moments, she was asleep while the Reynolds family was beginning to awaken.

~~~~~

After checking on her sleeping daughter, Elizabeth Reynolds began preparing mush and bread for the morning meal, always keeping Sarah in her range of vision. While she worked, she feared her heart would break. Her eldest daughter had been sick many times before, but this time was different.

John Reynolds stepped from the bedchamber pulling his suspenders over his shoulders. "Good Morning." He hurried across the room and kissed his wife. "How's Sarah?" he whispered.

"She's still sleeping," Elizabeth Reynolds said. "Her face is not as flushed as last night. I assume that's a good sign, but she's still extremely ill."

"I'll sit with her while thou finish breakfast and get the little ones ready for the day," John Reynolds said. "I wish I could stay home, but there is no one else working at the mercantile today."

Elizabeth Reynolds hurriedly ate a quick meal and tidied the house. Within minutes two-year-old Matthew began shaking the sides of his crib in the corner of the bedchamber.

"Good morning, sleepy head," she said. "Art thou ready for breakfast?"

"Eat... I want to eat," Matthew begged.

"It's almost time for thee to move to the big boy's bedchamber so the new baby can have the crib." Elizabeth Reynolds said as she lifted her son from the crib, hugged him, and set him on the floor. She took Matthew's chubby hand in hers and led him to the kitchen table. "I think I hear the others coming down the stairs."

While Elizabeth Reynolds seated Matthew at the table, Sarah rolled over and moaned. "Mama? . . . Mama?"

She ran to her daughter's side. "I'm here. How art thou?"

"I am hungry."

Elizabeth hugged her daughter with delight. "Praise God. Thou art better," she exclaimed. "I'll be right back with some mush and bread. I'll add a little extra sugar this morning to give thee more energy."

"Mama, didst thou stay with me all night?" Sarah asked. "It was like an angel was with me, holding my hand, and giving me food and water."

"No, dear," Elizabeth Reynolds replied squeezing her daughter's hand. "It was Rebekah who stayed with thee. God must have used her as thy healing angel."

~~~~

Day by day, Sarah's body began to strengthen and life within the Reynolds's household returned to a normal routine. A week later, they were able to dismantle her bed and move it back to the bedchamber Sarah shared with Rebekah and the younger girls. In its place, the Reynolds put a small cot in the corner for other short-term illnesses.

Late Fifth Day afternoon, Rebekah, Sarah, and the younger girls were working in the garden when the familiar wagon turned down the lane with two unknown women riding beside their father. Rebekah stood and used her hand to shield her eyes from the sun. She watched John Reynolds stop the horses near the front of the house, walk to the back of the wagon, and help the women to the ground. He took a heavy bag in each hand and the three engaged in a long conversation.

"Who dost thou think that is?" Sarah whispered to Rebekah.

"I don't know," Rebekah whispered back. "But I wonder if they are the traveling missionaries they were talking about at the First Day Meeting a few weeks ago. Thy father did volunteer for them to stay with us while they were in Philadelphia. I'm looking forward to meeting them."

Ann Bell

"I wish he hadn't done that," Sarah grumbled. "Our house is already too crowded."

Rebekah ignored Sarah's comments. "I've never met a woman missionary before. I don't understand how they can be led by the Inner Light to leave their home in London and come to America by themselves."

Sarah shook her head and handed her garden tools to Rebekah. "I'm going to the house to meet them. I am getting tired anyway. Thou can finish my row."

Rebekah sighed and bit her lip. She hurriedly finished Sarah's row, gathered the tools and the remaining seeds. She turned to the younger children. "I thank thee for all thy help. We are at a good quitting place; maybe we should all go in and help prepare dinner for our guests."

The girls entered the back door of the house at the same time John Reynolds opened the front door and motioned for the two women to enter. They watched as he set their bags on the floor in the corner and smiled at his wife.

"Elizabeth, I'd like you to meet Charity Jones and Hope Jamison. They just arrived in Philadelphia and needed a place to stay."

Elizabeth Reynolds looked up from her mending, smiled, and rose to greet them. "Welcome. It's nice to meet thee. I've heard so much about thee and was looking forward to having thee stay with us."

Both women smiled. "I thank thee for thy hospitality," Charity said. "We're looking forward to sharing the love of God around Philadelphia. It is such a beautiful city."

I'm certain thou wilt enjoy the peace and quiet of Philadelphia," John Reynolds said, unable to mask his pride. "William Penn's holy experiment turned out far better than anyone could have anticipated at the time."

John turned to his wife. "Elizabeth, on the way home the missionaries were telling me how the Puritans ran them out of Massachusetts. They barely escaped with their lives. They were grateful a kindly shipper was willing to bring them to Philadelphia with a load of merchandise."

"The Puritans just don't understand how we must follow the dictates of the Inner Light," Elizabeth Reynolds said. "They seem to think Quakers are listening to some kind of devil instead of God."

Hope Jamison nodded. "How true. There's so much about us they don't understand – like why Quakers consider men and women equal and how women can be missionaries as well as the men."

John wrapped his arm around his wife's shoulder. "I'm glad we're not Puritans," he said with a smile.

[93]

"They consider the man the autocratic head of the family and women only have the rights their husbands permit them to have. Personally, I enjoy decision-making together. Thou bring a lot of wisdom and insight into our family."

Elizabeth Reynolds beamed as her face flushed. "I'm glad thou respect the uniqueness and equality in which God created women," she said. "Because of that, I can follow the Inner Light of the Holy Spirit without fearing thy disapproval nor the disapproval of the Society."

"Thou art wise beyond words." John Reynolds looked around the room. "Where are the boys? We need to have them move their things into the extra room in the barn so the missionaries can use their room. They've always wanted to sleep in the hayloft of the barn close to their new horse, so this is a good time to do that."

"The last I knew, they were helping Moses fix the fence at the far end of the pasture. They should be back soon," Elizabeth Reynolds replied. "Rebekah and I will begin making supper; they should be back before we're finished."

~~~~~

After the evening meal, Mark and Adam could not wait to get to the barn to set up their temporary room. The missionaries unpacked their few possessions in the boys' bedchamber while Elizabeth Reynolds put Baby Matthew to bed. When these tasks were completed, the women returned to the living room.

Unsure if she should retreat to her own bedchamber or boldly remain with the family, Rebekah chose to remain and listen to the missionaries share their adventures.

During a break in the conversation Rebekah murmured, "Someday I'd like to go on missionary trips myself."

Sarah sneered and laid her needlework on her lap. "Thou?" she said sarcastically. "Thou still hast more than four years left in thy servanthood."

Rebekah's jaw tightened. "But someday I'll be free to chart my own course in life and I want to be able to make the right decisions and follow the Inner Light."

"Doesn't thou want to marry and have a family?" Sarah asked. "That is the greatest dream of girls in America."

"Perhaps," Rebekah said shyly, "but I want to be sure I'm doing the right thing. I don't want someone else to make that decision for me. I want to be led by the Inner Light the same as the traveling missionaries are."

Ann Bell

Charity Jones cleared her throat and smiled. "Rebekah, I'm glad thou art interested in serving God as a missionary. It's a noble, but difficult thing to do. When the time is right, God will lead thee."

Only Rebekah saw the demeaning glare Sarah projected toward her. *What do I do now? Do I risk the Reynolds's disapproval or do I try to find out what being a Quaker missionary is all about? I'm certain my father and mother would want me to look out for myself and not always have to be dependent on others.*

Rebekah took a deep breath and said, "Friend Jones, may I ask thee a question?"

"Certainly, my child," the missionary replied with a kindly smile.

"After thee was called to preach, what didst thou have to do to begin thy travels? How didst thou pay for thy food and transportation?" Rebekah asked softly. "Didst thou just pack thy bags and leave and trust God to provide?"

The missionary's laughter was gentle and understanding. "Oh no, it was not nearly that simple," she said. "There's an intensive process of obtaining what is called a traveling minute. People must first change themselves before going out to try to change others. There is a period of local nurture and testing of a vocal ministry. My home meeting regulates me and determines when, and if, I am

[96]

ready to travel to share the gospel. After I felt compelled to travel in the ministry, I had to appear before the ministry committee of my own monthly meeting to plead my case."

Rebekah nervously tucked a loose strand of hair back under her bonnet. "If I'm not being too bold to ask, what kind of things did the committee request of thee? If I ever heard the Inner Voice I wouldn't want people asking me questions I wouldn't be able to answer."

Charity Jones smiled. "When a woman is confident she is doing what the Inner Light commands, she doesn't have to be concerned about the questions others may ask," she said. "The committee I went before discussed my request in light of my health, family duties, and the strength and soundness of my ministry. Only after the local meeting believed all was well, were the quarterly and the yearly meetings consulted."

Rebekah wrinkled her forehead and paused. "That's a long ordeal to go through after someone has been called to preach. It seems like the Society doesn't trust the people who have felt called to become missionaries."

Charity Jones shook her head. "There's a good reason for that kind of interrogation," she said with a gentle voice. "Submitting to the questioning of the local and monthly meetings prevents men and women from wandering about, preaching doctrines

Ann Bell

not in accordance with Friends' beliefs. It tests the strength of the minister's sense of mission."

Rebekah hesitated, making sure she would remember each detail they were telling her. "That makes sense," she finally said. "If thou dost not think I am too bold to ask, I have another question. Do the missionaries have to pay their own passage to travel? If I ever heard the Inner Voice telling me to become a missionary I would never be able to go because I'm an indentured servant and will probably never be able to save enough money to leave Philadelphia."

Charity Jones gave Rebekah a reassuring smile. "Have faith in God and He'll direct thy path. After thou fulfill thy indentured servant contract, thou wilt be able to answer the Call if it happens."

"But if I do receive a call and the approval of the local meeting, how would I go about traveling from place to place?" Rebekah asked shyly. "Would I need my own horse?"

The missionaries exchanged knowing glances. "This is how the procedure works," Charity Jones explained. "Once a minister has been provided with what is called a minute to travel in the ministry, her home meetings are responsible for her expenses. The meetings she visits are expected to provide hospitality and money for the return voyage. Rest assured, Quakers abound with hospitality. The main problem is non-Quakers misunderstand our purpose."

"Friend Jones, I think I've felt the Inner Voice calling me to travel to Rhode Island to preach," Sarah interrupted. "I could go right away. Could I travel with thee and not go through all the questioning? I'm certain the elders would approve me. I am a good person."

Charity Jones shifted her attention from Rebekah to Sarah. An amused twist appeared in the corner of her mouth. "Thou need to continue to pray about it. Hope Jamison and I just came from Rhode Island where we faced a great deal of persecution. The people in that colony have never accepted the Friends. That is why William Penn started his Holy Experiment here in Philadelphia. Quakers are loved and protected here. One must be extremely strong to face the persecution of the Puritans."

From the corner of her eye, Rebekah noticed Sarah give her a jealous glare before protesting further. "I am very strong. My family just worries too much about my health."

"Sarah, I'm glad thy physical condition has improved." Charity Jones said. "My suggestion is to continue attending the weekly and monthly meetings. Fourth Day we will be speaking in the park to the non-convinced. Maybe thou wouldst like to join us. It is important for the Birthright Quakers to help the non-convinced seek the Inner Light.

Ann Bell

Nothing is more fulfilling than to see the non-convinced become Convinced Quakers."

Sarah wrinkled her brow. "I usually don't attend the meetings unless I have to. I hate to sit in silence and wait. I want to be doing things."

A knowing smile spread across the missionaries' faces. "Thy reaction is common among many young people," Charity Jones said. "The first discipline a Quaker must learn is to be silent and seek the Inner Light before doing the work of God. One doesn't have to become a traveling missionary to serve God. Thou can serve God by taking care of the sick, feeding the poor, and tending to the needy children."

Everyone sat in silence for several minutes. The embers burnt low in the fireplace. Finally, Hope Jamison broke the stillness. "I'm extremely weary and need to get some rest. Could I read a portion of scripture before we go to bed?"

"Most certainly," John Reynolds said. "We would be honored."

After she read scripture, Hope led the family in prayer. A sense of love and warmth engulfed the group. They exchanged embraces and each retreated to their individual bedchambers. Rebekah and Sarah tiptoed into the room they shared with the younger girls and slipped into their nightclothes without saying a word.

[100]

The girls lay in the dark for some time before Sarah whispered. "I don't understand why thou stayed to talk to the missionaries. Thou art not part of the family. Thou art just an indentured servant. I don't think the Inner Light would call an indentured servant to be a missionary when others more qualified are ready to go."

Tears filled Rebekah's eyes and she turned her head toward the wall. *I'm certain God loves me as much as He loves those who have had fewer difficulties in their lives. Why does Sarah say such cruel things? I've tried so hard to please her.*

Ann Bell

Five

Second Month 1717

"Rebekah, wake up. I need thy help," John Reynolds whispered, unable to mask his panic.

Rebekah rubbed her eyes and sat up in bed. Her employer's tall frame blocked the faint moonlight streaming through the window in the girls' bedchamber. She jerked to alertness. "What's wrong?"

"Elizabeth is having severe pains. I think the baby is coming."

Rebekah jumped to her feet. "But the baby's not due for another six weeks."

"That's what is frightening," he said as he retreated toward the doorway. "Get dressed while I awaken Adam and Mark. They'll have to take the horse to get Doctor Browning. I wish Moses was still with us, so the boys wouldn't have to venture out in the dark."

Rebekah heard heavy footsteps followed by two lighter ones run down the staircase as she pulled her gray linen dress over her head. The other three sleeping forms did not stir as she hurried from the bedchamber. The boys disappeared out the front door to the stable the same time as she stepped into the main room.

Bursting into her employers' bedchamber, Rebekah saw Elizabeth Reynolds lying on the bed perspiring and racked with pain. "How is she?"

"She's beginning to drift in and out of consciousness," John Reynolds said holding his wife's hand. "Take the lantern and go to the well and get more water."

Rebekah shuddered at the thought of making the long trip to the well in the dark, but her concern for Elizabeth Reynolds conquered her fears. Grabbing the lantern from the wall, she lit it and rushed outside. All was eerily silent except for the distant clopping of the horse bearing the two Reynolds boys. *Please, God, help us know what to do. Don't let Elizabeth Reynolds suffer or anything happen to the baby.*

Setting the lantern on the ground, Rebekah lowered the pail into the well. A distant splashing sound echoed up the deep shaft. In spite of the cold, sweat flowed down her forehead. It took nearly all her strength to turn the crank and raise the full bucket. Within moments, the shadow of the bucket was before her. Taking the lantern in one hand and the pail of water in the other, she hurried toward the house.

She set the bucket on the kitchen table and opened the door to the bedchamber; John Reynolds was still holding his wife's hand. "How is she?"

John Reynolds shook his head. "I don't know. I wish Doctor Browning would hurry. She's in a lot of pain."

"I remember when my brothers were born; the midwife needed a lot of boiling water," Rebekah said. "I'll fill the kettle and hang it over the fireplace."

Rebekah hurried to the kitchen and poured the water from the bucket into the black kettle on the hearth. After she stoked the fire and added more wood, she took the pail and returned to the well. When the pail was refilled, she hurried back to the house. While she was returning from the well bearing the third pail of water, she heard galloping horses in the distance. She waited on the path until the riders neared.

Doctor Browning jumped from his horse taking his saddlebag with him. He handed the reins to Adam and rushed toward the house. Rebekah tried to keep pace. "Thou must be Rebekah," he said. "Where can I find Elizabeth Reynolds?"

Rebekah motioned to him. "Follow me."

Doctor Browning took the pail of water from her and the pair sprinted up the path to the Reynolds's home. When they opened the front door, a loud moan from the bedchamber greeted them. Doctor Browning set the bucket beside the door and rushed to his patient's side.

Seeing the doctor, John Reynolds extended his trembling hand. "I thank thee for coming in the middle of the night. She seems to be slipping fast and is in a lot of pain."

Doctor Browning shook John's sweating hand while he patted him on the shoulder. "Wouldst thou mind waiting outside while I examine thy wife? Rebekah will be able to be my assistant."

John Reynolds nodded. "Let me know if there is anything I can do," he muttered with resignation. "I'm certain the children will need me. I'll awaken Sarah and help her start breakfast."

Through the coming hours, Rebekah remained by Elizabeth Reynolds's side, comforting her when she could, and following Doctor Browning's directions explicitly. By midmorning, Doctor Browning shook his head with frustration. "I'm sorry. I don't think I'll be able to save the baby. The best I'll be able to do is try to save the mother."

Within minutes the smallest baby Rebekah had ever seen was born. The newborn did not struggle for breath, but lay limply in the doctor's hands. "Get me the baby blanket from the baby's bed," Doctor Browning directed motioning to the crib in the corner of the room. He wrapped the baby gently in the blanket.

"Is the baby all right?" Elizabeth Reynolds whispered.

Doctor Browning took a deep breath. "I'm sorry, but your son's little lungs were not strong enough to work. He is with the Lord," he said solemnly.

Elizabeth Reynolds closed her eyes. "May I say goodbye to him?"

Doctor Browning laid the tiny bundle in his mother's arms. Tears rolled down her cheeks as she cradled the infant against her breast. In a few moments, she closed her eyes from exhaustion and the doctor took the premature infant from her. He gently laid the child in a wooden box that hours before had been under the bed, full of baby clothing.

The Reynolds family was huddled around the hearth when Rebekah and Doctor Browning emerged from the bedchamber. John Reynolds jumped to his feet. "How is she?"

"Elizabeth is sleeping now. She has lost a lot of blood, but I expect she will fully recover. However,

Ann Bell

she will need a lot of rest. All we can do now is pray."

"And the baby?" John Reynolds asked, scarcely able to control his quivering voice.

Doctor Browning cleared his throat. "It was a beautiful baby boy, but his lungs were not developed, and he did not take a single breath. I'm sorry. I wish I could have done more."

Each of the Reynolds children was crying as they followed their father into the bedchamber. They lovingly gazed at their sleeping mother. "Mamma's sleeping," two-and a-half-year-old Matthew whispered. "She's sick."

John Reynolds leaned down and picked up his youngest son. "Yes, thy mother is sleeping. We'll all need to take good care of her until she's better."

Matthew's eyes were wide with confusion. "When will the baby come?" he asked. "I want to see my new brother."

"The baby arrived this morning," John Reynolds explained, "but he couldn't stay. He went straight to heaven." A bewildered look crossed Matthew's face. "God will be taking care of the baby instead of thy mother." John Reynolds held his youngest son tightly against his chest, trying not to upset him any more than necessary.

The older children stood in silence, while the little ones wandered aimlessly around the room. John Reynolds did his best to comfort them, but tears ran unashamedly down his own cheeks.

Seeing that there was nothing more he could do for the sleeping mother, Doctor Browning turned to the grieving father. "Wouldst thou like me to make burial arrangements in the cemetery behind the meetinghouse?"

"I would appreciate that. I don't know where to begin in arranging burials," John sighed. "I thank thee for all thou hast done for us. I do not know what I would have done without thee." The men walked slowly to the door in silence. With his voice trembling, John Reynolds said. "Please come by the mercantile any day and I will pay thee with whatever supplies thou need."

~~~~

Elizabeth Reynolds remained in bed for the next month while Rebekah readily reorganized the household and assigned tasks to each one of the children, including little Matthew. Much to Rebekah's surprise, Sarah cheerfully attacked her tasks with enthusiasm and vigor. All traces of her long illness had faded into a blurred memory. Her resentment toward Rebekah seemed to subside.

Ann Bell

After fourteen months in America, Rebekah finally felt a part of the Reynolds family. However, every night her mind would drift back to her family in London. *How is my mother's health? How are my brothers? Are they going to school and learning to read? Are they learning a trade?* She would lie on her bed and pray for each one before falling asleep.

The weeks passed slowly. The buds finally began to appear on the trees and the wild flowers could be seen in the fields. Philadelphia became alive with spring-cleaning and gardening. Day by day, Elizabeth Reynolds regained her strength and started sharing in the family chores once again.

One Sixth Day afternoon when John Reynolds returned from work at the mercantile, he kissed his wife and hugged each of the children more enthusiastically than normal. "Richard Logan and I were talking today, and we both agree this is the most beautiful spring we've ever seen," he said as he lifted Matthew into his arms. "We thought it would be extremely pleasurable after the Society Meeting tomorrow to take our families to an outing in the clearing in the woods northeast of town. It's a beautiful location right on the Delaware River. It will do thy mother good to get out of the house and enjoy the fresh air."

The children gathered around their father. Excitement filled the room, "That would be perfect. I love going to the woods," Sarah exclaimed. "Rebekah and I could fix the food."

The boys' faces beamed. "Adam and I can take our fishing rods," Mark said. "We might be able to catch enough fish for the evening meal."

Lillian turned to her sister Mary. "We'll get to play with Ruth."

Elizabeth surveyed her smiling children one by one. "I don't think we have any disagreement in this family," she said with a laugh. "This will be my coming out day. It will be good to smell the fresh air again after lying in bed for over a month."

Everyone helped decide what to take to eat. Rebekah and Sarah worked in the kitchen far into the night preparing the food. An air of anticipation filled the house. The thought of an afternoon without work or study, to relax and enjoy the beauty of nature was a treat worth savoring.

Following the Society Meeting, the next afternoon the three Logans crowded into the back of the Reynolds's wagon along with the six Reynolds children and Rebekah. John Reynolds drove the horses down the narrow path to the clearing a few miles out of town. When they arrived, he found a large twisted shade tree with a low hanging branch to wrap the reins around. He had scarcely stopped the wagon before the children leaped from the sides. They scampered through the grass to the river flowing at the base of the hill. After being confined

[111]

during the long winter months, this was their first excursion to enjoy the coming of spring.

Naomi and John Logan insisted that Elizabeth Reynolds rest while the others busied themselves spreading out the blankets and arranging the meal. Before they had a chance to summon the family, Adam looked up from the riverbank and saw the food. He let out a shout, "Let's eat!" The children dropped everything and raced to the blankets.

Seeing his children's excitement, John Reynolds held up his hand to halt them. "One moment please," he reminded them. "Before anyone eats, we need to first thank God for our many blessings."

Instinctively, the children paused and bowed their heads while their father led them in prayer. When the prayer was completed, the children reached for the bread, cheese, fresh carrots, and apple pie. Amid a great deal of chatter and laughter, within minutes, the food was completely devoured.

For Rebekah, the fresh air seemed to add extra flavor to each bite of food she took. She watched Sarah lead the younger ones to the river where they took off their shoes and socks and began wading in the cool water. *The only thing more beautiful than Pennsylvania in the springtime would be a day in London with my family.*

Rebekah and Naomi Logan loaded the plates and utensils into the wagon while Elizabeth rested on the blanket. When they finished, Friend Logan motioned to her. "Rebekah, come and sit with us. There is something we'd like to discuss with thee."

What could this be about, she thought as she promptly obeyed and took a seat on the corner of the blanket. *Am I in some sort of trouble?*

Richard Logan stretched his long legs onto the grass. "Rebekah, tell me about thy brothers. Thou rarely speak of them."

Rebekah closed her eyes and tried to visualize what her brothers might look like now. Her eyes became distant. "Samuel was five and Joseph was seven when our father was killed," she said with a touch of melancholy. "Joseph was named after our father and looks much like him. Mother used to say that with his seriousness and hard work he would someday become a great leader in the Quaker Society. Samuel was always the fun loving one. He had a way of always making us laugh."

"Dost thou know where they are living now?" Richard Logan asked. "Has any one written thee?"

Rebekah shook her head. "When I left London, Martha Miller, one of the Friends in our Society who lived across the street from us, took them into her home, but I have not heard from anyone since that time. I hope they've been able to go to school. Learning to read was extremely important to our father. Why dost thou ask?"

[113]

"I'm in need of a couple boys to help around my store," Richard Logan said. "I'll be leaving for London on business soon and was considering checking with thy mother to see if they would also like to come to America as indentured servants. Thou would no longer have to be separated from thy family."

Tears filled Rebekah's eyes. She thought of her brothers, their constant activity, and their eager laughter. Having them close by was more than she could dare to dream. "I'd like that very much," she murmured. "I'll write a letter to mother and the boys that thou can hand carry and encourage them to come back with thee. I want them to know what a land of opportunity America is. When wilt thou leave?"

"I plan to depart within the next week and hope to dock in London by the first of Eighth Month," Richard Logan said. "I'll check with the Quaker Society there. I'm certain someone will know where to locate thy family. If all goes well, I'll have my business completed and be back home with thy brothers before Christmas."

Rebekah leaned over and embraced Richard, tears flowed unashamedly down her cheeks. "I could never thank thee enough. I'll pray every night for thy safe return with my brothers." Rebekah hesitated. A distant gaze blanketed her face. "Please give mother my love. I miss her so."

[114]

"I'll make sure thy mother is well cared for," Richard Logan promised, "and will check to see if there's money enough for her medicines. She has suffered greatly and deserves all the love and support the Quaker societies can give her."

After further plans were discussed, the adults spent the remainder of the afternoon stretched out on the green clover napping while the children fished or waded in the river. Rebekah laid on her back staring into the clouds. Each one took on the shape of a different animal as it drifted lazily across the sky. This was the most relaxed she had felt since her father was killed so many years before. Now there was a possibility of seeing her brothers again. Truly, God is good.

Richard Logan's voyage to London was uneventful. The seas were calm and there was suitable food for the entire trip. Four months after the spring outing in the woods with the Reynolds, he slipped quietly into the back seat of the High Street Quaker Society Meeting in London. He scanned the group wondering which one might have information about how to locate Mary Bradford and her two sons. He listened to the Friends pray, read from the Bible, and tell how God had answered their prayers, but the Bradford family was always paramount on his mind.

[115]

When the meeting was over, he approached the leader of the Society. "Excuse me," he began cautiously. "I'm Richard Logan from Philadelphia. Wouldst thou be able to direct me to someone who knows the whereabouts of Mary Bradford and her two sons, Joseph and Samuel?"

The short, balding man smiled and extended his right hand. "Welcome to our meeting. We are always anxious to have those outside our local meeting worship with us. My name is Joshua Evans. I may be able to help thee find Mary Bradford. If thou will join my wife and me for dinner and I will give thee the details I know."

"I thank thee for thy kindness. I would like that very much." Richard Logan breathed a sigh of relief and followed Joshua Evans down the path from the meetinghouse toward his waiting wagon.

~~~~~

After twelve weeks of food onboard ship, the tastes and smells of Phoebe Evans's home-cooked meal increased Richard Logan's appetite in a way he had not experienced since leaving home. He devoured three portions of thick stew, bread, and sweet cakes while continually thanking his host and hostess for their hospitality. The Evanses were anxious to hear news of the Quaker Society in Philadelphia. Although Richard Logan wanted to discuss the location and condition of the Bradford family, he patiently answered their questions about life in Philadelphia and the spiritual condition of their local meetings.

After the meal, Phoebe Evans cleared the table and washed the dishes while Joshua and Richard Logan retreated to the front porch. They continued sharing the activities of the London Society and the latest developments of the Philadelphia Annual Meeting for another half hour before they turned to the reason for the visit.

"Joseph Bradford was a fine man," Joshua Evans said. "He was willing to die rather than surrender his religious principles. It was a tragic situation. Since Joseph's death, his wife, Mary, has been moved from home to home to be cared for by different women of the Society. We are not certain where the boys are. Their daughter, Rebekah, went to America as an indentured servant and no one has heard from her since."

Richard Logan leaned back in his chair and smiled. "I'm well acquainted with Rebekah. She works for a good friend of mine named John Reynolds. Rebekah has been extremely concerned about her mother and brothers. Since I was coming to London on business, I promised her I would try to find them and bring her brothers to join her in Philadelphia."

Joshua Evans shook his head sadly. "Rebekah's mother will not be hard to find. She's now living with Widow Blackman just a few blocks from here." He paused and his eyes became distant. "But finding the boys would be more difficult. Soon after they went to live with the Miller family, the Millers were arrested on charges of failure to bow before the king and were sentenced to ten years in jail. The boys were taken to an orphanage and no one knows which one. There are scores of orphanages in London, and I wouldn't know where to begin to look for them."

"Orphanages are the worst place possible for any of our Quaker children," said Richard Logan. "We always look after our own and it's unfair for the state to take them away from our community." He set his jaw and took a deep breath. "I'll try to locate them, regardless of the cost."

The lines on Joshua Evan's face deepened. "The children were taken before we knew what happened to them," he said defensively. "One of our women was able to locate them soon after they were taken, but before we could get them back they were moved to another orphanage."

"Give me a few days and I'll see what I can do," Richard Logan said with determination. "In the meantime, the sun is beginning to set. I had better get back to the inn. I don't want to lose my way in the dark."

"Let me walk with thee," Joshua Evans offered. "I'm extremely familiar with the city."

"I thank thee for thy offer, but that will not be necessary. I think I'll be able to find the way myself." Richard Logan rose to leave. "I need a good night's sleep before I begin my search. They say child slave labor is rampant in London, but I will find them even if I have to turn this city upside down."

He paused to collect his thoughts. "My first stop is to visit with Mary Bradford and give her the letter Rebekah wrote to her. She needs to know what a wonderful young woman she reared."

"Let me know if thou find the boys," Joshua said as he walked Richard to the end of his street. "They deserve better than growing up in an orphanage."

~~~~~

Early the next morning, Richard Logan hurried down the cluttered, dirty, narrow street toward Widow Blackman's home. Dogs and chickens ambled in the pathway ahead of him. The smell of decaying food overwhelmed him. *No wonder disease is rampant here,* he thought. *I miss the wide, clean streets of Philadelphia.*

Stopping at a small, brown frame house on the corner, Richard rapped on the door. Moments later a frail, gray-haired woman opened the door. "May I help thee?"

"Art thou Friend Blackman?"

"Yes," the woman replied, cautiously surveying the tall stranger.

"Art thou caring for a woman named Mary Bradford?"

"Yes. How didst thou know?"

"My name is Richard Logan, and I am from Philadelphia. I know Mary Bradford's daughter, Rebekah, and bring a letter from her."

Widow Blackman's face broke into a broad smile. "Come in. Please come in. Mary will be extremely glad to meet thee." She motioned for her guest to follow her.

When he entered the small, yet tidy home, he was led to a small room in the back. A frail grey-haired form lay on a bed in the corner covered by a tattered quilt. Sister Blackman went to the window and opened the curtains. Narrow rays of light flooded the room through a soot-covered window. "Mary... Mary," she said softly. "Thou hast a guest from America."

The woman opened her eyes and tried to lift her head from the pillow. "Hello," she said with a puzzled look on her face. "How didst thou know who I am?"

"Hello." He reached out his hand to shake hers. "My name is Richard Logan and I'm from Philadelphia. I know thy daughter, Rebekah, and brought thee a letter from her. Wouldst thou like to read it or wouldst thou rather have me read it to thee?"

"Thou know Rebekah . . . Thou know Rebekah," the frail woman whispered excitedly. Tears filled her eyes and flowed unashamedly down her cheeks. "Please read the letter to me," she begged. "I haven't been able to see well since I've been ill."

Richard reached into his coat pocket and took out a crumpled envelope. He gingerly took it from the envelope and unfolded it with awe and reverence. He read the letter slowly and respectfully as if he were reading the Holy Bible itself.

Hearing the words of love and compassion from a young girl in a distant land who longed for her mother and brothers brought tears to everyone's eyes. In her letter, Rebekah begged for her brothers to join her in Philadelphia, the most beautiful place on earth. She poured out her love for her mother and gratefulness for the care she had given her when she was a child, in spite of the difficult circumstance.

A vibrant glow spread over Mary Bradford's pale face when Richard Logan finished reading the letter. "I can now die peacefully knowing my

Ann Bell

daughter is having a good life," she said. "I'm not able to travel to be with her, but maybe someday her brothers will be able to join their sister in America."

"Dost thou know where thy sons are living?" Richard asked.

Mary Bradford shook her head. "The last place I knew where they were was in an orphanage on Fifth Street. They were working long hours in a factory when one of the Quaker women accidentally ran across them. When she returned the next day to get them, they had been moved to another location and no one would tell them where they were."

Richard Logan had been warned of such news, but he refused to be deterred. "If I can find them, wouldst thou be willing to sign the papers so they could work for me until they reach the age of eighteen? I would make sure they went to school and got a good education," he said. "Education is an important part of our life in Philadelphia."

Mary Bradford took the Quaker gentleman's hand. Tears filled her eyes. "Thou art an answer to my prayers," she said. "I've lain on this bed month after month praying that someday my children would be together again. They deserve a better life than what has happened to them here in London."

"I'll do the best I can to help," Richard Logan promised as he patted the top of her hand. "Please pray for my search. It could prove to be most difficult."

"I will pray for thee constantly. I appreciate anything thou canst do to help," Mary Bradford said. The lines of worry and fear faded from her face as hope returned to her spirit.

Richard glanced out the dirty bedchamber window. "I'll return in a few days to let thee know if I found the boys or not. In the meantime, thou need to get some rest. It has been a very tiring day for thee."

Widow Blackman escorted her guest to the front door and thanked him profusely. Richard Logan returned the gratitude and stepped into a drizzling rain. He retraced his steps to the inn through litter-filled London streets. *Finding two young boys in a city of this magnitude would be like finding a gold coin on a sandy beach*, he thought. *However, I will give it my best effort. It is the only hope the poor family had to be reunited.*

Ann Bell

Six

London, Sixth Month 1717

Richard Logan walked silently down the narrow hallway of the Cross Bow Inn. The low rumble of snoring resonated through the thin walls of tiny rooms on both sides of him. *I hope none of the sleeping men are robbers,"* he thought. *All the money I have for restocking the mercantile for an entire year is in the lining of my coat. It would be easy for someone to overpower me and take it.*

The aroma of baking bread drew him toward the hearth in the dining room. As he entered, the innkeeper's wife was taking bread from the oven above the hearth. A scowl covered her face. "If you'd like some tea, bread, and cheese, sit at the table in the corner," she said dryly.

"I thank thee," Richard Logan replied. "I'm very hungry."

He crossed the room, pulled out the high-back chair from behind the bare wooden table in the far corner, and sat down. While he waited, he surveyed the humble surroundings. The cooking utensils hung on

Ann Bell

hooks around the fireplace. Shelves of food and dishes lined the wall next to the hearth. The innkeeper's wife hurriedly sliced freshly baked bread on a wooden table beside the hearth. The sound of snoring continued while the innkeeper's wife set a plate of food in front of Richard Logan without saying a word. The scowl had deepened on her face.

"I thank thee," he said. "This is very kind."

She nodded, but said nothing.

"Dost thou know where the Fifth Street Orphanage is?" he asked. "I'm trying to find two Quaker boys who were separated from their family two years ago."

The innkeeper's wife stopped and turned abruptly. "Yes, I know where the Fifth Street Orphanage is located, but you don't want to go there. That part of town is full of thieves and robbers."

"But I must find the boys," Richard Logan protested. "The family has suffered so much and needs to be reunited."

"If those boys have spent any time at all in the Fifth Street Orphanage you won't want to find them. It's a breeding ground for little criminals and pick-pockets."

"But these boys were from a good Quaker family. I am certain God would have protected them. Please, wouldst thou give me the directions?"

~~~~

A half-hour after leaving the inn, Richard Logan crossed the Thames River. As he neared Fifth Street, the stench from the garbage in the street became unbearable. He placed his hand over his nose and desperately wished he hadn't forgotten his handkerchief. Pigs wandered aimlessly about. Dogs snarled as he passed. Children delighted in playing in the mud. One threw a rock into a puddle and laughed when the mud splattered onto the leg of his trousers.

Gradually he made his way to the corner of Fifth and Baker Streets, where a large wooden house stood surrounded by a six-foot metal fence. Richard Logan took a deep breath and forced open the rusty latch on the gate. He cautiously approached the house and knocked on the door. After a long wait, a stern-looking man opened the door of the orphanage a few inches.

"Who are you? What do you want?"

"Good morning," Richard Logan said. "I'm trying to locate two boys by the name of Joseph and Samuel Bradford. Are they living at this fine establishment?"

"I've never heard of anyone by that name."

The door started to close. Richard Logan placed his boot in the crack. He reached into his pocket and took out a handful of shillings. "Now dost thou remember the boys?"

The door widened. The man's eyes sparkled while he counted the coins in Richard Logan's outstretched hand. "Hmmm... Now that you mention it, I do remember a couple of Bradford brothers. They were worthless and were moved to the orphanage on Thames Street several months ago. They were disobedient and will never amount to anything." He reached for the money in Richard's hand.

Richard handed the man the coins. "I thank thee for thy help," he said. When he turned to leave, a mangy brown dog came around the corner of the house growling and baring his teeth. His heart pounded as he increased his pace and focused on the metal gate. He had scarcely closed the gate behind him when the dog raced toward him and lunged at the gate, its teeth barely missing his hand.

Breathing a sigh of relief, Richard Logan trudged slowly down the same street, trying to regain his composure. *Are the boys really at the Thames Street Orphanage,* he pondered, *or was the man just trying to make a profit by taking the money?*

He wandered the neighborhood streets for another hour. He remembered seeing Thames Street soon after he crossed the river, but now he could not remember where it was. The streets seemed to wind in different directions, without reason. He wanted to seek directions from the men loitering in the nearby yards, but was afraid his Quaker attire would make him a ready target for mischief.

After two hours of wondering, Richard finally located the Thames Orphanage. He walked bravely to the front door and rapped loudly. Again, he was facing a stern-looking man in a doorway. "May I speak with the headmaster?" he asked politely.

"I'm the headmaster. What do you want?"

"Dost thou have two boys living here named Joseph and Samuel Bradford?"

The headmaster coldly surveyed him from head to foot. "What if there are?"

"I've been sent by their family to take them home."

The headmaster shook his head adamantly. "The boys are too valuable for me to lose. They put out twice the work than the others do. If I let them go, there will be a price."

Richard Logan felt rage rising in his chest. The children were being sold as common slaves, and he was trapped. He was again forced to delve into the money intended to be used to buy supplies. Without hesitation, he reached into his pocket, took out a handful of coins, and held them out. "I'm willing to buy their freedom."

The headmaster eyed the coins in Richard's hand. "That's not nearly enough."

He reached into another pocket and took out another handful of coins. "I think this should be enough or should I report thee to the officials for child slavery?"

The headmaster's eyes brightened, as he reached for the money. After counting the coins in his hand, he opened the door wider and motioned for Richard to enter. "Come into my office and I'll get the boys."

Richard Logan followed the plump, graying headmaster into an elegantly decorated room with floral carpeting, velvet drapes, and handcrafted furniture. He remained silent while the headmaster motioned for him to be seated on the padded chair by the window, and disappeared through a side door.

Fear and doubt began to stir within Richard Logan. *After taking the money, will he actually give me the Bradford boys or will he try to pass off any boys of the same age of the Bradfords? Would they have been abused as badly as the innkeeper's wife suggested? What if they're afraid to come with me?*

Time passed and no one reappeared. Fears continued to haunt Richard Logan as he shifted nervously in the chair as he watched out the window at the livestock roaming freely throughout the yard. Finally, twenty minutes later, the headmaster returned accompanied by two skinny boys with dirty faces and tousled hair.

Richard Logan examined their ragged clothes and sunken eyes. "Joseph? Samuel?" he asked.

The boys nodded; their faces expressionless.

Still not trusting that the headmaster brought him the right boys, he continued his questioning. "Dost thou remember what thy mother's name is?"

"Mary," they responded in unison.

"What was thy father's name?"

"Joseph. I was named after him," the eldest boy replied, unable to mask his pride.

"Didst thou have any other brothers or sisters?"

"We have a sister named Rebekah," Joseph replied softly. "She had to go to America after father died."

Richard Logan felt the lump in his throat grow. He stepped forward and tried to hug both boys at the same time while they stood motionless. "My name is Richard Logan from Philadelphia in far away

[131]

America. I know thy sister, Rebekah. I'm here to take thee to thy mother."

The boys exchanged bewildered glances. "Our mother is dead. How do we know who thou really are? Thou couldst be wearing Quaker clothes and using Quaker speech, but are not a Quaker in thy heart. Thou wilt probably beat us the way the others have." Joseph grew more defiant with each word.

"Thou can trust me. I am truly a Quaker like thy parents," Richard Logan explained. "If I wasn't, how would I know the names of thy family? Quakers always take care of their own people and I'm here to help thee. The officials deceived thy neighbors and took thee away when they went to jail. That is why thee ended up in an orphanage. The local Society has been looking for thee ever since."

The headmaster pointed toward the door and snarled. "Don't talk so much. Just go."

Richard Logan smiled at the boys. "Dost thou have any personal items thou need to get?"

The boys shook their heads. Their dirty, ill-fitting clothing spoke volumes.

"Let's be on our way to meet thy mother. She's anxious to see thee again."

Richard Logan opened the door for the boys, and followed them into the bright sunlight. A feeling of exhilaration enveloped him. *I've accomplished the nearly impossible. With the help of God, I was able to find Rebekah's brothers. It was truly a miracle.*

When they turned the first corner, Joseph mumbled, "Where art thou taking us? Our mother is dead. The headmaster told us so."

"No, thy mother is very much alive. A woman named Widow Blackman has been caring for her for the last few years. She is gravely ill and seeing her sons would be an answer to her prayers."

Samuel glared at him. "I don't believe thee," he shouted. "Thou just want to take us and make us work for you like everyone else has." With those words, Samuel glanced at his brother and started running. Joseph was fast on his heels.

Within a few yards, Richard caught up with them. "Boys, thou hast to trust me. I'm here to help thee."

The boys ignored him and darted right at the next corner. Richard increased his pace but to no avail. He was beginning to fall further and further behind them. His lungs burned and the calves of his legs tightened and ached. *Surely, God did not bring me this far to let me down now. If I lose the boys now they'll be lost to the criminal infested streets of London forever.*

Suddenly, a painful scream penetrated his perplexing thoughts. A few yards down the side

[133]

alley, he saw one of the boys on the ground and the other stooping over him.

Richard Logan raced to his side and knelt beside the mud-splattered, sobbing child. "Please let me help. What hurts? I'm truly here to take thee to thy mother."

Muddy water ran into the corner of Samuel's mouth. "M…m…my leg hurts," he stammered between sobs.

Richard Logan ran his hands carefully down both of the boy's legs. "Your legs do not seem to be broken, but it does appear thy ankle is sprained. When the sting goes away, I'll help thee stand." Richard sat in the mud, cradled the boy's head in his lap, and waited for a few minutes before he put his arm around Samuel's waist and lifted him to his feet. When Samuel put weight on his right leg, he again screamed with pain.

Ignoring his own discomfort, Richard Logan scooped the muddy boy into his arms. The mud from the boy's clothing was soon clinging to Richard's crisp, proper Quaker attire. Samuel laid his head against Richard's shoulder and continued sobbing.

"Things will work out," Richard promised as he stroked the boy's hair. "I'll take thee to the Cross Bow Inn and get thee cleaned up before I take thee to thy mother."

The boys said nothing as the trio trudged down the alley, turned left, and walked the five blocks to the Thames River. Before crossing the bridge, Richard Logan set Samuel on a large rock on the bank. "Let's rest for a few minutes. Thou both must be tired."

Joseph lay on the rocky bank, spread out his arms and legs and breathed deeply. "I am thirsty and hungry. It seems like we have been walking forever."

"I feel exactly the same," Richard Logan said and turned his attention to the younger brother. "Samuel, wouldst thou be more comfortable lying on the ground? I'd like to take another look at thy ankle."

Without saying a word, Samuel slid onto the ground. Richard carefully slipped the boy's shoe from his foot and gingerly touched the red, swollen ankle. Samuel grimaced each time Richard exerted pressure on the inside of the right ankle. "Looks like a mighty bad sprain. I'll need to carry thee the rest of the way."

Samuel nodded and closed his eyes.

Ann Bell

~~~~

For the next hour, time became a blur for the threesome. Finally, the inn came into view and they increased their pace. "Boys, this is the Cross Bow Inn where I slept last night. Maybe the innkeeper's wife will let us bathe. I will buy food for thee." Richard Logan said, shifting Samuel's weight in his arms.

Richard Logan rapped on the door with his foot. They waited in silence. Seconds seemed like hours. His body ached from the long walk carrying a seven-year-old child.

Finally, they heard a latch being lifted on the other side of the plank door and the innkeeper's wife appeared in the doorway. She surveyed the muddy boys. "So, you're back," she snarled. "I see you found the boys in the orphanage."

"Yes, God was good to us and I was able to locate them," Richard Logan replied, trying to ignore her briskness. "Samuel fell and sprained his ankle and isn't able to walk. May we have a room so we could rest, clean up, and have a warm meal?"

The scowl on woman's face deepened. "I should say not. I don't want thieving boys in my reputable establishment. You'll have to look elsewhere."

Richard felt his face turn red as he tried to control his anger. "These are fine Quaker boys who are in need of assistance."

"Not here. Not if they spent time at the Fifth Street Orphanage. Everyone knows that place is a training ground for thieves and murderers." With that, she stepped back and slammed the door.

The three exchanged exasperated glances. The sliding of the latch sent shivers down Richard's spine.

"What do we do now?" Samuel asked, scarcely able to choke back his tears. "I'm hungry. At least there was food to eat at the orphanage."

Richard Logan looked down at the boy in his arms with surprise. He had scarcely heard Samuel speak since the boys had run away from him after they left the orphanage. "Don't worry. I met a Quaker family at the First Day Meeting of the local Society. I had dinner with them and I'm certain they will help us. The bad thing is we will have to walk another half hour."

Both boys sighed with resignation. Richard hoisted Samuel onto his other shoulder. They turned and began trudging down the street once more. At least this part of town was not as dirty as the other side of the Thames, and the children and women in the yards they passed did not look upon them with suspicion. Richard Logan's arms ached from the

[137]

Ann Bell

weight of the injured child, but he dared not complain. He had to remain focused on the joy of finding the boys, not his physical discomfort. He had only walked this way once and he was not certain he would remember the way. The shadows were lengthening when they turned a corner by a well-groomed house. He breathed a sigh of relief. The house at the end of the block looked familiar. In spite of his fatigue, Richard Logan increased his pace. Suddenly a woman emerged from the house and came running toward them.

"Friend Logan, praise God. Thou found the Bradford brothers," Phoebe Evans shouted.

Her words echoed up and down the street. People began streaming from each of the houses along the street to see what the excitement was. Looks of confusion turned to expressions of joy as they joined their neighbor.

Within moments, Joshua Evans was running to catch up with his wife. "Congratulations for finding the boys," he shouted to Richard as he approached them. "Truthfully, I never thought thou wouldst be able to do it. Let me carry the boy." He lifted the child carefully from Richard's arms and examined the boy's mud-covered face and sunken eyes. "You must be Samuel."

The child nodded shyly, but did not speak.

Joshua Evens looked down at the boy trudging alongside Richard Logan. "Thou must be Joseph. I'm glad to have thee visit me. My wife will fix thee a warm meal and thou canst clean up and get a good night's rest."

A faint smile spread across Joseph's face, but he said nothing.

They slowly entered the Evans' yard followed by six curious neighborhood children. Joshua Evans turned to the children. "Please go back to thy homes. The boys need food and rest and I must tend to them. Tomorrow thou may come and meet them."

As soon as he entered the Evans' home, Richard Logan collapsed into a nearby chair. "We appreciate thy help very much," he said. "We're all extremely hungry and tired. The boys need to bathe and have a good night's rest before seeing their mother. She'll be excited to see them once again."

Joshua Evans set Samuel on a chair at the table and motioned for Joseph to sit across from him. The boys laid their heads on the table with exhaustion. Phoebe Evans handed each of them a cup of water and hurried to prepare a meal for her guests.

Joshua Evans pulled up his own chair and turned to Richard Logan. "We'll loan thee a hand wagon to pull Samuel to Widow Blackman's tomorrow. If the three of thee need a place to stay before thou leave

Ann Bell

for America, thou art welcome to stay with us. We have an extra room in the loft for the boys."

Joseph Bradford sat upright, rage flaring in his eyes. "Thou may be going to America, but Samuel and I are staying in London with Mother. Thou lied to us and tried to trick us. We should have stayed at the orphanage."

Seven

Philadelphia, Sixth Month 1717

The Reynolds family gathered around the supper table, each relaxing from their toils of the day. Rebekah filled a bowl with soup for each person and carried it to the table, setting one at each place. She had worked hard preparing dinner and had tasted it several times while it was cooking to make sure it was exactly right. At the end of the table, Elizabeth Reynolds was cutting a piece of freshly baked bread for each of the family. Rebekah thought it was unusual when Sarah got up and helped her without asking. From the corner of her eye, she thought she saw Sarah reach for the peppershaker, but she had turned to set a bowl in front of Lillian and did not give it another thought.

After John Reynolds said a blessing, each member of the family reached for a spoon and took a big bite of the vegetable soup. Suddenly, the strangest gasp escaped Adam's lips and he spit his soup back into his bowl as he grabbed for his glass of water. "Who made the soup? There's way too much pepper in it. It tastes awful."

Ann Bell

Rebekah watched as Sarah tried to choke back her giggles. "Rebekah made the soup. What's the matter? Don't thou like it?"

Elizabeth Reynolds scowled at Rebekah. "Thou must be more careful when thou cook," she said. "I'm truly shocked. Thou are usually an excellent cook."

Anger rose within Rebekah, but she said nothing. She lowered her head and avoided eye contact for the rest of the evening. *How does Sarah always get by with things like this? She's so sneaky, but no one seems to notice. Someday her nastiness is going to backfire and she's going to get what she deserves.*

Fortunately, the next day was Rebekah Bradford's free day. As was her custom by mid-morning, she meandered down the path leading to the river outlet a quarter mile from the Reynolds home on the outskirts of Philadelphia. This was a free day, and she could do whatever she chose. She treasured these moments of solitude. She could escape from the torments of Sarah Reynolds into her memories of life in London before her mother became ill, when her father was a contented cobbler. Tears filled her eyes as she pictured herself sitting on the floor of their humble home rolling a ball to her younger brothers. They had been so young and full of laughter before their world fell apart. Now, her father was dead. She didn't know if her mother was still alive or where her brothers were. Without her, what would become of them? Would they ever learn to read and become productive Quaker men?

On her free days, the first thing she wanted to do was take a bath. During the winter, the entire Reynolds family used the large metal tub filled with warm water placed near the hearth. With the lack of privacy, she was never able to relax and enjoy the luxury of being fully immersed. Even after working two years for the Reynolds, Rebekah's modesty prevented her from bathing until after the entire family was in bed, but today was different. She could take her time bathing undisturbed in the nearby river. She could bask in the warmth of the sunny morning.

Rebekah hung her bonnet, simple gray dress, and shift on the branch of a nearby tree along with a towel. Glancing around, she cautiously waded into the water with a small chip of soap from the supply she had made a few days before. Her body shuddered while it became accustomed to the colder temperature of the water. Slowly she stepped further toward the center of the river until the water was up to her chest. She relaxed as she inhaled the fresh summer air and leaned backwards, completely submerging herself. The cool water refreshed her hot, perspiring body as the sun beat down upon her.

When she resurfaced, she took the soap and began rubbing it over her mature sixteen-year-old body. So much had happened since she had left London. Not only had her body changed, but also her mind.

[143]

Ann Bell

She was no longer a scared little girl in a strange land, but a young woman uncertain of her future while still longing for a fragment of her past. She waded deeper into the water. A warm breeze blew through her wet brown hair.

Rebekah's thoughts drifted to pleasant moments after the last First Day Meeting. After the Meeting, she was surprised when Sybilla Master approached her and started a conversation. Within minutes, Sybilla had invited her to come to her home on her next free day. *I didn't think she knew who I was*, Rebekah mused. *Sybilla Master is a well-respected businesswoman and it is a great honor to be asked to dine with her. I wonder why she did it.*

Suddenly, a limb cracked behind her and muffled giggles echoed from behind a tree. She jerked her head toward the sound. "Who's there?" she shouted.

The laughter became louder.

"Who's there?" Rebekah demanded once again.

"Rebekah, when are you going to get out of the water?" a boy's voice chided. "We want to see you."

Rebekah knelt in the river until only her head was above the water. The sharp rocks at the bottom scratched her knees. She looked hard at the tree and recognized three of the neighbor boys who lived down the road from the Reynolds's home. "I'm not getting out until thou leave," she shouted back.

"We're in no hurry," the older boy replied. "We don't have to be home until it's time to do evening chores."

"Please . . . I must get out now. I told a friend I would meet her for dinner."

"Don't let us stop you," they taunted. "You are free to leave any time you like."

Rebekah remained immersed to her neck. Tears gathered in her eyes. "Please leave," she begged. "I have to go."

"Naaah. We want to wait and see if Quaker girls have real bodies under their dresses or if their skin has turned gray like the dresses they wear. Maybe I should take this dress back with me and see how it works."

Suddenly a tall lanky youth appeared from seemingly nowhere and raced across the field toward her tormentors. Rebekah gasped. "Oh no! Not another one of them."

"What are you doing?" the boy shouted. The tormentors blanched at the sight of their accuser.

Rebekah breathed a sigh of relief when she recognized the voice of Mark Reynolds. For the last two years, Mark had appeared to ignore her, but now he had wasted no time in coming to her defense.

"Get out of here," Mark shouted, "before I tell thy Pa what thou hast done."

The neighbor boys exchanged worried looks. "Don't tell. Pa will whip us!" the youngest one whimpered.

"Then get out of here," Mark ordered. He remained near the bank, hands on his hips until the neighbor boys raced across the field and disappeared from view.

When they were out of sight, Mark turned toward Rebekah. "I'll go down to the road and make sure they don't come back while thou get out of the water and dress."

Rebekah dried the tears from her eyes. "I thank thee," she said. "Thou art very kind. I don't know what I would have done if thou hadn't come."

"Quakers have to defend each other," Mark said, shrugging his shoulder. "People are always trying to give us a bad time. We have to let them know that just because we are against violence, we will not let people bully us. The neighbor boys are always trying to cause trouble somewhere."

Rebekah smiled. "I thank thee. Tomorrow I'll bake thee an extra apple pie for helping me."

"I'm looking forward to it. I love thy apple pies," Mark shouted over his shoulder as he raced to the top of the hill to make sure the boys weren't trying to sneak back.

When Mark was out of sight, Rebekah scrambled from the water, dried herself, and slipped into her clothes. She tucked her long brown hair under her bonnet and sat on a fallen log to slip on her stockings. Her hands trembled while she laced her shoes. *Why did they torment me? I have done nothing to them. Was it only because I am a Quaker? Would they have done it if I were not a Quaker?*

The summer breeze refreshed Rebekah as she walked the narrow road to Sybilla Masters' house. She never ceased marveling at the large, tidy homes of Philadelphia as compared to the cluttered ones in the poor section of London. She dared to wish to have such a home when her time with the Reynolds was fulfilled.

Rebekah spotted Sybilla Master's brick house that Elizabeth Reynolds had pointed out to her on the way home from the women's meeting on Fourth Day. She increased her pace, not wanting to keep Sybilla waiting.

Rebekah rapped on the door and waited nervously before it opened. Sybilla Masters greeted her warmly and motioned for her to enter. "Come in,

Rebekah. I'm glad thee could dine with me. We have so much to talk about."

"I want to thank thee for inviting me," Rebekah replied shyly. "I rarely get to go anyplace except to the Society Meetings."

"That's why I invited thee." Sybilla Masters placed her hand on Rebekah's shoulder. "I've watched thee at the Meetings and thou appear lonesome and in need of a friend."

Rebekah smiled as she stepped inside and surveyed the immaculate room. The furniture was carved of fine wood. The design was straight and simple without ornate additions, yet the quality of the wood defied its simplicity. The cooking utensils were neatly arranged around the fireplace and on the shelves on the far wall. A curtain in the back of the room separated the living area from what appeared to be the sleeping area.

"After we eat, I'll show thee my workshop." Sybilla Masters motioned for Rebekah to be seated on the wooden bench at the table by the fireplace. "First, I've prepared a special meal for just the two of us."

Sybilla Masters filled two bowls with venison stew, sliced four pieces of bread from a freshly baked loaf, and brought out a plate of food Rebekah had not seen before. Never had she tasted anything so exquisitely prepared. She tried to eat using all the social graces Elizabeth Reynolds had taught her, but she was fearful that her lack of social experience would be apparent to her new friend. "Thou art an excellent cook, Sybilla. What kind of food is this? It is like hominy only much better."

Sybilla Masters smiled. "I call it Tuscarora Rice. Instead of grinding corn between two large millstones, I discovered a way to use hammers to pound the corn into meal," she explained. "My husband and I went all the way to England to get a patent for my invention from King George. It turned out I was the first woman to obtain a patent on an invention."

Rebekah's eyes widened. "That's impressive. Thou must be extremely creative to do that. I would never be able to invent anything."

"What was unfair was that, even though I invented the process of cleaning and curing the Indian corn growing in several colonies in America, we had to take the patent out in my husband's name."

Rebekah shook her head. "That's not right. If thou hast the idea, thou should have the patent in thy name."

"Someday I hope the laws will change so women will have the same rights men have," Sybilla said. "The Quakers already recognize this equality but the non-Quakers have not accepted it yet. When we have to work with the secular laws, we have to do a lot of things we don't like."

[149]

Ann Bell

"If the patent is in thy husband's name, where is he now?" Rebekah asked. "Did he ever use thy method of grinding corn?"

"My husband set up a mill here in Philadelphia to make Tuscarora Rice. It was a very popular place until he died six years ago and his partner took over the business."

"I'm sorry," Rebekah replied softly. "It must have been a tremendous loss."

Sybilla Masters' eyes became distant. "It was. I was such a young widow and I missed him terribly. Fortunately, he had helped me set up my own hatmaking business before he died so I was able to be self-sufficient. I feel sorry for the Puritan women who are kept subservient to their husbands and when they die, the widows have to depend on others for support."

Rebekah wrinkled her forehead. "Why dost thou feel sorry for the Puritans? They're the ones who persecute us. I don't understand why they do that. We've done nothing to harm them."

"Rebekah, don't be too fast to criticize the Puritans. They just don't comprehend our way of life," Sybilla Masters said gently. "They can't understand how we can live in peace with ourselves and our God. They seem to emphasize the laws of God and not the love of God. I think that's why some of them persecute us."

[150]

Rebekah looked down. She felt her face flush. "I was persecuted today."

Sybilla Masters gasped. She laid her spoon on the table. "What happened? Quakers must take care of each other when we are confronted with challenges of the world."

Rebekah looked down and hesitated. "I don't want to burden anyone with my troubles." She took a deep breath. "Here's what happened. I was bathing in the outlet where the stream dumps into the river behind the Reynolds's house when the neighbor boys who lived down the road came and started taunting me. They wanted me to come out of the water so they could see if a Quaker girl had gray skin under her gray dress. They even threatened to take my dress I left hanging on the tree branch. I don't know what I would have done if Mark Reynolds hadn't come and chased them away. He threatened to tell their father."

Sybilla Masters shook her head. "No one likes being taunted about their religion, but in thy case, I don't think they were persecuting thee for religious purposes. I think they were just naughty boys who would have done the same to anyone, no matter what their religion was. I think I know which boys thou art talking about and they are always getting in trouble with someone."

Rebekah remained silent for a few moments. "I guess thou art right. They probably would have

Ann Bell

threatened to take any girl's clothes that were at the river bathing, regardless of their religion. They referred to me as a Quaker so I thought that was why they were there. In London, I heard many stories about Quakers being persecuted so I expected it from any non-Quaker who annoyed me."

"Being a Quaker in a Quaker colony is the safest place to be. Things may become difficult at times, but it is nothing like it would be in the other colonies."

Sybilla and Rebekah finished eating their meal in silence. Even though words were not spoken, a friendship was building between them. When they had finished, Rebekah thanked her for the delicious meal and helped Sybilla clear the table.

After the kitchen area was tidy, Sybilla said, "Come. I'd like to show thee my workroom. I spend most of my days here."

Rebekah rose and followed her into the workshop. She observed the huge vats and tables scattered around the room. Finished hats lined a far shelf. "Didst thou make all these hats?"

"Yes, I did," Sybilla Masters stated matter-of-factly. "I also invented a method to make hats from straw and Palmetto leaves that come from the West Indies. I received a patent for that process from King George. Of course, it had to be in my husband's name, as well. Now I weave hats from palmetto leaves, chips, and straw and sell them to local merchants."

"I wonder if I could be a businesswoman like thee after I fulfill my contract with the Reynolds, but I wouldn't know how to begin." Rebekah's voice trailed to a whisper as she finished her sentence.

"Thou must not worry about the details now," Sybilla Masters replied. "The Friends in the local meeting will help thee make the transition to independent living when the time comes. One person who could be a big help is Isaac Morris."

Rebekah raised her eyebrows. "Who is Isaac Morris and why would he be interested in helping me?"

Sybilla Masters laughed. "He's a prominent tailor in our Society. You must not have noticed him sitting on the other side of the room during the First Day Meetings. He has noticed you and would like me to introduce thee to him."

"I . . . I . . . I've never had anyone interested in me before," Rebekah stammered. "I don't know what to say."

Sybilla Masters laughed. "Rebekah, how old art thou?"

"Sixteen, almost seventeen."

"That's how old I was when I met William Masters," she replied. "We were married a year later. I was a widow much too soon."

Rebekah stood in silence. She had often dreamed about being an independent woman and didn't know if she would rather become a teacher, a businesswoman, or a traveling missionary. She had left the dreams of marriage to Sarah Reynolds. Finally, she turned her attention back to Sybilla. "I . . . I . . . I suppose I could meet him. It wouldn't mean I was betrothed or anything."

Sybilla Masters smiled. "I'm certain thou wilt like him; just give thyself time to consider all options for thy future."

"The future is uncertain for me, and life is too short. I'm afraid I'll make the wrong decisions," Rebekah said, and focused her attention on the mechanics of hatmaking to avoid any more uncertainties about the future.

For the remainder of the afternoon, Sybilla Masters showed Rebekah how she wove her hats. Words flew back and forth between the women nearly as fast as their fingers worked. Before Rebekah realized it, the sun was beginning to set in the west. She bade good-bye to her friend and promised to sit beside her during the next Society Meeting.

~~~~

Two days later Rebekah slipped away from the Reynolds family when she entered the meetinghouse and slid onto the bench beside Sybilla Masters. They smiled, nodded greetings, and bowed their head in silence. Rebekah pretended to pray. Her heart raced. Her eyes drifted to the men's section on the other side of the hall. She wondered which man was Isaac Morris. There were old men, young men, tall men, short men, handsome men, and not so handsome ones. Most of them appealed to her in a fatherly manner, but none stirred her heart.

Rebekah glanced at her friend. Sybilla, too, was scanning the men's section while pretending to be praying. Their eyes met. Sybilla looked down with frustration and shrugged her shoulders. She shook her head. "He's not here," she mouthed silently. Rebekah and Sybilla again closed their eyes as if in prayer, hoping no one had noticed their earthly distraction.

The following two First Days, Rebekah and Sybilla went through the same routine of searching the men's section, but to no avail. Isaac Morris was not present. After the meeting on the third First Day, Sybilla said to Rebekah, "I wonder what happened to Isaac. I hope he hasn't moved away. A month ago, all he could talk about was meeting the girl who worked for the Reynolds family; it's not like

[155]

Ann Bell

him to make any major changes without letting others know."

On the last First Day of Eighth Month, Rebekah slid onto the bench beside Sybilla. She smiled at her friend and bowed her head. Since Isaac Morris had not been in the men's section for the last three weeks she assumed it was not likely he would be there today, making it easier for her to concentrate on her prayers. Suddenly she felt a sharp nudge of an elbow in her ribs.

"Third row, second man from the left," Sybilla whispered before closing her eyes pretending to pray.

Rebekah lifted her eyes and cautiously glanced at the men's section. Her eyes widened. In the third row was a dark-haired man sitting with his face buried in his hands. She felt her heart start to race. Her eyes remained fixed on the third row. Unexpectedly, the dark-haired man rose to his feet and walked to the front of the meetinghouse.

"For those of you who do not know me, my name is Isaac Morris," he began in a loud tenor voice. "I just returned from a trip to Massachusetts. God has truly blessed me. I would like to share how He protected me from a band of thieves."

While he spoke, Rebekah was certain his eyes drifted to the women's side and stopped where she was sitting. Rebekah squirmed in her seat and looked to the floor. *This man is more handsome than Sybilla said. I wonder why I've never noticed him before.*

Isaac cleared his throat before continuing. "I was on the return trip with my wagon loaded with material and supplies for my tailoring business when three ruffians rode in front of me and blocked the trail. They had their pistols drawn and demanded I unload my wagon when a loud clap of thunder echoed through the woods and startled their horses. Two of the riders were thrown to the ground while the third was able to stay mounted and disappeared into the darkness."

Rebekah looked up. Again, she made direct eye contact with the speaker. *Why does he keep looking at me?* She tried to focus her eyes on the wooden plank beneath her feet, but too little avail.

Isaac paused, trying to choose his words carefully. "Amazingly, my horse remained calm. We raced toward the inn about two miles away. The rain was pouring down and the thunder and lightning was crackling around us. I thank God for sending the thunder at exactly the right moment and for keeping my horse calm when the horses of the ruffians were spooked. Truly, God does protect us from all evil. I will never doubt again."

With those words, Isaac returned to his seat and the congregation again sat in silence for several minutes. One by one, others stood and read

[157]

scripture or told how God had directed them or answered their prayers. Rebekah could scarcely hear what they were saying amid the pounding in her chest. *Why am I reacting this way? I've never even met this man.*

After the meeting, everyone filed silently from the hall. When Sybilla and Rebekah descended the steps of the meetinghouse, a voice from behind said, "Hello, Friend Masters. I was hoping to see thee today."

Sybilla and Rebekah stopped and turned. Isaac Morris had a broad smile on his face. "Greetings, Friend Morris," Sybilla responded. "It is good to see thee today. I liked what thou shared about how God protected thee while traveling. Truly thou art blessed."

"I'm extremely grateful for the Lord's protection. Without that protection I might not be here today," Isaac said. His eyes drifted to Rebekah and back to Sybilla. "I was hoping thou wouldst introduce me to the young lady beside thee."

Sybilla motioned to her friend. "Rebekah, I'd like thee to meet Isaac Morris. Friend Morris, this is Rebekah Bradford. Rebekah is employed with the John Reynolds family."

"Greetings, Friend Morris," Rebekah said shyly. "I've heard many good things about thee and was truly impressed with what thou shared today."

The trio continued talking as they walked slowly toward the fence where the horses and wagons were hitched. Suddenly an older woman called Sybilla Masters' name. Sybilla excused herself, leaving Rebekah alone with Isaac Morris. Conversation continued flowing easily between the two. After most of the other Quakers had returned to their horses and wagons, Isaac Morris became serious. "Rebekah, is there some time I can see thee again?"

Rebekah felt a warm glow in her face and hoped her blush was not apparent to anyone. "The Reynolds keep me busy most of the time," she replied quietly. "However, each week they do let me have the Fifth Day as a free day. On my days off, I usually go to Sybilla Masters' house and help her make hats."

"Good," Isaac said. "I'll stroll by Friend Masters' house next Fifth Day so we can visit again. She'll make an excellent chaperone."

Rebekah blushed and nodded as a familiar horse and wagon pulled to a stop next to where the two were standing.

"Come on, Rebekah," Sarah Reynolds shouted. "If thou want a ride home, thou had better hurry."

Rebekah bade Isaac Morris goodbye and hurried toward the waiting wagon. "I'm sorry I wasn't ready," she said as she seated herself beside Sarah.

"I became engaged in a conversation and didn't realize everyone else was ready to leave."

Sarah glared at her. "Why wert thou talking with a man? Didn't thou know thou still have to work for us for three more years?"

Rebekah swallowed hard. "I am fully aware of the length of time."

"That was Isaac Morris thou were talking to, was it not?" Sarah asked.

"Yes."

"If he is trying to court thee, he needs to know thou are not available for three years. However, I'm available right now. I'll have to meet him." Sarah tossed her head back in a show of defiance.

Rebekah bit her lip, but did not respond. While the wagon bounced along the ruts in the road toward the Reynolds home, tears welled in her eyes. *This is the first time I've talked with a man besides John Reynolds and Richard Logan and right away Sarah is making plans to create problems for me. I wonder what she'll try to do to get Isaac Morris's attention.*

Eight

Philadelphia, Tenth Month 1717

John Reynolds galloped his horse toward home. The crisp autumn air whisked around them. The few remaining leaves clung bravely to the trees and the fallen leaves swirled around the horse's hooves. Usually he sent a courier to carry information, but the importance of this news necessitated personal attention. When he learned the ship *Victoria* had been spotted in the bay, John Reynolds turned the management of his store over to his clerk and jumped onto his horse. Perhaps his friend, Richard Logan, would be on that ship.

When he reached home, he sprung from his horse, wrapped the reins around the hitching post, and raced inside. "Rebekah . . . Rebekah."

Rebekah looked up from the pot over the fireplace and hooked the ladle on the rim. "Friend Reynolds, I wasn't expecting thee for dinner until much later."

"I cannot stay," he said through huffs of breath. "The ship *Victoria* will be docking soon. Richard Logan might be on that ship. I'm going to the dock to meet him. I'm hoping he was able to bring thy

[161]

brothers with him. Wouldst thou like to come with me?"

Rebekah's eyes widened and her heart raced. "Of course I would. I've been praying for this day ever since I left London. I wouldn't want to miss their arrival for anything."

"Hurry and gather some bread, apples, and carrots for us to eat while I hitch the horse to the wagon." John Reynolds started to leave, hesitated, and turned to his eldest daughter who was sitting by the fireplace knitting. "Sarah, when thy mother gets home would thee tell her where we are? In the meantime, wouldst thou take over dinner preparations from Rebekah?"

Sarah stood and stepped toward the kettle where Rebekah had been working. "Yes, father," she said as she scowled at Rebekah.

Rebekah hurriedly prepared a food basket and joined John Reynolds waiting with the wagon in front of the house. As soon as she climbed onboard, John Reynolds snapped the reins, shouting "Giddy-up."

The mare maintained a steady pace through the streets of Philadelphia. Rebekah's heart pounded. *Will my brothers be on that ship? It is almost too much to expect. Richard Logan promised he would do his best to bring them back with him, but I have trouble believing it could really be possible.*

[162]

When they arrived at the dock, John Reynolds pulled the mare to a stop and wrapped the reins around a nearby tree. He helped Rebekah from the wagon and the pair joined the throng of onlookers waiting for the first person to appear on the gangplank. Within minutes, tired, haggard passengers began descending the shaking wooden plank. As the minutes passed, John Reynolds and Rebekah exchanged worried glances.

"Maybe Friend Logan was not able to return on this ship like he planned," John Reynolds said. "There's another ship due in about a month. Maybe he'll be on that one instead."

Rebekah's shoulders slumped. "I knew it was too much to hope for."

They stood in silence for a few more minutes. All the passengers appeared to be off the ship when John Reynolds took a few steps forward. "Wait . . . look! That might be Richard Logan starting down the gangplank now. There's a boy with him and it looks like he is carrying another."

"But my brothers aren't that big." Rebekah tried to shade the late afternoon sun with her hand. "Wait… wait…that is Joseph! He has grown so much I scarcely recognized him. Oh, I wonder what's wrong with Samuel."

Rebekah ran to the end of dock and waved frantically. "Joseph . . . Joseph. Here I am."

Halfway down the gangplank Joseph spotted his sister and increased his pace. He raised his arm limply in recognition.

Rebekah turned to John Reynolds. "What's wrong? Everyone getting off the ship looks sick."

John shook his head. "That's not uncommon. We were fortunate when we sailed from London. Only three died and few became seriously ill. However, sometimes if a ship runs into rough seas and the voyage is longer than expected, they run out of food. When that happens, diseases run rampant. I've heard of cases in which half those who leave England die before they arrive in America."

When Richard Logan and the boys reached the end of the dock, Rebekah and John Reynolds hurried to their side. Rebekah grabbed her brother and embraced him. Tears ran down her cheeks. "Joseph, Joseph. I'm glad thou art here. I missed thee so."

Joseph clung to his sister sobbing. "Rebekah, I never thought we'd make it. Everyone got sick. I was afraid Samuel would die before we got here."

Rebekah held her brother tightly against her breast. "I thank God thou made it. My prayers have been answered."

She turned her attention to her youngest brother in Richard Logan's arms. She stroked his forehead.

"Samuel, it's me . . . Rebekah. I'll take care of thee until thou art well."

The boy moaned and opened his eyes. "Rebekah, we made it," he whispered then closed his eyes and collapsed against Richard Logan's chest.

John Reynolds reached for the sick boy. "Let me take him," he said softly. "My wagon is over yonder."

Rebekah took Joseph's bag, wrapped her arm around his waist to help support his weight, and followed John to the wagon. "How's Mother?"

"She's even worse than when thou left. Widow Blackman is caring for her." Tears built in Joseph's eyes. "She said her greatest desire was to know we were together again before she died. We'll never see her again."

Rebekah pulled her brother closer to her. "She sacrificed so much for us. Her prayers have finally been answered. We are together again."

John Reynolds lifted Samuel onto the back of the wagon while Richard Logan helped Joseph and Rebekah in beside him. When the boys were comfortable, Richard Logan turned to his friend. "It will be a lot of work caring for two sick boys," he said. "Would it be an inconvenience if we borrowed Rebekah for a few days until the boys are better? She'd be a healing balm for her brothers."

[165]

Ann Bell

John Reynolds removed his hat, rubbed his head, and placed it back on his head. "That is the least I can do," he replied. "Thy family has helped us through many trials these last few years. Sarah can handle Rebekah's chores for a couple weeks."

Rebekah beamed with excitement while the Reynolds's wagon bumped along the cobblestones. She wrapped one arm around Joseph while she cradled Samuel's head in her lap. Unable to express their intense emotions, the Bradford children rode in silence, clinging to each other. In spite of the boys' illness, everything seemed right with the world.

When they stopped in front of the Logan's brick home, Naomi Logan raced out the door followed by eight-year-old Ruth close behind her. Richard Logan jumped from the wagon into his wife's waiting arms.

"Richard, welcome home. We've missed thee so. How was thy trip?"

"I missed thee too, Naomi. The trip was extremely difficult," he said, hugging his wife. "We were blown off course and it took us three weeks longer than expected. We ran out of food and many people contracted dysentery and died."

Naomi Logan glanced to the back of the wagon. "I see thou were able to find the Bradford boys and bring them back with thee. God was very good to thee."

Richard smiled. "It was indeed a miracle. The Inner Light directed my path to them. I'll explain the details later." He reached for their bags while John Reynolds lifted Samuel from the wagon into his arms.

"Naomi, the boys became extremely ill while they were on the sea. I knew thou needed help caring for them, so I asked Friend Reynolds to let Rebekah stay with us until they are better."

Naomi turned to John Reynolds, "I appreciate thy kind offer. Rebekah will be a great help to us. The children have a lot of reacquainting to do as well."

John Reynolds nodded and smiled. "Rebekah's a hard worker. I don't think we would be able to keep her away from her brothers until they're well anyway."

Naomi Logan turned her attention to the sick boys. "Come in. I'll make beds for thee by the fire. We have plenty of stew and bread to eat."

Within minutes, Joseph Bradford and Richard Logan eagerly devoured three bowls of stew apiece, relishing each bite as if it would be their last. Before long, Naomi had to remind them not to eat too much too soon or they could become sick at their stomachs.

Meanwhile, Samuel was placed on the cot by the hearth. Rebekah slowly lifted spoonfuls of soup to his lips interspersed with sips of water from a metal cup. Strength seemed to flow slowly through his body with each bite. After eating nearly a full bowl, he leaned back and was soon asleep.

When Richard Logan finished eating, he collapsed into his favorite chair by the fireplace and rested his head against the back. "Sometimes I feared I would never get to sit in this chair again," he said rocking back and forth. "But God was truly good to us. He protected us and brought us through a terrible ordeal. We have so much for which to be thankful."

~~~~~

For three days, Rebekah stayed close to her brothers' beds. By Third Day, Joseph had regained his strength and Samuel was beginning to respond to her loving care. Not since the death of their father and the separation of their family, had they experienced such love and concern.

After breakfast on Fourth Day, Naomi Logan called the boys to her side. "Joseph, are those the only clothes thou hast?"

"Yes, Ma'am. We both only have one change of britches and shirt, but they are now too small and torn."

Naomi nodded with understanding. "We'll have to do something about that. I know a tailor who does

[168]

excellent work. His name is Isaac Morris. Rebekah can take thee to his shop for a fitting."

Rebekah swallowed hard and choked back a cough. Naomi turned to her. "Dost thou know Isaac Morris? He attends almost every First Day Meeting."

"Y . . . Yes," Rebekah stammered. Hesitating she shifted her weight nervously. "Please don't tell John Reynolds, but I've been seeing him every time I have had a free day."

Naomi smiled. "Rebekah, do I sense a deep friendship developing? Wouldst thou like to tell me about it?"

Rebekah looked down. *Can I trust her with my secret I have shared only with Sybilla and Isaac?*

She cleared her throat. "Naomi, when I have a free day I go to Sybilla Masters' home and help her make hats. I'm becoming a very good hatmaker." Rebekah paused. She studied the plump Quaker woman's face. "While I'm there, Isaac Morris comes over with a basket of hand sewing. That way no one wastes time and we have a chance to be together." She hesitated. Her voice trembled. "Please don't tell the Reynolds or they might not let me have free days anymore if they knew."

An understanding expression spread across the older woman's face. "How interested in Isaac Morris art thou?"

Rebekah's eyes became distant and softened. "He's the most kind, understanding man I have ever known." She paused, trying to choose her words carefully. "He says he would like to marry me, but I do not know what to do."

"Hast thou not talked to the Reynolds about this? After all, thou art seventeen-years-old. Many girls thy age are already married."

Rebekah shook her head. "Sometimes I think perhaps Elizabeth Reynolds would understand, but if Sarah knew I was seeing Isaac, I'm certain she'd do anything possible to interfere and try to get Isaac to pay attention to her instead of me. She doesn't like anything I do and is always devising tricks to hurt me. I don't think John Reynolds understands how cruel she is to me."

Naomi walked around the table, slid onto the bench next to Rebekah, and put her arm around her. "Rebekah, I understand what thou art saying. I've known Sarah Reynolds all her life. She can be extremely manipulative at times. Yes, she's been ill several times, but she often fakes her illness to get her own way. Her mother knows what she's doing, but I'm not sure if John Reynolds realizes how conniving Sarah has become."

Tears started rolling down Rebekah's cheeks. Finally, someone besides Isaac Morris understood how she felt. "But what can I do?" she said. "I love Isaac and would like to marry him as soon as possible. I do not want to do anything that would hamper that possibility."

Naomi Logan hugged Rebekah. "Maybe I could talk with Elizabeth as friend to friend. Perhaps the two of us could come up with a solution. Never give up hope."

Rebekah's eyes widened. "I thank thee." She squeezed Naomi's hand while she wiped the tears from her cheeks with the back of her other hand. "I feel trapped and don't know what to do."

"Please don't feel that way," Naomi Logan said. "I'll do everything I can to help. Things have a way of working out in the end."

The older woman studied the boys resting by the fireplace. "Now, back to the original problem – thy brothers' new clothes. I have noticed thou art good handling horses. Wouldst thou be able to drive our horse and wagon to the tailor shop by thyself?"

Rebekah smiled. "I could give it a try. I've often driven the Reynolds's wagon," she said. "When wouldst thou like me to go?"

"What about this afternoon?"

~~~~~

After they finished their midday meal, Rebekah helped her brothers into the Logan's wagon. Samuel chose to lie in the back of the wagon while Joseph rode on the seat beside his sister.

"Rebekah, I cannot believe we're going to get two new sets of clothes," Joseph said. "We've always had to wear someone else's outgrown clothes."

"People are very generous in Philadelphia and many appear to be quite wealthy. During the ride, Joseph talked non-stop about the exciting new sights he was seeing on the streets of Philadelphia. His amazement with the city far surpassed Rebekah's first ride through Philadelphia. When they arrived at the tailor shop, he could scarcely stand still long enough for Isaac Morris to take his measurements.

When Isaac had finished taking his measurements, Joseph said, "Rebekah, Philadelphia is so different from London. May I walk around the neighborhood and look at the houses and shops while he measures Samuel?"

Rebekah looked at Isaac who gave her a mischievous wink. She turned back to her pleading brother. "Yes. Just don't go too far and get lost."

With that, Joseph raced out the door into the cool Eleventh Month weather. After the door closed behind him, Isaac turned his attention back to Samuel. "You look tired. I'll work fast in getting thy fittings so thou can lie down again."

True to his word, Isaac worked quickly in taking Samuel's measurements and recording them on a slip of paper. When he was finished, he laid the tape on the bench beside him, gently placed his arm around the boy's shoulder, and led him to the bed in the corner. Samuel immediately curled into a fetal position and closed his eyes. Isaac wrapped a quilt over the boy's frail body. Within moments, Samuel was asleep.

Isaac stoked the fire before pulling a chair next to Rebekah's. "We're finally alone," he said taking her hand in his, "and we don't even have Sybilla with us. I wish there was some way we didn't have to keep our relationship a secret."

Rebekah stared at the floor, trying to avoid Isaac's gaze. "I told Naomi Logan about us and about my problems with Sarah."

A furrow deepened on Isaac's forehead. "And what did she say?"

"She seemed to understand. She knows most girls are married when they are seventeen and thinks it is the most natural thing in the world."

"Women are always more sensitive to things of the heart," he said. "I'm glad thou told her. Telling John

Reynolds will be the real challenge. Maybe she can smooth the path a little for us."

"Naomi also realizes Sarah taunts me and uses her illness to manipulate others. She agreed to talk to Elizabeth Reynolds about my situation. I hope she can get them to understand."

"Half the people in our Society know how Sarah treats thee," Isaac replied, "but until her father accepts that fact, there will never be any change in thy situation."

The shadows in the tailor shop lengthened. Isaac and Rebekah basked in the company of each other, discussing their hopes and dreams for the future. "John Reynolds doesn't understand how his daughter treats me. He demands strict allegiance from his family and rarely sees fault in any of his children."

Isaac pressed Rebekah's hands against his lips. "I think it's time I quit trying to hide my feelings toward thee. I want to talk to John Reynolds myself. Maybe he'll let me buy thy indentured contract so we can be married sooner."

Rebekah stiffened. Tears filled her eyes. "Buying my contract makes me feel like a piece of livestock. The only way I can be free is if I'm bought or sold."

Isaac pulled her next to him. "I know that sounds cruel, but I'm afraid buying your contract is the only way we can obtain thy freedom early."

Rebekah shook her head and pulled back. "I'm living far better here than I did in London, but I still feel like a slave. I'm tired of meeting the demands of everyone in the Reynolds family whenever they want something done. I have no rights. Sarah continually uses her power to taunt me. I am trapped in a hopeless situation." Rebekah paused, the muscles in her chin tightened and tears gathered in her eyes. "However, I'd rather remain in servitude than to be bought and sold like a head of livestock."

Isaac stroked her cheek and wiped away a tear. "If it hurts thee that much if I try to buy thy indentured contract, I'll appeal to the goodness of John Reynolds's heart," Isaac said. "If he doesn't voluntarily release thee of the contract I'll appeal to the Monthly Business Meeting. Maybe they'll understand our desire to wed."

Rebekah leaned her head against Isaac's shoulder. "But what wilt thou do if they won't require John Reynolds to release me?" she asked softly. "I still have nearly three years left in my contract. Thou should not wait that long to obtain a wife."

"I would wait forever to have thee by my side. Thou art like a precious gem waiting to be unearthed."

[175]

Ann Bell

"But it's not fair to make thee wait that long," Rebekah protested.

"If I have to wait thirty years for thee, I will do so. While I wait, I'll spend my time building the biggest and best house in Philadelphia for thee," Isaac promised. "But I'm not giving up; I'm going to appeal to Friend Reynolds for thy hand in marriage."

Nine

Rebekah lingered over the supper dishes watching the snow whipping around the corner of the house and building into drifts outside the Reynolds's brick home. This evening was little different from many others. Each person silently concentrated on his or her own project while the fire crackled in the fireplace. The younger children worked on their school lessons while Sarah knitted scarves and mittens. Elizabeth Reynolds mended the children's clothes and laid them in neat piles beside her chair when she was finished.

Tears built in Rebekah's eyes as fear and doubt crowded her mind. *I hope I did the right thing to ask Isaac to wait a few months before asking John Reynolds to release me from my contract. I'm afraid Sarah will increase her taunting if she knows of my love for Isaac.* She studied her employer's face from across the room, but could not imagine how he might react to her unspoken wishes.

After working in silence for over an hour, John Reynolds laid the knife and the wood he was whittling on the table and turned to his eldest

[177]

Ann Bell

daughter. "Sarah, thou art of the age of marriage and yet thou dost not seem interested in finding a husband. Hast thou given any thought to marriage?" A dejected expression spread across Sarah's face. "Yes, Father. I'd very much like to marry, but I have not met anyone I feel would be suitable."

"That's understandable. Thou rarely go anyplace except to the meetinghouse." John Reynolds hesitated and took a deep breath. "I know of someone who might be interested in thee as a wife."

Sarah's eyes widened. A smile spread across her face. "Who could that be?"

"His name is George Nelson," John Reynolds said. "He's a good and stable man; any woman would be proud to be his wife."

"Hmm, that does sound interesting. Please tell me more."

With those words, the younger children looked up from their schoolwork, and Elizabeth Reynolds dropped her mending into her lap and looked at her husband with curiosity. Rebekah tried her best to hide her interest in the topic.

John Reynolds smiled. "George Nelson is thirty-five-years-old. His wife died in childbirth two years ago, leaving him alone with four small children. He's a wealthy man and his wife would be well provided for."

[178]

Sarah's face reddened. "He's only looking for someone to care for his children," she replied sarcastically.

"Don't be silly, Sarah. It's nothing like that." John Reynolds's nostrils widened and his eyes blazed. "He already has an old woman staying with them to take care of the children and do the housework. He's lonesome for female companionship and nothing more."

Sarah's lower lip protruded. "I was hoping to marry a handsome, dark-haired bachelor my own age. I don't want an old man with a ready-made family."

"But I don't know anyone who meets those criteria. That is purely a vanity wish," John stated firmly. "Quakers must be practical about the future."

An uncomfortable silence settled over the room. The younger children watched to see what their sister would say next.

Finally, Sarah said in a low voice, "What about Isaac Morris? I see him almost every First Day at the meetinghouse. I don't think he's married and he's very attractive."

Hearing those words, Rebekah dropped the clay plate she was drying. Everyone jumped when it broke into pieces that scattered around the kitchen floor.

"Rebekah, why can't thou be careful?" Sarah shouted. "Can't thou see we are having a serious discussion?"

"Sorry," Rebekah mumbled. She reached for the broom behind the door. Her hands trembled. *The moment I've feared ever since I met Isaac is upon me,* she thought. *Sarah is going to try to get Isaac's attention.*

Ignoring the tension between the girls, or perhaps not even recognizing it, John Reynolds turned back to his daughter. "That's an interesting idea. I forgot about Isaac Morris. He's a well-mannered young man and an excellent tailor. I'm certain he could support a wife and family quite comfortably."

John hesitated, stroked his chin, and shook his head. "Isaac Morris would be a good husband, but I don't know if he has anyone in mind for a wife. I've seen him carry a box of sewing into Widow Masters home several times, but I assumed he's there because of their businesses. If thou wouldst like, I'll speak to him on thy behalf."

"Father, if thou talk to Isaac, please don't let him know I'm interested in him," Sarah begged. "I want him to court me. Arranged marriages are so demeaning."

John Reynolds smiled and picked up his wood and began whittling again. "I'll be as discreet as I can."

~~~~

The following day Rebekah hurried through her morning chores. At mid-day, she turned to Elizabeth Reynolds. "If I work later tonight to make up my time, may I have a few hours of free time this afternoon?"

Rebekah held her breath as she waited for Elizabeth Reynolds's response. Never before had she made such a bold request. She could almost feel her employer studying her face searching for an answer and she tried to appear as casual as possible.

After what seemed like hours, Elizabeth said, "Certainly, as long as thy work is completed before thou retire for the evening."

Rebekah ignored her quizzical gaze. "I thank thee," she said and reached for her coat hanging beside the door. "I'll be back before the children are home from school."

Rebekah trudged through the freshly fallen snow trying to stay in the horses' tracks with her mind in turmoil. At times, the snow was nearly to her knees. It wasn't long before her toes became numb and her fingers tingled. She shivered from the cold. Tears rolled down her cheeks. *Please, God,* she prayed. *I have to get to Isaac before John Reynolds does. Please make a way that Isaac and I can wed. I love him and cannot imagine waiting another three years.*

When she arrived at the tailor shop, Rebekah beat frantically on the wooden door. Within moments, it flew open.

Isaac's warm eyes were a welcome sight. "Rebekah, what's wrong? Please come in. It's much too cold for such a long walk."

Rebekah trembled as Isaac escorted her to the fireplace and helped her remove her coat. He placed a rocking chair next to the open flame. "Sit here and warm thyself. Thou must tell me what is so serious thou ventured out on such a wintry day?"

Rebekah wiped the tears from her cheeks, blew on her frostbitten fingers, and rubbed them together. She took three deep breaths. "John Reynolds is going to visit thee sometime this week."

Isaac smiled. "Why is that? Didst thou finally get enough courage to tell him about our love?"

Rebekah shook her head adamantly. "Oh no, it's nothing that easy." She stopped short. How could such a simple statement be so hard to say? "John Reynolds told Sarah that George Nelson might be interested in her as his bride, but she wasn't interested. She said she wanted to have thee as a husband."

Isaac burst into gales of laughter. After a few seconds, he noticed Rebekah's pained expression and instantly aborted his amusement. "I'm sorry," he said. He took her cold fingers in his. "Sarah Reynolds is the last person I would want to share my life with. She's manipulative and spoiled. If her father does suggest marriage, I'll tell him thou art the one I love and want to marry, even if I have to wait a hundred years."

Rebekah smiled as she gazed into Isaac's dark eyes. *Truly, this is the man of my dreams.* Tears from the cold turned into tears of love. "Dost thou really mean that?"

"Of course I mean it. Thou art the only woman I would ever consider as a wife," he said. He pressed her hand against his lips. "In fact, tomorrow I'm going to look at some land on the west side of town where I can begin building the biggest, best house in town for us to raise a family."

Just as she laid her head upon Isaac's shoulder, a loud banging on the front door interrupted them. They exchanged worried glances. Isaac hurried to the door and opened it. "Friend Reynolds, do come in. What brings thee here this frosty day?"

John Reynolds stomped the snow from his boots and stepped into the tailor shop. A look of shock spread across his face. "Rebekah, what art thou doing here? Why art thou not home helping Elizabeth?"

Rebekah felt the back of her neck turn warm, not knowing what to say. She hesitated searching for the right words.

Not waiting for her response, Isaac said, "Rebekah trudged all the way here through the snow to tell me of Sarah's interest in me."

A puzzled expression spread across John Reynolds's face. "But why would she be concerned about that? She has work to do at home."

"Rebekah and I love each other and desire to marry. We've been waiting for the right time to tell the world about our love."

The corner of John Reynolds's mouth turned upward and his eyes began to twinkle. "I was suspicious of that. I've noticed thy hurried conversations after meetings and wondered about Rebekah's frequent visits to Sybilla Masters' home."

"That's true," Isaac confessed. "While Sybilla and Rebekah made hats, I often brought my hand sewing and joined them for a day of work and conversation."

Rebekah's eyes widened as she listened to their conversation. She watched Isaac study the merchant's lined face. *Where will this conversation lead? Surely, John Reynolds will understand our love. I have worked extremely hard for his family.*

The seconds dragged by until Isaac spoke. "I realize Rebekah has been a great help to thy family and she still has more than two years left on her contract. If I found someone to take her place, wouldst thou consider releasing her so we can wed as soon as possible?"

John Reynolds shook his head; furrows deepened on his brow. "Rebekah was brought to Philadelphia at great personal expense. Not only was her passage provided, but long-term care for her ailing mother. I think it's only fair she completes her contract."

"But what if I bought out her contract?" Isaac pleaded. "Thou couldst hire someone else to do her chores."

"Money is not the point; personal responsibility is," John Reynolds said curtly. "A Quaker must honor their word. I need Rebekah to help my wife. It would take weeks to train someone else and it would be extremely disruptive to my family."

Isaac Morris set his jaw. "If that is thy stand, I will appeal my case to the Monthly Business Meeting of Friends."

Isaac turned to Rebekah. She could not hide her feeling of betrayal and felt tears gather in her eyes. Isaac had done exactly what she had asked him not to do. She was being bargained for. He had broken his promise to her.

John Reynolds interrupted the awkward silence. "Rebekah, I don't want to deny thee happiness. I just need thee to be true to thy word and fulfill thy contract. In the meantime, I'll allow time for thee to spend with Isaac and will try to interest Sarah in George Nelson."

"I thank thee," she murmured, scarcely able to control her conflicting emotions.

John Reynolds turned to Isaac. "In two years thou wilt have my blessings to marry Rebekah. That is the only fair way."

Isaac shifted his weight and cleared his throat. "I understand thy point of view, but there has to be a way to make Rebekah happy without having to wait that long. I'll still appeal to the members of the Monthly Meeting for an immediate solution to the problem. It is not right she suffers so."

John Reynolds walked toward the door. "Do what thou must," he said. "But I am certain they will agree with me. Have a good day."

When the door closed behind her employer Rebekah exclaimed, "Isaac, thou dost not understand how I feel. I love thee and want to marry thee, but I don't want to feel I'm being bought like a head of livestock. I must fulfill my contract in spite of my love for thee. Her tone was short and full of pain."

Isaac took Rebekah in his arms. Remorse covered his face. "I'm sorry. I didn't mean to hurt thee. When Friend Reynolds said 'no' I became too impulsive. I should have accepted his answer as God's Will for our lives. If thou dost not want me to appeal to the Monthly Meeting of Friends, I'll wait as long as necessary."

Rebekah pulled back and took his face in her hands. "Isaac, more than anything I want to be free to marry. My father taught me to be true to my word, regardless of the consequences. That is the Quaker way." Tears ran unashamedly down her cheeks. "Please do not plead our case; I must fulfill my obligation in spite of my love for thee."

Isaac's voice softened. He held her even closer. "Rebekah, I love thee. Thy integrity to fulfill thy contract in spite of thy personal desires makes my love for thee even stronger. In two years I will move thee into the biggest, best house in Philadelphia built by my own hands."

True to her word, Rebekah returned to the Reynolds home that afternoon before the younger children were back from school. She hummed her favorite hymn while she prepared the evening meal. *The*

worst is over, she thought. *Although John Reynolds will not release me from my contract, he knows Isaac and I plan to marry as soon as possible. I can now trust him to discourage Sarah from pursuing Isaac.*

That evening while Rebekah went about her routine chores, Sarah spent her customary time in her chair by the fire knitting. When she heard her father's footsteps on the porch, she rushed to the door to meet him.

"Father, didst thou talk with Isaac Morris today?" Sarah asked, unable to mask her enthusiasm. "What did he say? Is he interested in me?"

"Yes. I talked with Isaac Morris this afternoon," he said flatly.

"Is it arranged?" Sarah said eagerly. "Has he noticed me at the meetinghouse? Might he be interested in marrying me?"

John Reynolds shook his head. "No . . . Isaac wants to marry Rebekah."

Sarah's face turned ashen. She gasped for breath and collapsed into her chair. "Thou must be teasing me. Rebekah has to work for us for another two years. Surely thou art not planning to release her from her obligation."

"No," John Reynolds replied firmly. "A contract is a contract, but Isaac Morris loves Rebekah and is willing to wait for her as long as necessary."

Sarah buried her face in her hands. Uncontrollable sobs shook her shoulders. "Father, how could thou let them marry? It's not fair. I want to marry Isaac Morris. Rebekah is just a poor indentured servant from London."

"Sarah, listen to thy selfishness," John Reynolds said angrily, ignoring her crying. "I had nothing to do with their relationship. Fate, God, and Sybilla Masters brought them together, not me."

Her eyes widened. A look of shock spread across Sarah's face at her father's burst of anger. "But what am I supposed to do? Remain single all my life?"

John Reynolds crossed his arms and scowled at his eldest daughter. "Thou couldst at least meet George Nelson. Thou wilt never know if thou wilt like him if thou dost not meet him."

Sarah's sobs became further and further apart until they finally ceased. She wiped her eyes with the sleeve of her gray dress. "If I can't have Isaac Morris, I don't want anyone," she muttered and stormed from the room. "I'll find a way."

The following morning there was no discussion as of the outburst the night before. After the younger children left for school, Elizabeth Reynolds turned to Sarah. "I have a lot of work to do at home today; wouldst thou go with Rebekah to the market. She will have the list of supplies. Some may be heavy and she'll need help loading the wagon."

Sarah scowled. "If I must," she relied sharply, "but I'm not good at handling horses. Rebekah will have to do that."

"That should not be a problem; Rebekah has always been excellent with the horses. Just help her load the wagon." Elizabeth went to the window and pulled back the curtain. "There she is now. It didn't take her long to harness the horses. Hurry and get on the wagon. I'm certain thou wilt have a pleasant time in town."

"Yes, Mother," Sarah said dryly as she took her shawl from the hook by the door and wrapped it around herself. She trudged to the waiting wagon and climbed aboard without saying a word to Rebekah.

The puddles from the rain the night before splattered around the wagon as the horses plodded down the road. When they reached the edge of town, Rebekah broke the silence. "Shall we go to the feed store first?"

"If we must."

Rebekah turned the team down a side street when she reached the feed store, she pulled wagon to a stop. "Wouldst thou hold the reins while I go inside and buy the oats? The owner usually loads it in the wagon for me so thou may not need to even get down."

Sarah watched as Rebekah took a broad step to avoid a puddle as she alighted from the wagon. Much to her surprise Isaac Morris appeared around the corner riding his gray mare. *I can make her look ugly and foolish. When Isaac sees her, he'll laugh and have no interest in her.* With that, Sarah snapped the reins on the horses' rears and they took off with a jolt.

Water splattered over Rebekah and she instinctively jumped backward. Her foot hit a loose branch in the road, causing her to fall face first into the mud.

Sarah's laughter was short lived, as Isaac jumped from his horse and raced toward them. "What hast thou done?" he shouted.

Isaac knelt in the mud beside Rebekah as she struggled to get up. "Art thou hurt?"

Tears streamed down her mud-streaked face. "My arm hurts," she moaned.

Isaac ran his hand gently over her left arm. "I'm afraid it might be broken. Let me help thee into the back of the wagon. I'll drive the team to Doctor Browning's office and have it examined."

Without saying another word, Isaac gently lifted Rebekah onto the back of the wagon, tied his horse to the hitching post nearby, climbed onto the seat of the wagon, and took the reins from Sarah's hands. "Thou should be ashamed of thyself."

Tears streamed down Sarah's face. "I'm sorry. I'm so very sorry. I didn't mean for Rebekah to be hurt. I just wanted her to look foolish. I'm certain no one will believe me."

Isaac said nothing as he raced the horses and wagon towards the doctor's office. The expression on his face said that any chance of him ever being interested in her would never happen.

Fortunately, Rebekah's back was turned and she did not see what I did, Sarah thought. *Ever since she came to live with us, I've never liked her, but I'd never intentionally injure her. What kind of a person am I? I wonder if Isaac will tell her what really happened.*

~~~~

For the next month, Rebekah's left arm remained bound in a sling made from a kitchen towel. Every time Sarah looked at her guilt overwhelmed her. She willingly did Rebekah's chores without a complaint. *Will Isaac tell my parents what I did to Rebekah? What will they do to me if they find out?*

At first, Sarah was relieved that her parents did not seem to know what had happened, but gradually the feeling turned to dread. *What kind of an evil person would do such a thing to another human being? Will I ever be able to make amends for what I did?*

One night Rebekah retired early, Sarah turned to her father. "Father, I have been doing a lot of thinking. I have changed my mind." She took a deep breath. "I would be willing to meet George Nelson and see if he is as kind as everyone says he is. However, I want to make it clear from the beginning, I don't want to be a ready-made housekeeper and mother."

John Reynolds's tense face muscles relaxed. "That is a wise decision, Sarah. I am certain thou wilt approve of him. He is an honorable man. I will visit with him tomorrow."

As the winter months turned into spring, Rebekah continued spending her free days helping Sybilla make hats while Isaac brought his hand sewing to the hat shop. Each week Rebekah became more and more proficient in the craft of weaving. She took pride in the tightness and design of her weave.

One warm Fifth Month afternoon, Rebekah's fingers gingerly flew in and out amid the stalks of straw as her mind dwelt upon her future. They worked in silence for several minutes before she turned to Isaac and said, "When I was on the ship crossing to America I was sure I wanted to someday become a teacher, but now I'm not sure what I want to do when I am free. I enjoy helping Sybilla make hats, and I am thinking perhaps I would like to open a hat business myself someday."

Isaac first smiled and then started to laugh.

A puzzled look spread across Rebekah's face. "Why is that funny? Dost thou not think I am capable of handling a business?"

Isaac laid the fabric on the floor and knelt beside her. "Rebekah, my love, on the contrary," he said. "I've watched the way thy fingers manipulate the straw and the satisfaction thou hast every time thou completes another hat. I've been making plans I haven't shared with anyone. Wouldst thou and Sybilla be able to leave thy work for a short while? I'd like to show thee the progress on our house."

The two women exchanged curious glances, nodded at each other, and laid their work aside without saying a word. With mystified expressions on their faces, they followed Isaac. He helped them climb into his wagon and pulled himself onto the seat beside Rebekah.

Isaac snapped the reins. "Off we go," he shouted. "My secret will now be disclosed." The horse's hooves clopped against the hard-packed cobblestone streets while the trio waved to friends and acquaintances they passed on foot and horseback.

Excitement built within Rebekah. *This is the first time I'll get to see my future home. I wonder why Isaac is acting so mysteriously.*

When they turned right at the end of Market Street, the frame of a large house loomed before them. Rebekah gasped. "Is that it?"

Isaac's chest expanded with pride. "Yes, this is our future home," he said. He pulled the horse to a stop, jumped down, and wrapped the reins around a low branch. He first helped Sybilla alight from the wagon, before reaching for Rebekah and gently lifting her to the ground.

"Thou wilt have to use thy imagination," he said. He led them into the uncompleted house. "The frame is nearly finished, but I may have to hire a bricklayer to help me. It's just too much of a job, and I don't have all the skills necessary to complete that portion of the construction."

Rebekah's eyes widened. "It is so big."

"I promised thee the biggest, best house in town, did I not?" Isaac gave a teasing grandiose bow and motioned for her to step over the front door frame. "Come inside, and I'll give thee the grand tour."

Isaac pointed over his head. "Upstairs there will be three rooms, one for the boys, one for the girls, and one for company or hired help."
"The rooms are huge," Sybilla said with a laugh. "You must be planning for many children."

"The more the better," Isaac said and turned his attention to the main floor. "The room to the right of the fireplace will be our bedchamber, and the room to the left will be my tailor shop. It will have its own separate entrance. I don't want my customers interfering with our children."

Rebekah walked across the wooden floor taking in the enormity of the area. "I can scarcely believe the size of these rooms." She stepped into a room on the far right of the living room. "What will this room be?"

"That will be the hatmaking shop," Isaac said. "I know it looks large now, but within a few years I'm certain thou wilt have a thriving business and it will become much too small. I'm planning for both our businesses to expand and prosper along with our family."

Rebekah threw her arms around Isaac. "I thank thee . . . I thank thee . . . I cannot believe this. I simply cannot believe anyone would go to this much work for me."

"Thou art worth all this work plus so much more," Isaac assured her. "By the time we wed, I'll have a mansion prepared for thee."

~~~~~

After realizing Isaac Morris was unavailable for her, Sarah Reynolds began to change. She accepted the fact that perhaps her father's suggestion was worth exploring. Little by little, she discovered George Nelson was far more attractive than she imagined and his four children had taken an instant liking to her. Whenever she visited the Nelsons, the elderly housekeeper not only took care of the children, but also pampered her. By Sixth Month, Sarah Reynolds and George Nelson were betrothed and planned to say their vows in Eighth Month.

While Sarah's affections grew toward the entire Nelson family, her antagonism toward Rebekah diminished. The entire Society recognized the change in her. Sarah began showing interest in the concerns of others and not just her own. She appeared to become more interested in spiritual things and listened to the speakers at the meetings.

The night before she was to marry and move into the Nelson home, Sarah tiptoed to the side of Rebekah's bed. "Rebekah . . . Rebekah," she whispered.

[197]

Rebekah rolled over. The moonlight streaming through the opened window reflected around Sarah's trim body. "Dost thou need something?" Rebekah muttered through her grogginess.

"Can we talk?" Sarah sat on the side of the bed, not waiting for an answer.

Rebekah sat up and propped herself against the headboard. "Certainly. What dost thou want to talk about?"

"I'm getting married tomorrow and I am both excited and frightened. I'm going to miss thee," Sarah said. "Even when I mistreated thee, thou were always cheerful and continued to serve us in spite of everything. I'm truly sorry for the way I treated thee. I wish I had the same kind of faith thou hast."

Rebekah sat upright. Her back stiffened. *What do I say? I do not have the faith she thinks I have and I did not take her unkindness graciously. I may not have said anything, but my thought life was anything but God pleasing. I don't have the faith she thinks I have.* She took a deep breath.

"Honestly, thy words often hurt me deeply. I always wanted to be thy friend, not thy enemy." Rebekah reached for Sarah's hand. "I forgive thee for all the harsh words. I want to put this behind us and be genuine friends."

Sarah's back stiffened. "Rebekah, thou dost not know what I did to thee, or thou wouldst not be as willing to forgive me."

The full moon casts shadows through the window onto the bed they were sitting. The younger girls turned in their beds across the room. "I don't understand. What didst thou do that was so terrible I could not forgive thee?" Rebekah whispered.

Sarah took a deep breath. Her voice trembled. "Remember a couple years ago, when thou had a broken arm?" Tears began streaming down Sarah's cheeks. "I snapped the reins hoping the wagon would splash mud on thee so thou wouldst look foolish to Isaac. I did not intend for thee to fall and get hurt. I was jealous and wanted Isaac to be interested in me instead of thee. Now that thou know the truth, thou wilt never speak to me again and I will not blame thee."

Rebekah took Sarah's hand. "I was suspicious something like that had happened, but I was never certain. I did notice after that day thou began treating me differently. God has forgiven me of many impure thoughts and actions, how can I not forgive thee."

Sarah continued crying as she wrapped her arms around Rebekah and held her close. "I thank thee for forgiving me. Thou art like an angel to me. I want our relationship to start anew from this time forward. I know thou hast a bright future with Isaac."

Rebekah wiped the tears from Sarah's cheek with her hand. "I can hardly wait to share my life with Isaac. I wish thee a long and happy life with George Nelson. I only wish I were the one marrying tomorrow."

The two young women clung to each other, the years of hostilities and misunderstanding fading. Finally, Sarah pulled back and looked kindly into Rebekah's eyes. "As my parting gift, I'm going to try one more time to convince Father to release thee from thy contract so you can marry sooner."

Ten

Philadelphia, Second Month 1720

An eerie atmosphere engulfed Rebekah as she followed the Reynolds's family into the meetinghouse. Something was different, but she could not identify what. She automatically turned and followed Elizabeth Reynolds to the women's side of the hall and took a seat on a hard bench in the back row. Instead of the usual peaceful hush among the congregation, there was an intense cloud of sadness in the room. Tears were streaming down several women's cheeks while the men were bowed with grief.

Finally, one of the leaders arose. "Many of thou may already know our beloved founder, William Penn, was paralyzed with a stroke in 1712 while living in England." The gray-haired Quaker reached into his pocket and took out a tattered envelope. "The Society has just received a letter from William Penn's wife, Hannah, dated the thirtieth day of the Seventh Month, 1718. Somehow, the letter has been delayed in crossing the ocean. Hannah Penn writes, 'My poor Dearest's last breath was fetched this morning.'"

A gasp echoed through the hall as each person received the news. The elderly Quaker leader finished reading the letter filled with love and admiration and returned to his seat. The mourners continued to sit in silence, each lost in his or her thoughts and grief. Although William Penn's final years had been spent away from the colony, he had been their ever-present guide and protector. He wrote constantly, providing them with spiritual, moral, and legal guidance.

Finally, a middle-aged man in the back row arose and walked to the front. "William Penn was our Governor and he merits our love and honor for years to come. We must regard his memory when we consider the blessings and ease we have enjoyed under his government."

Each person in the congregation nodded in agreement as the speaker took his seat.

In time, Richard Logan stood. "Word of William Penn's death has already reached the Indians, and they are also mourning for the one they loved and call Onas. I just received a package from their chief. They want to send Hannah Penn skins to make a garment suitable for traveling through a thorny wilderness without her guide."

Richard Logan took a handkerchief from his pocket and wiped his eyes. "William Penn was a man who walked unarmed and unafraid among the Indians and easily made friends with them. He built this great colony on the belief in freedom of religion and democracy in government. William Penn never sought success for himself, but success for ideas. Today, the religious liberty he struggled and suffered for we take for granted as part of our inheritance."

While the members of the Society gave testimony of the influence of William Penn, pride in her Quaker heritage overwhelmed Rebekah. Her years of being an indentured servant began to make sense to her. She had been working for the common good of the community. Without accepting this period in her life, she never would have had the opportunity to live in peace in the city of William Penn. She was truly a part of history, a part of a Holy Experiment. She pondered what her life would now be like if she were still living in the poor, smoky section of London.

~~~~

Rebekah Bradford took her homemade calendar from the wall and made a large X through the date Third Month 2, 1720. Her freedom date was slowly approaching. On the sixteenth of Ninth Month, she would have fulfilled her indentured servant contract with John Reynolds and would be free to marry Isaac. She lay on her bed and gazed at the stars through her bedchamber window. Tomorrow would be her free day and she could go to Sybilla's home to make hats, but more importantly, Isaac would meet her there. *How I treasure those few precious hours with my beloved. I'm blessed not only to have a man who truly loves me, but a female friend whom I can trust with my innermost thoughts.* She fell asleep imagining herself living in the large house Isaac was preparing for them.

The morning rays from the sun bounced across Rebekah's face causing her to awaken. She bolted upright. *I must get to Sybilla's house as early as possible. Isaac promised to show Sybilla and me the progress he was making on the house. I can hardly wait.*

She slipped into her gray dress and bonnet and tiptoed down the steps. At the landing, she paused. Elizabeth Reynolds had already prepared breakfast and the younger children were hurrying through their meal so they would not be late for school.

The entire Reynolds family has changed so much since I joined them nearly five years ago, she thought. *Sarah is happily married. It's hard to believe Mark is now sixteen and works with his father in the mercantile while Adam helps there after school. Mary and Lillian have grown into little women and now help with the household chores. However, the biggest change of all is Matthew. He is far from the chubby baby he was when I arrived, but an active seven-year-old.*

"Good morning, everyone," Rebekah said brightly. "It looks like it is going to be a beautiful day."

The children looked up and returned her greeting.

"The weather is perfect," Elizabeth Reynolds said as she continued sweeping the floor around the fireplace. "Art thou going to Sybilla's again today?"

Rebekah took a wooden bowl from the shelf, and filled it with mush. "Oh, yes. Last week she received a large order for hats from a merchant in Germantown so I promised I would be there early today to help her."

"Be very cautious in that neighborhood," Elizabeth said. "I heard there's an outburst of smallpox and parts of that section of town are quarantined."

Rebekah stopped eating and shuddered. "Smallpox is such a dreadful disease."

"If thou see any quarantine signs anyplace near Sybilla's house, please come home immediately," Elizabeth Reynolds reminded her.

Rebekah nodded. "I'll be careful." She left the table and rinsed her bowl in the basin on the counter. Taking a light shawl from the hook beside the door, she bade the family farewell.

The birds were singing in the treetops while Rebekah walked through the tree-lined streets of Philadelphia. She had been waiting all week for this day. Her heart soared when she thought about seeing Isaac again. Dear, sweet Isaac had become

Ann Bell

her greatest source of support and encouragement. She basked in the knowledge that he had been working extra late in the evenings to complete the house before their marriage. Truly, that house was a labor of love for her, a poor Quaker girl from the poorest district of London.

Rebekah's sense of contentment lessened when she turned onto Sybilla's street. The first house had a quarantine sign nailed to the front gate and on the door. Two houses down, on the other side of the street, was another sign. Forgetting her promise to Elizabeth, she continued onward. In the next block, the signs seemed to be on nearly every other house. Fear enveloped her and she began to run. She stopped suddenly in horror. Tears rolled down her cheeks when she saw a white sheet of paper hanging from the doorframe of Sybilla's home.

What's wrong? Surely, Sybilla is not sick. She has always been the strong one. She pounded on the door. "Sybilla . . . Sybilla," she shouted. "Art thou all right? Can I come in and see thee?"

A plump middle-aged woman garbed in a gray dress and white bonnet opened the door. "Who art thou? Please do not come any closer. Art thou a friend of Sybilla's?"

Rebekah choked back her sobs that were beginning to shake her entire body. "She's a very dear friend of mine. I come every week to help her make hats.

She cannot be ill, I just saw her First Day at the meetinghouse."

"I'm sorry but Sybilla is very sick," the woman replied dryly. "She has smallpox. For three days she has been delirious with fever."

Rebekah's voice trembled. "Will she be all right? I want to see her."

The woman's large frame blocked the doorway. "We cannot let anyone see her until the scabs have come off. If she survives, it will be at least three weeks before she can have visitors."

"Wh . . . Wh . . . What does thou mean? If she survives?"

The woman shook her head. "I am sorry. We cannot risk the spread of this horrible disease."

Rebekah shuddered as a loud, delirious moan resounded from the house. She pictured her best friend lying on what could be her deathbed racked with pain and she could not go to her side and comfort her.

The older woman cringed. "Please excuse me. Sybilla needs my attention. If she comes to, I will tell her thou were here and left thy regards."

Unable to control sobs, Rebekah turned and trudged slowly down the street. *This cannot be. It has to be a bad dream. I will awaken soon to find everything as it was before. Sybilla cannot die. She's my best friend.*

Tears rolled down her cheeks and seemed to freeze to her face. She scarcely knew where she was going. Dogs barked around her, but she paid no heed. Wagons and horses clopped down the street, yet Rebekah did not look up to wave to her friends and neighbors.

From seemingly nowhere, she felt a gentle hand on her shoulder. "Rebekah, hast thou heard the news?" a strong, gentle male voice asked.

Rebekah stopped. Through blinding tears, she looked up and saw her beloved. "Isaac, it's awful. Sybilla has smallpox and may die."

"I know. I was there earlier this morning. Come with me to the tailor shop where thou can cry. They say tears can wash the soul."

In the solitude of Isaac's simple tailor shop, Rebekah cried for the remainder of the day. She not only cried for Sybilla, she cried for her dead father and ill mother. She cried for her friends she left behind in London. Tears not shed five years before now flowed freely. Isaac fixed her lunch and held her hand, but nothing took away the pain. By late afternoon, Rebekah's tears were spent. The emotional strain had left her body weak and limp.

Isaac's face was tense and worn. "Let me give thee a ride home so thou can get some rest. I'll explain to Elizabeth Reynolds what has happened."

~~~~~

A large crowd of Friends gathered at the cemetery behind the Market Street Meetinghouse to say farewell to Sybilla Masters. Rebekah's grief was inconsolable. Isaac remained constantly by her side, but she rarely felt his presence. She fluctuated between grief and despondency. Years of pain exploded within her. Words of comfort were of no avail.

After the funeral and a brief service in the cemetery, Rebekah leaned against the front corner of the wagon. Outside of the day her father was killed and the day she said goodbye to her mother in London, this was the worst day of her life. She prepared the evening meal in silence. While the others made small talk around the table, Rebekah could scarcely eat. When the evening chores were finished, she retired to her bed without speaking to anyone.

Rebekah's pillow was soon wet with tears. She tossed and turned well into the night. Usually she arose with the first ray of sunlight, but the next morning she did not drift into a restless sleep until the sun was rising over the disease-weary city.

Understanding her grief, Lillian and Mary tiptoed from their upstairs bedchamber and quietly did Rebekah's morning chores before they left for school. Elizabeth checked on Rebekah every few hours, but let her stay in bed for the remainder of the day, hoping the rest would ease her pain.

As the days passed, Rebekah's grief did not lessen. She cried for her lost friend while she went about her routine chores. She had trouble concentrating on what she was doing and often found herself staring mindlessly into space. Late the next week, Isaac came to the Reynolds' home to take her for a wagon ride. He tried to remind her of his love, and more importantly, of God's love in the hopes of lifting her spirits. However, his words could not penetrate her overwhelming grief. Rebekah continued to sink into a deeper state of melancholy and depression.

Other Friends of their Society also noticed the change in Rebekah's mental state. On a hot Seventh Month afternoon following a First Day Meeting, Richard Logan approached the Reynolds family as they walked to their wagon. "Friend Reynolds," he said. "Wouldst thou and thy family like to join us for an outing by the river in the clearing northeast of town? Naomi fixed enough food to feed half the city. Rebekah has not had a chance to see her brothers since Sybilla's death. Perhaps spending time with them would help lift her sadness."

John Reynolds surveyed the faces of his family. His wife nodded with approval, while his children looked on with pleading eyes. "We would be honored to join thee," he said. "The fresh air and company would help us all. We'll follow thy family in our wagon."

John Reynolds helped his family into the wagon and climbed in himself. He took the reins of the horses, slapped the reins on their hindquarters, and shouted for them to start. Cautiously he followed the Logan's freshly painted wagon through the wide streets of Philadelphia. Rebekah slumped on the bench in the back of the wagon. The warm summer breeze evaporated the tears on her cheeks and a faint smile crossed her face. Although she felt trapped in the depth of depression, she began to realize how much she had neglected her brothers. She watched the wind tousle her brothers' hair in the wagon ahead of them. Memories of their years together in London were reawakened. *"Lord, forgive me for being so caught in my own grief that I've neglected my own family. Please help me regain the joy of living."*

When the Reynolds and Logan families arrived at the clearing, the boys unhitched the horses and led them to the river to drink the cool water. Elizabeth Reynolds helped Naomi Logan lay blankets on the ground and arrange their lunch while the younger girls played tag in the grass.

Rebekah leaned against a massive oak tree while her brothers sat at her feet. Conversation flowed easily among them; and was occasionally

[211]

interrupted by gales of laughter. In spite of her grief, Rebekah could not help but share in their joy.

The boys talked about what they had learned in school. Faraway places and climates were fascinating to them. After experiencing the differences between London and Philadelphia their curiosity was peaked as to the other parts of the world, and the different varieties of plants, trees, and animals that grew there. Both Joseph and Samuel agreed they wanted to explore the world when they completed their indentured servant contract.

Rebekah told her brothers about her upcoming marriage and her plans for the spacious home Isaac Morris was building for her. In a rare burst of excitement, Joseph grabbed his sister. "How exciting! I really like Isaac and to think he loves thee enough to wait two years for thee and spend time building a large house for thee."

In the midst of their gaiety, Samuel became serious. "I wish mother could be here with us," he said. "We are all doing exactly what she prayed for, and yet she'll never know."

A somber expression spread across Joseph's face. "We don't even know if she is in London or in heaven. However, whatever we do we can always feel her presence."

Rebekah nodded. "I know. If she's in heaven, she already knows how much God has blessed us. I only wish she could have known Sybilla. Mother would have been impressed with how much she accomplished in her short lifetime."

A shout from near the wagon interrupted their intense conversation. "Time to eat."

Everyone raced toward the blankets laden with food. Richard Logan held up his hand indicating for them to stop and join him in a short prayer.

After the prayer, the food was quickly devoured and the children hurried to the river to play. Rebekah went back to the massive oak tree to rest. She lay on the ground and closed her eyes; for the first time since Sybilla's death, she felt relaxed and at peace.

Richard Logan stuck a blade of grass in his mouth and squatted on the ground next to his friend. "John, to be honest, there was an ulterior motive for me inviting thy family here today." He paused as he lowered himself to a sitting position on the ground. "I have a business proposition I'd like thee to consider."

John Reynolds studied his friend's weatherworn face. A twinkle appeared in his eyes. "I was

Ann Bell

suspicious of an ulterior motive. Do I dare ask what it is?"

"It could benefit both of us and Rebekah," Richard replied. "Since Sybilla Masters' death I have had customers begging me to continue selling the straw hats she made. Rebekah is probably the only person in Philadelphia who knows how to make them. I would be willing to buy Sybilla's house and workshop if thou wouldst release Rebekah at least two or three days a week to make hats for both our mercantiles."

John Reynolds listened intently, paused, and stroked his chin. "Hmm. An interesting proposition. I too have been deluged with requests for Sybilla's hats." He sat in silence for a few minutes. "Since Sarah left home and the other children are old enough to share in the chores, I'm in a better position to release her. I could allow Rebekah to make hats three days a week. She only has six months left in her contract anyway. If we do that, we could have a monopoly on the hat business in Philadelphia."

"Then thou art amiable to the idea?"

John Reynolds glanced at his indentured servant relaxing under the tree and turned back to his friend. "I told Rebekah I would not release her from her contract for marriage because I needed her, but now I'm considering releasing her part-time for another business arrangement. It makes me look inconsistent in my dealings."

Richard Logan shook his head. "Not really. Rebekah signed an agreement to work for five years, regardless of the type of work involved. Keeping one's word is an important lesson all Quakers must learn and abide by."

"That's true. However, I feel a little uncomfortable about presenting this option since I stood firm on Isaac's request. I will agree to this arrangement only if Rebekah is willing."

~~~~

Rebekah pretended to be asleep as she lay on her blanket straining to hear the men's conversation. She tried not to react even though joy overflowed within her. *John Reynolds saw her as a real person, rather than merely an indentured servant. He understood her internal conflict.*

John Reynolds and Richard Logan left the blanket and walked to the oak tree. "Rebekah, art thou sleeping?" John Reynolds asked. "We have a question to ask thee."

Rebekah opened her eyes and sat up. "What is the question?"

The men sat on the grass beside her. "Wouldst thou be willing to make hats in Sybilla's shop three days a week?" John Reynolds asked. "If Friend Logan

[215]

Ann Bell

purchased Sybilla's hatmaking shop and equipment, I would release thee from thy household chores. If we did this, both mercantiles could continue selling that style of hat. Thou art the only one in Philadelphia who knows how to make them."

Rebekah could hardly contain her excitement. "I would be honored to continue Sybilla's business. Making hats would keep her memory alive."

"I'm glad thou feel that way," Richard Logan said. "Wouldst thou be willing to teach the trade to thy brothers? They could work as thy helpers until they are proficient in hat weaving as well. We want to make sure Sybilla's method of hatmaking will not be lost."

Rebekah pictured her younger brothers' stubby fingers and smiled. "I'll do my best, but it may be years before they can develop the dexterity to entwine the straw tightly enough."

"I'm certain it will come with time," Richard Logan said. "But until it does, they could help by setting up and preparing the materials. If it is agreed upon, I'll contact the administrator of Sybilla's estate and we can begin working on this project right away."

The following evening, while the Reynolds family sat on the front porch enjoying the fresh summer air, a wagon turned into their lane and approached their front yard. Everyone strained to see who it was. Within moments, Isaac Morris was bounding toward them. "Good evening," he greeted. "It was too hot to work on the house, so I rode over to see if Rebekah and the children would like to go for a wagon ride and see the progress of the house."

Rebekah rushed to his side. "I'd love to see the house again. I have so much I'd like to talk about with thee."

"May I come too?" Mary begged.

Isaac Morris looked at Elizabeth, who was watching the encounter with obvious amusement. "Only if it is agreeable with thy mother," he said.

Before their mother could respond, Lillian interjected, "May I come too?"

Elizabeth Reynolds nodded and smiled. "Of course. Just remember thy manners."

Lillian took Rebekah's hand and skipped toward the wagon with Mary close behind. Isaac lifted the girls into the back of the wagon before he helped Rebekah onto the seat in the front. The sun glistened off the hide of Isaac's black mare when he slid into the seat beside her. With a shout of "farewell" to the remaining Reynolds and a "giddy-up" to the mare, Isaac slapped the reins against the mare's hindquarters.

Ann Bell

As they rode along with the wind whipping through their hair, Isaac reached for her hand. "Rebekah, thou appear to be happier this evening than I have seen thee in a long time. I'm glad to see my old Rebekah back. What happened to bring about the change?"

Rebekah raised her head and looked lovingly into Isaac's eyes. "I'm sorry I withdrew the way I did. I could not bear the loss of Sybilla. She was not only my friend, but also a mentor and guide. I missed her so, but it wasn't fair to thee that I withdrew into my own sorrow."

"Sybilla was a remarkable woman," Isaac said. "The city of Philadelphia is a much better place because she lived here. It is very normal to grieve for her."

"I wanted to do something to show the world how much she meant to me, but I didn't know what." Rebekah paused and shielded her eyes from the glowing western sun. "That is, until last First Day. That is when I received a new direction for my life."

A panicked look spread across Isaac's face. "I hope I am included in that direction."
Rebekah laughed and squeezed Isaac's hand. "Of course, thou art a part of that direction. I'll be the happiest woman in the world when I can spend the rest of my life with thee. "

Isaac pulled her slim frame against his shoulder. "I promise to do everything in my power to make thee happy. But answer me this, what is the new direction thou received?"

A smile spread across Rebekah's face and a twinkle appeared in her eye. "The Reynolds and the Logans had a picnic together after the First Day Meeting. Richard Logan told me his customers are constantly requesting Sybilla Master's style of straw hat. He offered to buy her house and workshop so I could continue making her hats."

"But what about thy contract? Did John Reynolds agree to release thee? He was very stern about not releasing thee to marry. He insisted a Quaker must always fulfill their contract and keep their word."

Rebekah smiled as she remembered the intense emotions when they first approached John Reynolds with their desire to marry. Nothing would have moved him from his position at the time. "Surprisingly enough, he let me make the decision," she said. "Their offer was one I couldn't refuse. It is what I wanted to do after we were married and now I get to begin work six months before I finish my contract."

Isaac squeezed her hand. "What exactly did they propose?"

"John Reynolds agreed to let me have two or three free days a week to work in Sybilla's shop and Richard Logan agreed to buy Sybilla's house, shop, and equipment. They even want me to teach my brothers the skill so the trade secret would no longer be locked in one person's head."

By the time they finished discussing the new development in their lives, they had arrived at their destination. Isaac stopped the wagon in front the nearly completed brick house. Mary and Lillian bounded from the back of the wagon before Isaac had a chance to help them, their eyes wide with awe. "Friend Morris, didst thou build this all by thyself?"

"Most of it," he said with unmasked pride. "Several friends helped me with the stonework on the fireplace, laying bricks, and lifting the beams to the roof. Dost thou like it?"

Mary pushed open the front door and ran inside. "Oh, yes. It's huge," she exclaimed. "Can I come and stay with thee after thee and Rebekah are married?"

"Thou most certainly can. I built rooms for everyone." Isaac hesitated and winked at Rebekah. "When we have a large a family of our own, we'll always be able to make room for special people like thee."

Mary and Lillian giggled and chattered excitedly while Isaac showed them the upstairs bedchambers, Rebekah's future hatmaking shop, and his tailor shop. "I've never seen a house this big before," Lillian said. "It's beautiful."

When they entered the tailor shop Isaac Morris said to Rebekah, "The tailor shop is finished and ready to move into. I wanted to purchase Sybilla's equipment for thy shop in the back, but I have all my money invested in this house. I'm glad Richard Logan was able to obtain it for thee; it will make our dreams come true more quickly."

Rebekah took Isaac's hand. "I'm grateful for everything that's being done on my behalf. It has restored my faith in God and assured me God had not abandoned me after all."

Hand-in-hand, the couple continued walking through the house. When they finished the tour, Rebekah asked, "When dost thou plan to move thy shop here from its present location?"

"I'd like to move the shop to this location in two or three weeks. I've more than outgrown my old tailor shop. It's so crowded I never seem to be able to find what I need."

Rebekah smiled as she remembered the last time she and Sybilla had been in the crowded, cluttered tailor shop. "Thou wilt not know how to work in a spacious, organized room."

Isaac laughed and gave her a playful hug. "My next project will be to collect enough furniture to fill this house. After the shop is moved, I can begin sleeping and preparing my meals here as well."

Mary and Lillian amused themselves by wandering around the living area and making suggestions where they felt the furniture should be placed. Mary was convinced a spinning wheel had to be to the right of the fireplace since that was where her mother kept hers, while Lillian thought it should be in the corner.

When the sun faded below the horizon and pink and red streaks spread across the western sky, the foursome climbed into the wagon and headed toward the Reynolds's home. The cool evening breeze brushed across their faces. Rebekah laid her head upon Isaac's shoulder. In six months, she and Isaac would be wed and living in their own home with her own business in a connecting room and his on the other side of the house.

When the wagon approached the Reynolds's home, Mary pointed to a sign on the front gate of the neighbor's house. "Rebekah, there's a sign on the Clark's front door. I think it says 'Quarantined.' Do they have smallpox? Dost thou think my friend Margaret will die like Sybilla did?"

Ann Bell

Eleven

Rebekah gazed out the front kitchen window while she continued slicing apples. If she hurried, she could have the dessert ready for the evening meal. In the distance, she saw two girls trudging down the lane. The smaller one seemed to be supporting the larger one. She laid the knife on the counter and raced out the front door. "Lillian, what's wrong?"

Lillian's eyes were wide with fear. "Mary's sick. She can barely walk."

"Let me help her," Rebekah said. She wrapped her arm around Mary and supported as much of her weight as she could. "She's much too heavy for thee."

"Mary turned red this afternoon in class and kept her head on her desk until school was over. No one realized how sick she was and everyone left as soon as school was over," Lillian said. "She hardly knows what is going on. I've had to support her all the way home."

[225]

When Mary stumbled over a rock, Rebekah lifted her into her arms and carried her the rest of the way to the house. Every muscle strained from the heavy load as Rebekah stepped onto the porch, but she barely noticed it. She felt strength she never knew she had.

Suddenly the door flew open in front of them and Elizabeth Reynolds appeared. "Rebekah, what happened? I was upstairs and didn't see them coming," she said as she held the door open. "Lay Mary on the cot in the corner."

When Rebekah got Mary to the cot, Elizabeth lifted her daughter's shoulders from Rebekah while Rebekah straightened the girl's body and together they gently lowered Mary.

"Rebekah, wouldst thou get a basin of cold water and a cloth?" Elizabeth said as she unfastened her daughter's dress and surveyed her back. "Oh, no! There are faint red spots. I hope this isn't smallpox."

Rebekah set the basin of water on a table beside the cot. "Wouldst thou like me to take the horse and get Doctor Browning?"

"Yes, please do," Elizabeth Reynolds begged. "There have been too many cases of smallpox in this area. Mary had been with Margaret right before she got sick, so it's possible that Mary got it from her."

Rebekah raced from the house to the barn. She took the bridle from the hook, adjusted it in the horse's mouth, and threw a blanket over his back. There was no time to use the heavy saddle. She stepped her foot on the railing and threw her other leg over the horse's back. Within moments, she was galloping the horse as fast as she could down their lane and across town to Doctor Browning's office.

When she arrived, she slid from the horse and tethered him to the hitching post in front of the building. The last patient was leaving when she burst into his office. "Doctor Browning, come quickly. Mary is ill."

The doctor put his hand on Rebekah's shoulder and motioned her to a nearby chair. "Sit down and rest. Thou art exhausted. I'll get thee a glass of water and thou can refresh thyself while I retrieve my bag and signs."

Rebekah wrinkled her forehead. "What kind of sign wouldst thou need to come to the Reynolds's house to see Mary? Thou have been to our house many times before."

"If Mary has smallpox, the entire household may need to be quarantined," he said as he disappeared into the back of the building.

[227]

Rebekah leaned her head against the back of the chair and sipped her water. *Quarantined? They can't quarantine us. I won't be able to see Isaac. I am supposed to start making hats on the next Second Day in Sybilla's shop.*

Doctor Browning appeared in the front of the office and motioned for Rebekah to follow him. His brown mare was now tethered next to Rebekah's. He helped her onto her horse and climbed onto his. The shadows lengthened when the pair galloped their horses toward the Reynolds's home. While Doctor Browning wrapped the reins of his horse around the tree limb and hurried up the path to Elizabeth Reynolds who was waiting at the door, Rebekah returned her horse to the barn. By the time Rebekah had returned to the house, Doctor Browning had his diagnosis.

"Elizabeth, I regret to tell thee, but thy suspicions are correct. Mary does have smallpox. It's in the early stages so I don't know how severe it will become. I'm afraid I'll have to quarantine thy entire family."

Elizabeth Reynolds could not mask her inner panic. "But what about our men folks? They haven't been around Mary these last few days. They need to keep the mercantile open. Our livelihood depends on it, and people depend on them for their supplies."

Doctor Browning hesitated and scratched his chin. "Maybe if they do not come home during thy quarantine period, and avoid close contact with the people who come into the mercantile, they won't be contagious."

Elizabeth Reynolds slumped into a kitchen chair and cradled her head in her hands. "There's a storeroom in the mercantile big enough for the three of them to sleep," she said. "If I gather food and clothing for them, wouldst thou deliver it to them and explain the situation?"

The doctor closed his bag and joined Elizabeth at the kitchen table. "I'll do whatever I can to help. My first concern is if thou and Rebekah will be able to handle all the work of such a large place and care for Mary. It would be much easier if thy freedman was still here to help."

"I know it will be difficult," Elizabeth said, looking at their indentured servant who was already preparing the evening meal beside the fireplace, "Rebekah is a hard worker and I'm certain we will be able to manage."

Rebekah shuddered. *How will I be able to survive three weeks without seeing Isaac? He was the only one who gave her the courage to carry on.*

Isaac Morris laid his saw on the tree stump beside him when a galloping horse entered the yard of his future home and a rider jumped to the ground.

[229]

Ann Bell

"Friend Reynolds, what brings thee out so late in the afternoon? Wouldst thou like to come in and see the house and share a cup of tea?"

"Oh no. I cannot stay long. I am a bearer of bad news," he said, his brow wrinkled from concern.

Isaac's face blanched. "Is it Rebekah? Is she all right?"

"I hope so, but there's no way I can know for sure. Mary contracted smallpox and my home is quarantined."

"If thy home is quarantined, how art thou able to be out and about? Art thou breaking the health rules? I've heard stories that they lock people in jail for breaking quarantine."

"Doctor Browning brought food and clothing from the house and told me not to go home until the quarantine is lifted. I have no way of knowing how serious the situation is. The older boys are with me, and Matthew is with his mother. I could lose the rest of my family and I would have no way of helping them."

Isaac Morris slumped onto the ground and leaned against a tree. "I hope Mary will be all right. I cannot bear the thought of Rebekah quarantined with someone with smallpox. She was so devastated after losing Sybilla I don't think she'll be able to withstand any more pain. I must go to her."

John Reynolds knelt beside Isaac. "Thou cannot go. We must curtail this evil disease, even if it means great personal sacrifice."

"I cannot stay here in comfort and do nothing when the one I love could be in peril." Isaac slammed his fist against the side of the tree. "I just cannot do it."

"Isaac, God will give thee the strength to endure whatever lies ahead. We must look out for the common good of the colony. All we can do now is pray for them."

"I have to do something for my Rebekah or I'll lose my mind."

"Maybe thou couldst prepare Sybilla's shop so Rebekah could begin working there as soon as she's out of quarantine. It'll take several days to clean the house. I could take some of the unneeded clothing and household furnishings from the house to the mercantile and sell them. We could use that money to buy more hatmaking supplies."

Isaac became somber. *Dear God, he prayed, please give me strength. I know Friend Reynolds is right. I must learn to better trust God.* After a long silence, he turned back to his friend. "It's agreed upon. Tomorrow, I'll begin cleaning and arranging Sybilla's home and hatmaking shop. Rebekah will

Ann Bell

be pleased when she sees it. After what she has been through she'll need all the help she can get."

~~~~

Three weeks after Mary's diagnosis, Doctor Browning returned to the Reynolds home. Rebekah was walking across the yard with dry clothes from the line when he rode up. "How's everyone, today? I hope Mary is better and no one else has become ill."

Rebekah hurried to the path to join him. "Good day, Doctor Browning. Come in and see," she said as she led the way to the house. "Mary appears much better, but something is wrong with her eyes. For a while, she even had scabs on them."

He unlatched the door and held it open for Rebekah. Mary was sitting in a chair by the window with a blank stare on her face. Doctor Browning knelt beside her. "Hello, Mary," he said. "How art thou today? Thou look much better than the last time I saw thee."

"I feel better," Mary mumbled.

Wouldst thou lie on the cot for a few moments so I can examine thee?"

Mary obediently rose from her chair and walked hesitantly toward the cot. The doctor spent several

[232]

minutes examining the girl's body. Elizabeth and Rebekah exchanged worried glances until the doctor spoke. "Mary, it appears thou art one of the lucky ones. Thy scars have healed nicely. I can declare thee healed and will lift the quarantine immediately. However, I want to look at thy eyes more closely. I do not like the looks of the scars around them."

For the next few minutes, Doctor Browning held a different number of fingers at different heights and locations around Mary's head. Much to Rebekah's and Elizabeth's chagrin, Mary's responses were wrong about ninety percent of the time.

Finally, Doctor Browning pulled up a chair next to the cot and took Mary's hand. "Mary, I'm afraid smallpox has done permanent damage to thy vision. I don't think thy eyesight will ever improve."

Tears began flowing down Mary's cheeks. "If the smallpox went away, my vision has got to come back as well. I want my papa," she cried, burying her head in her hands. "When can he come home? He'll be able to make everything right. He always has."

Doctor Browning patted Mary's shoulder as he exchanged pathetic glances with Elizabeth Reynolds. "I'll go directly to the mercantile and tell thy father the news," he said. "I'm certain he'll be here shortly. He's been anxious to be with thee during thy long illness, but we couldn't risk him spreading the disease further."

[233]

~~~~~

Mary Reynolds was one of the last victims of the smallpox outbreak in Philadelphia that year. In spite of her poor vision, life in the Reynolds household returned to normal. Within a week, Rebekah was working at her freshly renovated hatmaking shop with Isaac hovering nearby. Not only was she making hats for both the Logan and Reynolds mercantiles, but also people from across Philadelphia began stopping at the shop to leave orders.

Rebekah was getting use to the new normal and anticipating her future as the wife of Isaac Morris, when her peaceful inner tranquility was shattered during a First Day Meeting. Rebekah was sitting in her typical bowed posture, waiting for a word from the Inner Light, when suddenly, Rebekah's thoughts were interrupted by a familiar woman's voice.

"Greetings, seekers of the Inner Light. I am Charity Jones," she began. "I bring greetings to thee from the High Street Society in London. My friend, Hope Jamison, and I just returned to America from England. I am pleased to report the Quakers in London are standing strong in the midst of adversity. Because of that, they are being richly blessed. More than three years ago, we lived within thy midst at John Reynolds' home and shared God's love and peace with thy Society. Recently we have been led back to encourage thee to follow the Inner Light within instead of thy own physical desires."

Rebekah took a deep breath. The memory of her internal struggles concerning becoming a missionary resurfaced. *How strong is my faith? Do I love God more than I love Isaac? Will I have to choose between a life with Isaac Morris and a life serving God as a traveling minister like Charity Jones and Hope Jamison?* An image of her beloved flashed before her. *What if after I am married I become fully convinced of my calling to be a traveling minister, will Isaac accept that calling and permit me to go?*

From that moment onward, Rebekah continued her spiritual struggle. She read from her family Bible each day and started a spiritual journal with the scraps of paper John Reynolds brought home from his mercantile. Each day she poured out her love for Isaac and her love for God. Could she continue to love both, or would she have to give up her beloved to follow the Inner Light?

During the remainder of the summer, Rebekah's brothers took turns assisting her in the work area and establishing a small store in the living room of Sybilla's house. Samuel's job was to talk to the customers who entered the store and help them decide which hat they would like to buy.

Late one afternoon Samuel came bursting into the room where Rebekah was bent over a vat soaking straw. "Rebekah, there's a strange man here who's interested in buying a hat. He keeps asking me all kinds of questions about how they're made. I don't know what to say."

"Don't worry, I'll help him," she said. She dried her hands on a towel and hurried to the front room. A lean, gawky young man was examining the details of a hat with intense interest.

"May I help thee?"

"I've never seen hats made like this. Are you the one who makes them?" the stranger asked.

"Yes, I am. Wouldst thou like to try one on?"

The stranger tried on several hats with absolute glee. "I don't have enough money to buy one today," he said downheartedly, "but I'll be back as soon as I can save enough. Would you mind explaining how you make such fine hats?"

Rebekah smiled with pride. "My friend, Sybilla Masters, taught me," she said. "Come to the shop in the back and I'll show thee what I do."

For the next half hour, Rebekah demonstrated the techniques involved in the making of her specialized straw hats. She was enthralled by the stranger's intellect and quick wit. When he turned to leave he said, "I want to thank you for your time and hospitality; it was extremely enlightening. I apologize I don't even know your name."

"My name is Rebekah Bradford," she said, "but in less than a month I'll marry Isaac Morris so my name will be Rebekah Morris. And what might thy name be?"

He bowed low. "It is nice to meet you, Rebekah Bradford," he said. "My name is Benjamin Franklin. I've just arrived in Philadelphia and am familiarizing myself with the surroundings. This city is a fascinating place with many new and exciting things happening around every corner. Your shop is a definite rarity. Thank you for your hospitality. I'll be back when I have enough money to purchase a hat."

Rebekah stood in the doorway watching the strange young man walk down the street and turn the corner. *There is something unusual about that man,* she mused. *He is different from the men I've met at the meetings. I wonder if he's a Quaker. He does not talk like one.*

~~~~~

The week before their marriage, Isaac Morris appeared in the doorway of the hatmaking shop. An amused smile spread across his face. "Rebekah, thou hast already outgrown this shop. I don't know how Sybilla ever worked in this cramped space.

[237]

Thou definitely need to have larger accommodations."

"I agree the shop is crowded," Rebekah said and shrugged her shoulders. "But I don't know what else to do. Richard Logan owns the building and all the equipment and supplies."

"Maybe we should talk to him and try to work things out. I've recently accumulated a little money; maybe he'll let me buy the hatmaking equipment for thee. Without the equipment, Richard Logan could sell the house to someone else and make a profit."

Rebekah studied the soft eyes and strong chin of her betrothed. "Thou wouldst do all that for me?"

"Of course, I'd do anything for thee. I love thee with all my heart. Nothing is too good for thee."

Isaac watched as Rebekah completed the hat she was working on. When the supplies were all returned to the shelf, she locked the door of the house and walked hand-in-hand with him to the waiting wagon.

The first hint of autumn was in the air and the ride across town was exhilarating. With each block, Rebekah became more pensive. *For years, it had seemed as if time stood still, but now my contract with the Reynolds is almost fulfilled and I'll soon be a free woman and the bride of Isaac Morris. Why do I feel afraid? Am I doing the right thing by marrying Isaac and not becoming a traveling missionary like Hope Jamison and Charity Jones?*

Ann Bell

Twelve

Philadelphia, Sixth Month 1720

Rebekah sat on the back row at the First Day
Meeting, her head bowed and in deep conversation
with herself. *I deeply love Isaac Morris. I've never
met anyone as wise and kind as he is, and I want to
spend the rest of my life with him. Yet, Charity
Jones and Hope Jamison were willing to leave their
loved ones to spread the Word of God. Hope
Jamison leaves her beloved husband behind and
travels for several months before she sees him
again. Would I be willing to do the same? God has
been good to me. He has brought me to a new land
with more opportunities than I ever thought
possible. Soon I will be free to make all my own
choices. After being controlled by others all my life,
will I be able to make the right choices on my own?*

Rebekah scarcely noticed when, one by one, three
men and one Quaker woman stood to speak about
how the Inner Light was leading them. Their
audible voices were drowned out by two voices
struggling within her.

Ann Bell

Rebekah, thou should follow the example of Charity Jones and Hope Jamison and become a traveling missionary to spread the love of God.

No, Rebekah. Thou would best serve God by marrying Isaac Morris and bearing him many children.

But Rebekah, God has blessed thee in many ways; thou must serve Him full-time to show Him how grateful thou art for what He has done.

Rebekah's thoughts were interrupted when she noticed the other attendees were filing from the meetinghouse in silence. She was one of the last out the door and squinted while her eyes adjusted to the bright sunlight. When she reached the middle of the yard, she searched for the Reynolds family. *There are only four more First Day Meetings in which I'll be riding home with them,* she thought. *I wonder what will happen next.*

"Rebekah....Rebekah," a familiar voice shouted from behind her.

She turned as Sarah Nelson came hurrying toward her and embraced her warmly. "Rebekah, how art thou? I have missed thee so. I'm anxious to learn of thy marriage plans."

Rebekah smiled and returned the embrace. "Sarah, it's good to see thee again. I've been doing very well. Didst thou know that I've been working two days a week for thy family and three days at Sybilla's hat shop? It's amazing how many people want to buy that style of hat."

"My father told me about the hat business. How wonderful for everyone." Sarah reached down and took the hand of a small child who had raced to her side. "I'm going to have to go, but please come visit me on thy next free day. We have so much to talk about."

"I'll do that," Rebekah promised as Sarah went to join her husband.

~~~~

"Rebekah, wouldst thou like a cup of tea?" Sarah asked as the two young women gathered around Sarah's kitchen table during Rebekah's next free day.

Rebekah hesitated. This was the first time she had visited her friend and former nemesis in the home Sarah now shared with her husband, his four children, and their aging housekeeper. Rebekah watched the children playing near the fireplace while the housekeeper worked in the garden in the backyard. *What a perfect life of peace and tranquility. Sarah seems like a different person. Gone is the constant pout that was so familiar to me during the last five years. She has truly become a beautiful person, both inside and out.*

[243]

Rebekah quickly turned her attention back to her friend. "If it is no problem, I would love to have a cup of tea," she said.

Sarah poured the steaming tea into two cups and placed one before her friend. "Rebekah, I'm concerned for thee. I thought thou were planning to wed Isaac Morris in the Ninth Month, but at the last First Day Meeting, thou looked sad. What was wrong? It is a time thou should be glowing."

Rebekah felt her face flush and looked down. She ran her index finger around the rim of her cup. "Was it that obvious?"

Sarah reached for Rebekah's hand and squeezed it. "Yes, it was. I could see thee from the corner of my eye and thou appeared to be in a full sweat while the room was chilly that morning."

Rebekah hesitated. She had not shared her innermost thoughts with another woman since Sybilla died. Was this a time to change? *Since Sarah's marriage to George Nelson, she appears to be an entirely different person. Surely, I can trust her now.* She took a deep breath. "I was trying to listen to the Inner Light, but all I could hear were two distinct voices screaming back and forth within my head."

An expression of understanding spread across Sarah's face. "I have had that experience many times," she said. "What were the voices saying?"

Rebekah took a deep breath. "One voice said that since God had blessed me, I should give up my dreams of marrying Isaac Morris and become a traveling missionary. The other voice said I would be pleasing God if I married Isaac as planned. It was a horrible struggle."

"It sounds like it was terribly confusing," Sarah said. "I'm certain thee will soon know which voice is the Inner Light and which was the voice of darkness. I remember the time Charity Jones and Hope Jamison stayed at our home several years ago. At that time, I thought the Inner Light was leading me to become a traveling missionary. Do you remember what they told me?"

Rebekah smiled as memories stirred within. "I think I can almost quote Charity's exact words. 'One does not have to become a traveling missionary to serve God. Thou can serve God by taking care of the sick, feeding the poor, and tending to the children of the poor.'"

Sarah sat quietly, watching Rebekah struggle with her plans for the future and her love for Isaac Morris and the Almighty God.

Finally, Rebekah lifted the cup of tea to her lips. The warmth of the liquid brought a special calm and relaxation to her body. "That is the answer. Now I'm certain I hear the Inner Light speaking to me and not the enemy."

"And what is the Inner Light saying?"

"I feel God wants me to go ahead and marry Isaac. He has worked hard to build a house and a hatmaking shop for me. Our love is deep and pure. It would be sinful if I disappointed him now. I will serve God best by being the best wife, hatmaker, and hopefully someday a mother."

~~~~~

The first rays of sunlight streamed into the upstairs bedchamber of Rebekah Bradford on the Seventeenth Day of the Ninth Month, 1720. When she awoke, she sprang to her feet. This was her day of liberation. Her indentured contract had been fulfilled. This was also the day of her marriage to Isaac Morris. She hurriedly packed her few possessions into a small chest.

The last thing to be packed was her most treasured possession, the family Bible. She ran her fingers over the tattered leather edges with longing. *This is the most important day of my life and mother is not here to share it with me. I don't know if she is even alive. Mother sacrificed a great deal so the boys and I could have a good life in America. If there is ever a way, I'm determined someday to visit London and find out what happened to mother and share my gratitude with those who cared for her.*

The day was busy with activities. Rebekah gathered the remainder of her belongings and loaded them into John Reynolds' wagon. She took one last stroll around the yard, the garden, and the barn. For years, she thought this day would never come, yet when it did, she was surprised by the melancholy that enveloped her. *In spite of the hard work the Reynolds required of me, they treated me well. I have heard horror stories about the indentured servants of some non-Quakers. The plight of the Africans is even worse. In spite of my rebellious spirit, I was truly blessed.*

She hugged each of the Reynolds children and made each one promise to visit her often. She thanked Elizabeth Reynolds for all her kindness and turned to John. "I thank thee for all thou hast done for me. I don't know what would have happened if thou had not hired me as an indentured servant and brought me to Philadelphia. Even when I wanted to get out of my contract early, thou were right in having me fulfill it. A Quaker must always be true to their word, regardless of how difficult it may be at times. I'll always be indebted to thee."

Late that afternoon a small congregation of Friends gathered at the Market Street Meetinghouse to watch Rebekah Bradford and Isaac Morris say their marriage promises to each other. The service ended with many prayers for their health, happiness, and well-being. Truly, the presence of God was felt in that simple service of love and commitment.

[247]

When Rebekah turned to greet the congregation, she lost her serious sense of decorum and screeched with excitement. There in the back of the meetinghouse was a familiar face. The young woman looked much older and more tired than she remembered, but it had to be her.

"Priscilla," she shouted and ran down the aisle and fell into her former shipmate's arms. The two women held each other and cried for several minutes, ignoring the groom and the guests around them. "How did thee find me and know this was my wedding day?"

Pricilla pulled away, but continued holding both of Rebekah's hands. "I wanted to find you sooner, but our circumstances changed when we got off the ship. Life was very difficult. The land my father thought he had purchased actually belonged to another. He was swindled out of his entire investment. However, he was able to obtain a tract of land in Indian country and start a small farm."

"How terrible," Rebekah exclaimed. "What did thy family do?"

"We had to work doubly hard just to survive. I rarely got to town. Six months ago, a small band of Indians raided our farm and burned our house and barn. Father and Peter were killed when the burning roof collapsed while they were leading the horses out of the barn."

"How sad. They were both such good people." Rebekah gasped. "What didst thou do without them?"

Pricilla hesitated and swallowed hard before she answered. "Mother and the girls and I had to walk all the way to Philadelphia. No one would help us until we came to a Quaker meetinghouse. We'll be forever grateful for their help. Someone knew of a small dwelling where we could live. Mother started taking in laundry to help buy food. We had to work long hours to make ends meet."

A sense of guilt enveloped Rebekah. On the ship, she had envied Priscilla because she had a family, plus better clothing and food to eat. However, Priscilla's life on the frontier had been much harder than she could have imagined as an indentured servant. The Smith family did not deserve this kind of a life. "I am sorry to hear this," Rebekah said. "Life has not treated thee fairly. Is there anything I can do to help?"

Priscilla looked up at Isaac, smiled, and turned back to her friend. "Just be happy with your new husband," she said. "I married a wonderful man last week. I want you to be as happy as I am. My husband was in the tailor shop yesterday when Isaac told him of his upcoming marriage. I had told my husband all about you and the hours we spent together on the ship *Good Hope*. While Isaac was describing his betrothed, my husband was certain it had to be you. There were few other girls our age on that ship. I had to come today to see for myself."

Rebekah could scarcely contain her excitement. "I'm so glad thou found me. It makes the best day of my life even better."

Rebekah turned to her groom who waited patiently behind her. She formally introduced Isaac to her friend and proceeded around the room introducing Priscilla to the other guests at the marriage ceremony. When Priscilla saw John Reynolds, she rushed to his side. "John Reynolds, I would know you anywhere. You were so good to my family onboard and were such comfort when my baby brother died."

John Reynolds wrapped a protective arm around Priscilla and introduced her to his family. Years of hardship seemed to melt away as they exchanged news of their families. Meanwhile, Rebekah and Isaac spent nearly an hour receiving well wishes amid much levity and lightheartedness. After all the guests were greeted, Isaac helped Rebekah into his wagon and waved goodbye to their friends. Their new life together had finally begun.

Rebekah Morris lived blissfully in her new marital state while the seasons changed from spring to summer and then to fall. She basked in the responsibility of being in control of her own home. Not only did her hatmaking business thrive, but also her cooking skills. Rarely a week went by without friends and relatives gathering around their spacious kitchen table for a mouth-watering meal. Rebekah became one of the first women in the neighborhood to take food to an ailing neighbor.

After Christmas, Rebekah began feeling more tired than she had ever felt in her life. *It must be the long hours of working in the shop,* she reasoned. She continued pushing herself to her limit of endurance. While the demand for her hats continued to grow, she continued ignoring her physical discomfort in an effort to produce more hats faster than ever before.

One evening while Rebekah and Isaac warmed themselves around the fireplace, Rebekah sighed deeply, laid her knitting in her lap, and turned to her husband. "Isaac, I've been extremely tired lately and I don't think I can continue this pace much longer. But I'm afraid the hatmaking business will suffer if I slow down."

"Rebekah, my love, I've noticed the change in thee, and have become extremely concerned. Thou hast been working much too hard. Thou need to rest more and take care of thyself."

Rebekah reached for Isaac's hand and smiled meekly. "I think it's more than overwork," she said. "I think I'm expecting a child."

[251]

Isaac leaned over to embrace his wife. A smile spread across his face. "Rebekah, I'm so happy. Except for our wedding day, this is the most exciting thing that has ever happened to us. When dost thou think the baby will come?"

"Probably the middle of the summer. I'm not exactly sure."

"Maybe thou should not work on your hats until after the baby is born," Isaac said. "Bending over the vats will not be good for thee and thou wilt need all the rest thou can get."

"I'm feeling better than I did a couple of weeks ago," she protested. "Other women can work until the day their baby arrives and I want to do so as well."

Isaac took Rebekah in his arms, cradled her head against his chest, and caressed her hair. "I understand thy feelings, but I don't want anything to happen. Listen to what thy body tells thee. When thou begin to tire, promise me thou wilt go to bed and rest."

~~~~~

As the weeks passed, Rebekah felt less tired in spite of her expanding waistline. Isaac not only maintained his tailoring business, but helped with the heavy lifting in the hatmaking shop as well. In spite of the difficulty of bending over the vats to soak the straw, Rebekah maintained a steady work schedule. She often wondered why others complained during their pregnancy when she was feeling the healthiest she had ever felt in her life.

The first day of Eighth Month was one of the hottest days of the summer. It began like any other day, but in mid-afternoon, while sitting on a bench weaving a hat, Rebekah began to suffer severe abdominal pains. She hurried to Isaac's tailor shop. "Isaac, I think the time may be close. Wouldst thou get the midwife? If Sister Martin is not available, Elizabeth Reynolds said she would help when the baby is born."

Isaac wrapped his arm around his wife and led her to the bedchamber. "I wouldn't consider having anyone except a doctor deliver our children. Too many things could go wrong."

"After a rough first few weeks, I've had an extremely easy pregnancy," she protested. "I shouldn't have any problems with the delivery." When another pain shot through her abdomen, Rebekah stretched out on the bed. She grimaced before continuing. "When Elizabeth Reynolds and the other women I knew lost their babies, it was because they were almost past childbearing years. I am young and healthy. What could possibly go wrong?"

Isaac shook his head. "I'm thankful for thy good health," he said. He wiped the perspiration from her forehead, "but I insist on having Doctor Browning with us. Get some rest and I'll be right back."

Rebekah tried to sleep, but the pains were becoming stronger and more frequent. She clutched her fist with pain. *I wish Isaac would hurry. I know there isn't anything he can do for me, but I would like to hold his hand every time I have a pain.*

Within a half hour, she heard two separate sets of footsteps on the front porch. Isaac flung open the door to the bedchamber. "How art thou doing, my love?"

Rebekah grimaced. "I think the baby will be here soon. The pains are intense and close together. I am glad thou brought the doctor."

Doctor Browning greeted Rebekah and turned to her husband. "Isaac, maybe thou should wait in the other room while I check Rebekah. I will let thee know if I need anything."

Isaac kissed her on the lips and retreated from the bedchamber. The hours passed and the skies darkened outside while Rebekah's pain intensified. "When will the baby come?" she asked between pains. "This is taking much too long. Is something wrong?"

Doctor Browning forced an unconvincing smile. "It shouldn't be long now. Some babies just take longer getting here than others."

After five long hours, a baby boy was born. Doctor Browning cleaned the baby, wrapped him in a quilted blanket Rebekah had made for her firstborn, and laid the child in his mother's arms. In spite of her fatigue, Rebekah smiled at her new child and lovingly stroked his cheeks. "My precious, precious son. He is a true blessing from God."

Isaac hurried into the bedchamber and leaned over to kiss his wife and stroke his son's sallow cheeks. "We have such a beautiful son."

"I know," Rebekah murmured proudly. "What wouldst thou like to name him?"

Isaac paused. Even though they had discussed this many times before, in the intensity of the moment, he could scarcely remember their final decision. Several faces of family and friends flashed through his mind. "I'd like to name him Christopher Adam after my father," he whispered. Seeing the fatigue on Rebekah's face, he wiped the perspiration from her brow. "Thou hast worked hard. Lie back and rest."

Rebekah closed her eyes while Isaac took the bundle from his wife's arms. He studied his son's face for several long moments. "Doctor, is

Ann Bell

something wrong? The baby's breathing seems very shallow."

Doctor Browning took a deep breath and frowned. "The next few hours may be critical," he said.

"What's wrong with our son? Are we in danger of losing him?"

The doctor shook his head. "It is too early to say. His breathing is not as strong as most newborn's. I want to stay here through the night and keep an eye on him."

Isaac's shoulders slumped. He handed his son back to the doctor. "By all means," he said. "I'll make a warm meal and tea for thee. If there's anything thou need, I'll get it for thee. Just please save our baby. Rebekah could not bear the loss."

"All we can do now is to wait and pray," the doctor said, shaking his head.

Rebekah fell into a heavy, deep sleep, but the night passed slowly for the two men. They watched the baby's labored breathing. They tried to get Christopher to swallow a few drops of warm water, but to no avail. He continued to lie limp in their arms.

The first ray of light shone through the Morris bedchamber window when Rebekah awakened. She could hear the two men talking in the next room. "Isaac, Isaac," she called weakly.

Isaac glanced at his son lying in a box next to the doctor beside the fireplace, the furrow on his forehead deepened. A bluish tinge had penetrated the baby's thin skin. With six long strides, Isaac was across the room. He opened the door to the bedchamber, rushed to his wife's bedside, and took her hand.

"Isaac, why is the doctor still here? Is something wrong?"

Isaac took a deep breath. "Christopher is having trouble breathing so Doctor Browning spent the night. He's going to have to leave when it gets lighter but he'll have someone come to help with the baby."

Tears built in Rebekah's eyes. "But our son is beautiful," she protested. "How could anything be wrong?"

Isaac sat on the side of the bed, took his wife's hands, and pressed them against his lips. "Our son is in God's hands," he assured her. "Just remember, whatever happens, I'll always love thee and will remain at thy side."

Rebekah began sobbing. "Please bring Christopher to me. I want to hold him."

Ann Bell

Isaac leaned over and kissed her gently on the lips. "I'll tell the doctor," he said, "and he will bring Christopher to thee."

Isaac went to the door and motioned to the doctor. Doctor Browning tiptoed into the bedchamber carrying the baby and laid him in her arms. "Thou hast a beautiful son, Rebekah," he said gently. "However, he's still fragile and is having trouble breathing."

A cold chill shuddered through her body when she ran her fingers over her baby's soft skin. "Is he going to be all right?"

The doctor shrugged his shoulders and shook his head. "I hope so. He made it through the night, so that's encouraging, but he's still not out of danger."

Rebekah clutched her firstborn child to her breast and wept while her husband and doctor looked on. "I was there when Elizabeth Reynolds lost her baby, but I was able to handle that because her baby was so tiny." She ran her fingers across her son's face, trying to memorize each tiny feature. "Christopher is the most perfectly formed newborn I've ever seen. He has his father's dark hair and strong nose with high cheekbones along with my dimples and square face. It just doesn't make sense that he can't breathe right."

"We must place the baby in God's hands and pray His will be done," Doctor Browning tried to reassure her.

Isaac's voice trembled. "Everything is going to be all right," he said with tears in his eyes. "God has been good to us and has cared for us this far; He will not let us down now."

Rebekah forced a smile. "I know, but it's so difficult."

Doctor Browning took Rebekah's hand. "I must leave now," he said. "I have other patients to see today, but I will ask Elizabeth Reynolds to come and help care for thy son."

Time passed slowly. Within a half hour, Elizabeth Reynolds arrived at the Morris' spacious home. She rushed to Rebekah's side. The women held each other and exchanged tears. Words could not express their grief. Only a mother who has lost a child would understand the pain involved. Finally, Rebekah lay back against her pillow, weak from emotional exhaustion. Elizabeth Reynolds and Isaac exchanged worried glances while Rebekah's sobs slowly subsided and she fell into another exhausted sleep.

Seeing that Rebekah was asleep Elizabeth put her hand gently on Isaac's arm. "Please try to get some rest thyself. Thou look exhausted. I'll take care of the baby."

"I don't want to leave my wife's side. If she awakens she'll think I've abandoned her." He hesitated while his eyes studied his wife's sleeping form. "There is plenty of room on the right side of the bed. I'll lie down beside her."

Elizabeth Reynolds nodded. She cradled the baby in her arms and slipped from the room. Every few minutes she tried to put a few drops of warm milk into the baby's mouth, but Christopher would not swallow and the nourishment dribbled down his chin. While the baby napped, Elizabeth made a hearty meal that could feed the three of them for several days. Silence filled the home for most of the day.

When the shadows began to lengthen at the end of the day, Isaac appeared from the bedchamber and sniffed the air. "That smells delicious. I hope we'll be able to get Rebekah to eat." He moved closer and studied his newborn son sleeping in Elizabeth Reynolds's arms. "I'm worried about Christopher, but I'm even more concerned about Rebekah," he said. "If something happens, will she slip into a deep depression like she did when Sybilla died?"

Elizabeth Reynolds laid the baby back into his box and went to stir the soup in the pot on the fireplace. "I share that concern. No man can possibly feel the intense loss a woman feels when she loses a child."

Isaac opened the cupboard and began assembling utensils and dishes. "I want to have a tray of food ready for Rebekah when she awakens. She hasn't eaten since yesterday."

Elizabeth Reynolds nodded. "While I wait for her to awaken, I can decorate her tray with garden flowers. She has always loved flowers. Maybe that will cheer her." She hurried to the garden while Isaac filled Rebekah's bowl with the thick, creamy soup.

When she returned, Elizabeth placed the freshly picked bouquet in a jar on the corner of the tray. "Isaac, let me take it to her," she said quietly. "As much as she loves thee, this is something only a woman can understand. Wouldst thou keep trying to get a few drops of nourishment into Christopher while I am with Rebekah?"

Solemnly Isaac handed the tray to her, picked up his son, and cradled him in his arms. "I love thee, little one," he said. "Please don't leave us. I just met thee, and I am already overwhelmed with love."

Across the room, Elizabeth quietly opened the door to the bedchamber. "Rebekah," she whispered. "I made a big pot of soup. It's very tasty, even if I say so myself."

Rebekah opened her eyes, but they remained glazed and distant. "I thank thee, but I'm not hungry."

Elizabeth Reynolds sat on the edge of the bed holding the tray. "Thou hast to eat so thou can regain thy strength," she pleaded.

"How can I eat when my baby is dying?"

"That's the very reason thou must eat," Elizabeth stated firmly. "Thou must regain thy strength in order to face the challenges of life. Isaac is also hurting. He cannot bear to see thee suffer. Thou must strengthen thyself for his sake."

Rebekah shook her head.

Persistently Elizabeth lifted a spoonful of vegetables to the young mother's lips. "Here, let me help."

The warm aroma melted Rebekah's stubbornness and she opened her mouth to receive the nourishment. Savoring its rich flavor, she slowly took one bite after another.

When the bowl was empty, she sunk back onto her pillow and whispered. "I thank thee. That tasted better than I expected." Rebekah forced a smile and reached out her hand. "Wouldst thou ask Isaac to come to me and bring Christopher with him?"

"Certainly," Elizabeth said. She set the jar of flowers on the nightstand and left the bedchamber, closing the door behind her.

When she entered the living room, Isaac looked up from the rocking chair. "How's Rebekah?" he asked while he wiped the drops of warm milk from the chin of his son. "Did she eat anything?"

Elizabeth smiled. "She ate the entire bowl. We had a little talk and she asked thee to come to her and bring the baby. I think it is a positive sign."

"I'll be forever indebted to thee. I could never have done it myself."

"Rebekah's a strong woman," she said. "She just needs to be reminded of that during difficult times."

Isaac carried the limp child into the bedchamber. He tried to mask his concern in seeing his beloved lying pale and distraught with red, puffy eyes. "How art thou?"

"I am not important," she said sharply. "The important thing is how Christopher is doing."

Isaac swallowed hard. "My beloved, I'm afraid we might lose him. He is so fragile." He laid the baby gently into his mother's waiting arms. "We must be brave and trust our little one into God's hands."

Rebekah cradled her firstborn tight against her bosom. "I know," she whispered.

"Christopher will soon be taken from us." She paused while she watched the child's breathing become slower and slower. "At first I thought I could never live with the thought of my precious child lying in the hard, cold ground. However, knowing Sybilla and father are in heaven to greet him, I think I may be able to release him from my heart if it must come to that."

Tears rolled down Isaac's cheeks. "Rebekah, I love thee more than I can ever express. Thy words have taken the sting from my heart. Thou art the bravest, wisest woman I know."

That evening Rebekah continued cradling Christopher in her arms, while Isaac lay on the side of the bed watching the labored breathing of his son in his wife's arms. The hours passed and the candle flickered on the nightstand. Just before dawn, he noticed the baby's color change and his body become rigid.

"He is gone," Isaac whispered tenderly. "Christopher is now in the arms of Jesus."

Although Rebekah thought she was prepared for anything, her body began to tremble, and her face turned ashen. Clutching her fist, she screamed. "No! I will never let anyone take Christopher from my arms. I will not be able to go on without my baby."

Thirteen

Rebekah leaned over the workbench in her hatmaking shop. Her fingers craftily wove the strips of straw as tears ran down her cheeks. *Why did my little Christopher have to die before he even had a chance at life? Is God punishing me for not becoming a traveling missionary and preaching His Word? Should I not have followed my heart's desire to marry Isaac? If I had not married, I wouldn't feel this unbearable pain.*

Rebekah pushed the unfinished hat aside and buried her head in her hands. Uncontrollable sobs escaped her lips. *How can I go on like this? Do I have to do something to win God's approval? Isaac must never know I question my inner calling and faith or even my marriage. I would never do anything to hurt him.*

Heavy footsteps thumped across the porch and the front door opened. Rebekah dried her face with the sleeve of her dress and took a deep breath. She forced a smile and went to greet her husband.

Isaac opened his arms and she walked into his warm embrace. She laid her head against his chest.

[265]

"Rebekah, what can I do to ease thy pain? Thou suffer from grief far too much. Wouldst thou like to visit the graveyard with me?"

Rebekah shook her head. "I must force myself to move forward. I took flowers there yesterday and spent some time. I'll go tomorrow with fresh flowers. I want to spend the remainder of the day with thee."

Isaac smiled. "I'd like that very much. I'll bring my sewing into thy shop and we can share these precious hours together. I know we can trust God to get us through this pain."

Rebekah lowered her eyes. "I fear I'll never get over losing my son."

She looked away and retreated into her own thoughts. *I hope Isaac will never learn of my questioning our faith. He thinks I follow the Inner Light with complete trust and confidence.*

~~~~~

The next few days passed uneventfully. The Morrises spent the early evenings sitting on the front porch watching the neighborhood children play in the street. Fourth Day evening Isaac was finishing the day's tasks in his shop while Rebekah made herself comfortable in the fresh evening air. She laid her head against the back of the rocking chair. *Life is finally falling into place*, she thought. *In spite of everything, God has been good to me. He's blessed me with a loving husband, a beautiful home, and a prosperous business. I'm thankful God understands my anger and questioning. I'll have to try to put my doubts behind me and let Isaac know how much I love him. I cannot continue in my pit of despair, It isn't fair to Isaac.*

With a smile on her face, she left her chair and went to Isaac's tailor shop. She found him fitting a wool coat over a mold. "This room is much too cluttered," she teased. "I don't understand how anyone can possibly work in such a mess."

Isaac looked up and laughed. "This looks almost as cluttered as thy shop. It's a sign of four years of growth and hard work." He paused, looked around his shop, and became serious. "You're right; it is time I do something about it. I scarcely know where to begin."

"You've had to cram too much material into a small space," Rebekah said. "The only thing that could help this clutter would be to knock down the walls and make the room bigger, but that's not practical."

"Hmmm." Isaac stroked his chin. He stood from the bench and walked to the far wall. "That's not a bad idea. I would not have to knock down the entire wall; I could just add a double door and add another room onto the back. I could use the back room for storing fabric and finished garments and the current

Ann Bell

shop could be used strictly for sewing, cutting, and displaying clothing."

Rebekah studied her husband. The smoothness of the face of the man she loved was beginning to show faint creases around the eyes and brow and a few strands of grey graced his temples. "Wilt thou have the time to build the addition? Thou art already too busy with thy tailoring."

"I have been considering my options for a while, but thou have given voice to my thinking. Maybe it's time to act." Isaac took a seat on the workbench and motioned for her to join him. "What dost thou think of me hiring an apprentice? If I only worked part-time in the shop, I could have an addition finished before winter."

Rebekah slid onto the bench beside her husband. She took both his hands in hers and squeezed them. "That's an excellent idea. I could make advertising signs and put them around town. I'm certain John Reynolds and Richard Logan would let us put them in their mercantiles. I could also nail them to some of the prominent trees along the way."

"I thank thee for offering to help," he said. "I know thou art extremely busy, but thou hast much better penmanship than I."

With those encouraging words, Rebekah retreated to their living room. She took out a quill pen, ink, and paper, and began to work. Time flew rapidly.

One by one, bold letters appeared on each sheet of paper. Two hours later, she had completed eight decorative signs and held them up for her husband's approval.

"Beautiful work. They'll definitely attract attention," he said. "When thou art ready, I'll hitch the black mare to the wagon for thee."

Rebekah waited on the front porch while Isaac led the mare and wagon to the front of the house. She climbed onto the wagon and took the reins from her husband. She loved the sense of independence the horses provided while she rode the streets of Philadelphia. In spite of the brisk autumn wind, she relished the vibrant colors around her. The promise of hope was in the air.

When she arrived at the Reynolds's Mercantile, Rebekah jumped from the wagon and rushed inside. John Reynolds was assisting a customer while eighteen-year-old Adam was standing on a stool restocking shelves nearby.

When the customer left, John Reynolds came from behind the counter. "Good afternoon, Rebekah. What brings thee out this fine day?"

She smiled and handed him a sheet of paper. "I'd like to put this sign on the wall by the door, if I may."

John Reynolds wrinkled his forehead. "What does it advertise?"

"Isaac has decided to hire a tailor's apprentice and I've made several notices to display around town. I hope he'll be able to find one soon; he has other interests he'd like to pursue."

From the corner of her eye, Rebekah noticed Adam nearly drop a jar he was placing on an upper shelf. He stepped from the stool and rushed to the counter. "I'd like to become a tailor's apprentice. May I apply, Father?"

John Reynolds eyes widened as his forehead wrinkled. "I thought thou were happy working at the mercantile. In a few years, I was planning on turning the store over to thee and thy brothers."

Adam looked down and took a deep breath. "Mark likes this kind of work. Matthew is too young to know what he wants to do when he grows up. As for me, I'd rather be making things with my hands than selling merchandise and keeping records."

The store became quiet. Rebekah thought she could hear both men breathing. Which one would be the first to break the tension?

Finally, John Reynolds broke the silence. "Adam, I don't want to force anyone in my family to choose a profession they do not want. If thou art interested in becoming a tailor's apprentice, ride back to the

Morris' house with Rebekah and talk with Isaac. I'll stop for thee on my way home from work at the end of the day."

Adam beamed. "I thank thee, Father. Thou wilt not be disappointed." He turned to follow Rebekah to her wagon. "If this works out, I'll become the best tailor's apprentice in Philadelphia."

"I am sure thou wilt," Rebekah said as they approached the wagon. She climbed up the side of the wagon while Adam took the seat beside her. "I guess I'll not need these signs after all," she laughed as she handed the posters to Adam and slapped the reins on the rump of the horse. Within ten minutes, she turned onto Market Street.

When Rebekah and Adam neared the Morris home, Isaac rushed outside. A puzzled expression spread across his face. "Hello Rebekah…Adam. That didn't take long. Didst thou get all the flyers distributed already?"

Rebekah leaped from the wagon into her husband's waiting arms. "I didn't put up a single poster, but I did get thee an apprentice."

Isaac looked at her quizzically, but did not respond, while Adam walked around the wagon and joined the couple. "Hello, Friend Morris. I'm here to apply for the position of tailor's apprentice."

Isaac smiled. "This is a big surprise," he said. "If thou wilt help me get the horse into the stable we can go inside and discuss it. I'm looking for a hardworking lad such as thee."

For the remainder of the afternoon, Adam listened attentively while Isaac provided an overview of the tailoring business. He examined the different types and colors of fabric in Isaac's inventory, the tools necessary to turn that fabric into clothing, and the finished garments Isaac had completed with meticulous care. Following Isaac's directions and patterns, Adam cut out three simple women's aprons and painstakingly sewed them together. While he was finishing the last apron there was a rap on the tailor shop door.

"Good afternoon, Friend Reynolds," Isaac Morris said and motioned for his friend to enter. "Do come in. We were expecting thee."

"Greetings, Friend Morris. I thank thee for talking with my son. I was extremely surprised when he showed interest in becoming a tailor's apprentice."

"Thou have a fine son with a lot of potential for becoming an excellent tailor some day. He has a tight, controlled stitch and good visual acuity for sizing. The rest is easy to learn."

John Reynolds surveyed the room before focusing on his son, who had just risen from a flat-backed chair surrounded by baskets of needles, pins, and scissors on one side and white fabric on the other. "Hello, son," he greeted. "Thou look happy. What dost thou think of the tailor business?"

Adam smiled. "I've never felt such joy as I did while I was creating these simple aprons. If thou wouldst approve, I'd like to become Isaac's apprentice."

John Reynolds set his jaw. The muscles in his neck tightened. He took a deep breath. "If that is what thou want, thou have my blessings to become a tailor's apprentice. If God has given thee such skills, thou must use them. However, I will miss thee at the mercantile."

~~~~

Adam Reynolds learned the tailoring craft quickly and within weeks had mastered the fundamental skills. Having someone handle the basics of the shop, Isaac Morris spent every free moment of the day with a hammer and saw in his hand. He contacted a bricklayer to help with the exterior of the addition. By the first week of Twelfth Month, the construction was complete.

Rebekah marveled at what her husband had accomplished in a short time. She had done everything she could to help, but many tasks she was not strong enough to do herself. About the time the addition was complete, she noticed increasing nausea and weariness. Assuming it was from overwork, she ignored the symptoms. However, after a few weeks, she changed her mind.

Early one morning after Rebekah set a bowl of porridge before her husband, she joined him at a chair next to him at the kitchen table. "Isaac, my beloved, I believe I'm going to have another child."

Isaac took her hands and pulled her close to him. "Rebekah, I'm so happy for thee. I know how badly we both would like a child, but why art thou not smiling?"

Rebekah gazed into her husband's gentle eyes. *No one had such an understanding husband as she had.* She paused as she weighed the impact of her words carefully. "I'm both excited and frightened. I want a family of our own, but I cannot bear the thought of losing another child."

Isaac kissed her forehead lightly. "God will protect thee and our child, but please take it easy during this pregnancy. We need to hire a young girl to help thee with thy heavy chores."

Rebekah felt her heart pound. Emotions from former years enveloped her. "I don't want to be responsible for making an innocent girl feel as a slave the way I did."

Isaac shook his head. "Our arrangement will not be the same as an indentured servant. We'll hire someone, pay her a fair salary at the end of every week, and provide her with room and board. She'll be free to leave any time she chooses."

Rebekah rested her head on her hands for a few moments, her eyes heavy with fatigue. "That seems reasonable. After I finish my order of hats for today, I'll make signs advertising the position. Tomorrow I can post them around town before I go to the cemetery."

Isaac's back straightened and his voice deepened. "I cannot let thee ride around town in a wagon until after the baby is born. There are too many potholes in the streets and we cannot risk the baby coming early. When thou art finished with the signs, I'll take them around myself."

Three weeks passed after Isaac Morris posted the signs around Philadelphia and yet no one responded to their advertisement for a maid. Since Rebekah was forced to rest more frequently, she became further behind in her work. Whenever they could, her brothers came and helped, but their small fingers were unable to do the intricate weaving Rebekah did. Isaac did many of the routine household chores. She tried to hide her fatigue, but was becoming more and more exhausted with each passing day.

One late afternoon while Rebekah was resting on the bed, she heard a faint rapping on the front door. When she opened the door, she was shocked to see a dirty, tattered young girl. "May I help thee?"

"I . . . I . . . saw a sign at the mercantile that you needed a maid," the frightened girl stammered.

Rebekah choked back a gasp. A mental picture of how she must have looked to Naomi Logan when she first got off the ship from England flashed before her. She stepped aside and motioned for the young girl to enter. "Come in," she said. "Wouldst thou like to sit and have tea and biscuits, while we talk about it?"

The girl followed her to the kitchen table. "Thank you," she mumbled. "I haven't eaten since yesterday."

Rebekah poured a cup of tea and took three large biscuits from the bin. She set the food before the girl and took the chair across the table. "What is thy name?"

"Hilda . . . Hilda James. I'm from Salem, Massachusetts."

Rebekah watched the girl devour a biscuit in four bites and empty the cup without seeming to take a breath. *Did I once look that pathetic? We could truly be doing this child a favor by providing her a way to take care of herself.* Trying to put the girl at ease, she said, "How didst thou get to Philadelphia? Didst thou come with thy family?"

Hilda hesitated. Her eyes focused on a plank of the floor under her feet. "I walked and begged for rides in the wagons of merchants who were traveling to Philadelphia."

"But why wouldst thou risk such a dangerous trip alone?"

Tears built in the girl's eyes and she wiped her nose with the sleeve of her dress. "People started saying terrible things in Salem about me and I was scared. I had to get away before something awful happened. They might have killed me like they did the women they thought were witches."

Rebekah wrinkled her forehead. She could scarcely believe what she was hearing. "I'm sorry. That is unbelievably cruel. I don't blame thee for wanting to leave," she said. "But why didst thou come to Philadelphia? Wouldn't Boston have been closer?"

Hilda looked up timidly. "A traveler told me about the Quakers. He said they practice love and kindness in Philadelphia. He said that someone would take pity on me and help me even if I wasn't a Quaker."

Rebekah smiled and reached across the table to pat her on the hand. "The traveler was right; we will help thee, but if thou art not a Quaker, what faith art thou?"

"I'm a Puritan." Hilda hesitated and looked down once again. "Some people say I'm a witch, but that isn't true."

Rebekah shook her head in disbelief. "Why would someone say such a silly thing as that?"

"It was all a crazy misunderstanding." Hilda took a deep breath and studied Rebekah's demeanor. "It all started when the minister of the church ran over a dog with his wagon. Everyone thought the dog was dead and wanted my father to bury it. He brought the dog home and left to dig the grave. While he was gone, I saw the dog's tail move. I begged my father to let me keep the dog and take care of it. He didn't want me to, but finally reluctantly agreed."

"For a week, I stayed up nights forcing food and water into the animal. I made a tiny splint for its lower leg and he learned to walk on it. I named the dog Lazarus because it was as if he rose from the dead. However, since the people in the church thought the dog was dead, they were convinced I was a witch who brought the dog back to life."

A worried expression spread across Hilda's face while she continued to study Rebekah. "I hope you don't believe I have the power to bring dogs back from the dead. That dog really wasn't dead when my father brought it home."

Rebekah smiled. "Of course I don't believe such foolishness. You have a very special gift from God. With thy healing touch, thou wouldst be a welcomed addition to any family. We would be pleased and honored to have thee help our family and will pay thee a reasonable wage along with room and board."

~~~~~

The weeks flew by in the busy Morris household. Adam Reynolds not only learned to design and construct the garments, he began selling them to his friends and neighbors as well. When Isaac finished the addition onto the tailor's shop, he began expanding the hatmaking shop. Since the hat business was also increasing Rebekah's brothers took turns helping her in the shop, while Hilda took care of the household duties.

Hilda was the first one up in the mornings and the last one to retire in the evenings and rarely stopped to rest throughout the day. Rebekah tried to work by her side, but fatigue engulfed her by mid-day. She was not accustomed to seeing other people do her work. She had spent years being annoyed when Sarah Reynolds watched her work without helping and now she felt as if she were doing the same thing.

One afternoon when Rebekah noticed the perspiration on Hilda's forehead, she motioned at a chair across the kitchen table. "Please take a break and come and sit with me." Hilda poured a glass of cold water for each of them, set a glass in front of Rebekah, and sat in the designated chair. A puzzled look spread across her face.

"Hilda, why dost thou work so hard?" Rebekah asked. "Thou dost far more than what is expected of thee."

Hilda looked down and squirmed restlessly in her chair. "More than anything I want to please thee and Isaac Morris. You were so good to take me in when I had nowhere else to go. I literally owe you my life."

Rebekah shook her head. "Just because we helped thee does not mean thou must feel as if thou must be a slave to us for life. Let's agree that thou wilt not work more than nine hours a day. Some days it may be a little more and some days less. When thy work is done, take time to relax, walk around the neighborhood, or meet with friends."

Hilda looked at Rebekah with appreciation and deep respect. "I don't know how to thank you," she said. "When my own Christian people turned me away, you were willing to take me in. I will always be grateful to the Quaker people. You have demonstrated what true Christian service is about."

"Please remember one thing," Rebekah said. "In God's eyes thou dost not have to work to proof thyself worthy. God loves thee just the way thou art. He was the one who made each one of us."

After their conversation, Rebekah felt a bond with Hilda that she had never felt before. She could identify with Hilda's feelings of wanting to please her employer, but never certain if she was pleasing them or if they were merely tolerating her.

Each day Rebekah rested in bed several more hours than normal. The remainder of the day she would sit in a chair weaving the hats that were too intricate for her brothers' stubby fingers. Often while she was working on the hats, she noticed Hilda watching her. After several days of noticing this interest, she asked, "Wouldst thou like to learn to weave hats?"

Hilda's eyes brightened. "Could I?"

"Certainly," Rebekah said. "Maybe later, if thou become good enough, we could develop a partnership."

From that day on, Hilda would hurry through her household chores so she could learn the hatmaking business. Samuel and Joseph taught Hilda the preliminary processes of preparing the straw and Palmetto leaves, and Rebekah taught her how to weave.

One day while resting on a cot near the fireplace, Rebekah examined Hilda's most recent hat. *I'm amazed at the dexterity of Hilda's fingers*, she mused. *If I'm not always able to work on the hats, Hilda would be able to continue Sybilla Masters' legacy. I wonder if Hilda's skill will provide opportunities for me to pursue other interests. Is God leading me in another direction?*

After she finished breakfast on the last day of the month, Rebekah began feeling labor pains. At first, she ignored them, but they soon became too intense and she went to lie on the bed.

Seeing Rebekah laying on the bed clutching her fists, Isaac hurried to her side. "Is the baby coming?"

"Yes, I think so. Wouldst thou stay by my side? I need thy support," she said and grimaced as another sharp pain shot across her back.

"Let me talk with Adam and I will be right back."

Isaac rushed from the bedchamber to his tailor shop. "Adam, wouldst thou ride to Doctor Browning's home and ask him to come right away? Rebekah is about to give birth."

Without hesitation, Adam jumped from his chair and grabbed his coat. "I'll have the doctor here within a half-hour."

Time passed slowly for Isaac as he held his wife's hand. One minute she would be talking cheerfully about her dreams for her child and the next she was grimacing with pain. Every sound of hoof beats on the street increased their anticipation of Doctor Browning's arrival.

True to his word, Doctor Browning rushed into the Morris home with Adam twenty minutes later. Having experienced the birth of a previous child, Isaac retreated to living room while the doctor checked Rebekah. When she was comfortable, Doctor Browning requested Hilda to gather the supplies he would need for the delivery and returned to the bedchamber to be with his patient.

Everyone communicated in subdued whispers throughout the evening. Isaac paced around the living room, unable to concentrate on even the most minor tasks. Time passed slowly. Finally, after one loud agonizing scream from Rebekah, a lusty infant cry resounded from the bedchamber.

Doctor Browning carefully cut the cord connecting mother and child and began cleaning the newborn. He smiled as he held the newborn in his hands. "That is one healthy set of lungs we're hearing," he assured Rebekah. "Thou hast a fine baby boy."

Hearing the cry, Isaac rushed to the door of the bedchamber. "How are they?" he said loud enough to be heard through the door.

[283]

"They're both doing fine," Doctor Browning assured him. "In a moment thou can come in and see thy beautiful new son."

Doctor Browning wrapped the infant in the white clothing Rebekah had prepared for her first child who never had a chance to wear it. He invited Isaac into the bedchamber, laid the infant in his arms, and retreated to the kitchen.

Through exhausted eyes, Rebekah watched her husband's pleasure in seeing their baby wail with frustration. He walked to her side and gently laid the baby in her waiting arms. "Welcome William Matthew Morris into the world. Thou hast done a fine job."

Tears of joy filled Rebekah's eyes and rolled down her cheeks. Her new son lay in her arms crying loudly. "That sound is music to my ears," she said and closed her eyes, falling into an exhausted sleep.

News of the beautiful, healthy son born to Isaac and Rebekah Morris spread quickly throughout Philadelphia. The entire Society of Friends rejoiced with them. Food and gifts arrived from people they scarcely knew. They overwhelmed with gratitude and love for God and each other. Rebekah's fears evaporated into a pool of joy whenever she gazed into the eyes of her newborn son.

Motherhood came naturally to Rebekah. Little William was a good-natured child, with a smile for anyone who would pay attention to him. Rebekah would take his basket into the hatmaking shop with her when she worked on hats. Her days passed quickly and she scarcely noted the melting of the snow and the budding of the trees.

When William was two months old, Rebekah approached her husband while he was working in the tailor shop. "Isaac, the weather is getting warm and the baby is healthy, I'd like to go to First Day Meeting with thee tomorrow. It has been more than six months since I've been able to attend. The women of our Society were very good about visiting me during my pregnancy, but it's time I rejoin them. I miss the strength I received from sharing their quietness and prayers."

Isaac laid his sewing on the table beside him. "I was thinking exactly the same," he said. "Thou need to get out of the house, plus I am anxious to show off my new son."

Rebekah watched a familiar twinkle appear in his eyes. She laughed, acknowledging his pride before becoming serious. "Dost thou think Hilda would like to come with us?"

Ann Bell

Isaac raised one eyebrow. "We could ask her, but we have to remember she's a Puritan, not a Quaker."

"I keep forgetting that. She's so kind and gentle I think of her as if she were one of the Friends."

Rebekah left Isaac's tailor shop carrying the basket holding her baby, returned to her own shop, and pulled a chair next to where Hilda was working. She sat in silence for a few moments watching the girl's fingers fly in and out around the base of a hat. "Thou dost beautiful work," she said. "Any person would be proud to wear one of thy hats."

Hilda straightened her back, laid the hat on the table, and turned toward Rebekah. "Thank you," she said. "I enjoy making these. I don't think they have anything like this in Massachusetts."

Suddenly William began crying. Rebekah took her son from his basket, hugged him against her bosom, and rocked him back and forth in her arms. When William quieted, Rebekah turned her attention back to Hilda.

"Hilda, thou have scarcely been out of the house since thou came to stay with us. I know thou are not a Quaker, but wouldst thou like to go to First Day Meeting with Isaac and me tomorrow?"

A glow spread across Hilda's face that Rebekah had never seen before. "I'd like that very much. Since my own church people shunned me, I was beginning to feel I was unacceptable to God. You have shown me what true Christian love is."

"I'm certain thou wilt feel God's love and acceptance when thou sit in the silence of our Society Meeting. God heals our inner turmoil and pain through the stillness and peace of worshipping together."

"I will be up early to prepare breakfast so there will be enough time for me to tidy the kitchen before we leave," Hilda promised.

The next day, Rebekah felt refreshed and excited as their wagon bounced along the rutty streets of Philadelphia to the meetinghouse. There had been so many changes to the neighborhood since she had been in this part of town. During the meeting, she relished sharing both the peaceful silence with her Society of Friends and the spoken words of hope and encouragement. Truly, God had blessed her with more than she could ever imagine.

After shaking hands with fellow worshipers, a crowd of women and children gathered around the Morrises to admire their new baby. Both parents beamed with pride.

"We've missed having thee at our meetings," Naomi Logan told Rebekah after most of the well-wishers had departed. "There have been many changes during thy absence. I don't know if anyone

Ann Bell

has told thee we have established an Alms House three buildings south of here. The women take turns working there. When thou art stronger and the baby older, we would love to have thee join us."

"What didst thou have to do to prepare the Alms House and keep it going?" Rebekah asked. "I may not be able to do much for a while, but if there is any way I can be of service, I will try my best."

Naomi took a deep breath. "First we had to clean up an old house and prepare a storeroom for foodstuffs. After that, we set up a space where the needy could choose free used clothing and prepared a room for travelers to spend the night. This coming week, we'll be receiving more clothing that will need to be sorted and mended. We can use all the workers we can get for that project."

Rebekah gave her husband a questioning look. He smiled and nodded.

"I'd love to help," she replied. "I have been cooped up in the house for six months and the change would do me good. Hilda will be able to keep the hat business going for a few hours while I'm away."

"Of course thou can bring Little William with thee," Naomi said. "There will be plenty of women there to help care for him."

Rebekah hesitated. "I do have one concern. I'd love to help, but I'm concerned William will contract a disease from the helpers or the people seeking help. Is it worth the risk?"

Ann Bell

Fourteen

Philadelphia, Sixth Month 1724

Rebekah Morris folded *The American Weekly Mercury* and laid it in her lap. "Isaac, I wish there were something we could do about the Indian affair. Europeans are going into their lands, robbing, and killing them. Isn't there something we can do to stop that kind of mistreatment?"

Isaac shook his head. "I wish there were a way to stop it," Isaac said. "But most people in the colonies have no idea what is happening on the frontier. I hadn't realized how complex the Indian problems had become until Andrew Rittenhouse started a newspaper. At least the Quakers are trying to live in peace with the Indians."

"While I was working at the Alms House yesterday, we loaded a wagon of food and supplies for the Quaker men to take to the Indian settlement. They reported that disease is ravaging the tribe and many are dying. The Indians are angry because they claim they never had such diseases until the Europeans came to their land and want them to leave as soon as possible."

[291]

"That's true. I've heard the same thing," Isaac replied. "Beside the diseases, with the French inciting the Indians against the English, I can see a big conflict coming for everyone. The English want to move into the Indian lands to build their homes and farm the land while the French want to use the land strictly for trapping and hunting. I'm afraid the Indians will soon be caught up in fights they are not a part of. It has been rumored the King of England will raise our taxes to support an army to protect the land they are claiming for themselves."

Rebekah frowned. "Won't that leave us Quakers in a dilemma? Since we don't believe in war, is it right to withhold taxes from the king and go against the scripture that says to 'Render unto Caesar the things that are Caesar's?' If we pay the taxes, the money will be used to wage war against the Indians."

"Rebekah, thou hast summarized the problem well. If we don't address this issue now, our little William will grow up in a very frightening world."

"I wish there were something we could do to keep peace with the Indians before things get out of hand."

Isaac sat in silence for a few moments. "Thou art doing thy part by supporting the work of the women in the Society by preparing food and supplies for the Indians. However, I feel I need to be doing more to help the Indians. I have an idea I'd like to pursue if thou wouldst agree."

Before Rebekah could respond, William began crying in his cradle in the corner. Rebekah instinctively rose to comfort him. She picked him up, cuddled him close to her bosom, and carried him back to her chair. "How can thou help the Indians?" she asked Isaac.

"I think I could make a difference by running for the Pennsylvania Assembly. Laws protecting the Indians need to be made, and the laws we already have need to be enforced or changed."

"Isaac, that is a great idea. Thou hast always been good at examining problems from different perspectives," Rebekah exclaimed. "I remember them telling how William Penn once had a treaty with the Delaware Indians; but no one seems to be paying attention to it any more. The Indians claim Penn had promised that all paths should be open and free to both Christians and Indians, and both groups should be comfortable in each other's homes. They agreed neither group should believe false rumors about the other."

Isaac sighed. "That's exactly right. William Penn had a great relationship with the Indians, but he's dead now and the non-Quakers are taking over our colony. People have forgotten the very principles the colony was built upon."
Rebekah could not hide her concern. "Dost thou think the Quakers will be pushed off our own land the way the Indians are being pushed from theirs?"

Ann Bell

"I pray not," Isaac said, "but non-Quakers are gaining control in the Pennsylvania Assembly. That's why Quakers need to be politically active; otherwise we'll lose our freedom to live in peace and solitude."

Rebekah studied her husband's strong features. The hair on his temples was graying and the creases on his forehead were deeper, but to her he was even more handsome than the day they first met. "I agree thou should run for political office. Our colony needs thy wisdom."

Isaac paused. "One thing concerns me about serving in the Assembly is that I'd be away from thee and Little William for extended periods of time. We've never been separated since we've been married."

Rebekah squeezed his hand and gazed into his dark brown eyes. "I'd be willing to make the sacrifice, knowing that through thy efforts our children can grow up in peace and tranquility." She hesitated as a puzzled expression spread across her face. "There is one thing that has always bothered me. How can Quakers sit in the Pennsylvania Assembly without taking an oath of office?"

Isaac gave a dry laugh and shook his head. "The English Parliament and the Quakers have been fighting over that for decades. They finally came up with an Affirmation Act about three years ago that satisfied all sides. Now all we have to say is 'I do

[294]

solemnly, sincerely, and truly affirm' whatever we agree to do."

"I'm certain someone will challenge that method in the near future as well," Rebekah replied.

The remainder of the evening, the couple completed their routine chores before retiring. After turning in, Rebekah tossed and turned in her bed as sleep eluded her. Her mind raced in many different directions. *Truly, America is the land of opportunity. A few years ago, I was a tattered indentured servant barely able to walk off the ship Good Hope and now in a few weeks I might be the wife of a Pennsylvania Assemblyman. In spite of the noble attempts of William Penn, there are so many problems facing the colony. How will all these changes affect our children and us? Will they have the same opportunities we have had?*

~~~~

Isaac Morris's campaign for the Pennsylvania Assembly began slowly, but gradually he became more active. He talked with the other Friends at the Men's Monthly Business Meeting and received unanimous encouragement to run for office. Instead of riding his horse to the mercantile, Isaac chose to make the long walk, taking every opportunity to stop and introduce himself to each person he passed. His tall, lean figure was soon a common sight around the colony.

[295]

One evening, the late Eighth Month breeze cooled the steaming streets of Philadelphia as the Morris family finished their evening meal. Rebekah cleared the table while William slept in his crib. Isaac stepped outside, took a deep breath, and returned. "It's beautiful outside. Rebekah, wouldst thou like to take an evening stroll with me? I don't think Hilda would mind watching William while we are gone."

Rebekah gave a questioning glance to her maid and new business partner.

Hilda nodded. "I don't mind at all," she said. "I have a lot of mending I'd like to finish this evening. I'll just stay close to his crib. Go and enjoy yourselves."

Rebekah removed her apron while Isaac took his hat from the peg by the door. She basked in the rare moments she had alone with her husband. While they walked, they talked about the changes the influx of new people was bringing to their beloved city. The streets now extended several blocks further in all directions than they did five years before.

When they neared the town square, a crowd had gathered around three men and a woman in stocks. Rebekah drew back in horror. "I wonder what they did. And to think we have such public humiliation here in Philadelphia."

Isaac grimaced as he surveyed the scene. "When William Penn founded this colony we didn't have to worry about crime, but the Pennsylvania Assembly keeps revising our criminal code. Wait here and I'll talk to the guard."

Rebekah watched from under a maple tree while Isaac approached a guard. She strained for a hint of understanding while the men talked intently. When they were finished, Isaac returned shaking his head. "I'm almost afraid to tell thee what happened," he said. "It is so unfair."

"What happened?"

"Two men are here for burglary, but the other man and woman have a very sad story."

Rebekah frowned. "Thou knowest how much I hate to see people mistreated. Please give me the details."

"The woman was married to a cruel man who continually beat her; when she finally could take no more, she ran away."

Words tumbled out of Rebekah's mouth before she had a chance to think about what she was saying. "Good for her."

Isaac shook his head. "By law it is sometimes not that easy. I have never told thee this because I do

Ann Bell

not believe it is right. Under the civil law, a wife is considered the legal property of her husband and he has a right to her services. Despite what the circumstances might be, if an unhappy wife runs away, all her husband has to do is advertise in the newspaper announcing his intention of prosecuting anyone who knowingly gives her shelter."

"I've seen those advertisements in *The American Weekly Mercury*." Rebekah's voice quivered. "I thought those ads only applied to fugitive servants and slaves; I didn't realize it also applies to wives. That is definitely not the Quaker way of doing things."

Isaac put his arm around his wife and took her hand as the pair surveyed the sorry situation from a distance. "Few people are cruel enough to apply that law, but this husband was. He not only had his wife arrested, but the head of the household where she was hiding was also arrested and put in stocks."

Rebekah's eyes widened as tears streamed down her cheek. "I wonder if I can buy their freedom. It's not right that they are treated this way in a Quaker colony."

Isaac reached into his pocket and took out of handful of coins. "That is a good idea. I'm going to talk to the guard and see if I can get them released. He seemed like a reasonable man. If I can get them released we can take the woman home with us until she finds a safe place to live."

Rebekah smiled through her tears and nodded. "I hope thou wilt be able to free them. It's extremely cruel, and not a Christian way to treat other human beings, regardless of what they've done."

Rebekah and Isaac approached the guard who neither moved nor spoke. He gave Isaac a severe questioning look as they neared. Isaac opened his hand full of coins and in a soft voice said, "Wouldst thou be willing to release the man and woman into my care?"

The guard remained expressionless, stiff, and erect. Fear mounted in Rebekah. *Will they arrest us for bribing a guard?*

After a long, tense moment, the guard reached out and took the money without saying a word. He lifted the plank on the stocks and released the woman and man. When the man was free, he stood, thanked Isaac, and disappeared into a crowd of bystanders.

When the woman's head and feet were released, she slumped to the ground. Instinctively Rebekah knelt beside her. "Hello, my name is Rebekah Morris. I would like to help thee. Come home with me and I'll provide food, water, and a place to rest. Thou have been through a great deal."

"Thank you," the woman said weakly.

Ann Bell

"Art thou able to walk or should we get a wagon?" Rebekah asked.

The dirt-splattered woman forced a smile and tried to rise to her feet. Rebekah wrapped her arm around her shoulder to help support the woman's weight. "I think I can walk, but I have no way to repay you."

"Thou dost not have to repay us. We take great pleasure in helping others. Hold my arm and I will help thee walk. We do not live far from here."

Slowly the three trudged toward the Morris home. Rebekah studied the weak, struggling woman. As they turned the corner onto Market Street, she looked up at her husband. "Something has to be done to protect women. It's not right that they can be treated like slaves, depending on their husbands' whims. Men should not be punished because they aide a woman in distress. Dost thou think the officials will come after thee for helping?"

Isaac's jaw tightened and his eyes stared straight ahead. "If this woman's husband tries to prosecute me for helping her, I'll defend her rights in a court of law. This kind of injustice is the reason why I want to become an Assemblyman."

~~~~~

As Election Day approached, Isaac spent even more time walking the streets of Philadelphia meeting and greeting the people and asking for their support. He listened to everyone's concerns – the Indian cause, taxation, the treatment of indentured servants and slaves, and the status of women, public safety, health, and poor streets. The list seemed endless. With each new concern, Isaac became overwhelmed by the enormity of the challenge before him. After many hours in prayer, he received the assurance God was with him and would provide the courage and wisdom to carry on.

When the votes were finally tallied, it was obvious the people of Philadelphia recognized his multifaceted abilities, and Isaac Morris won by a wide margin. That night the young couple's lives changed forever.

Isaac Morris attended all the neighborhood and community meetings he could and Rebekah accompanied him whenever possible. At first, she loved the social whirl in which she was thrust. Although she continued wearing her basic gray dress and white bonnet, she secretly admired the expensive clothing shipped from England that other Assemblymen's wives wore. She enjoyed the gaiety and the wide variety of sweet foods served. However, within weeks, the excitement of constant social functions began to wear thin. The contrast

[301]

between her work in the Alms House and extravagant lifestyle of some of the Assemblymen was too painful to consider.

One night while they were preparing for bed, Rebekah asked, "When is the Assembly going to begin working on ways to help the Indians and slaves? I've enjoyed the gala events, but nothing seems to be done. No one seems concerned about the sick and the poor."

Isaac sighed and lifted his head from his pillow. "I wish I knew. The governor sent from England does everything he can to make things difficult for us. There is even a rumor floating around that he is trying to disqualify all Quakers from the Assembly. It will take a while for him to accomplish that, but I'm certain it will happen sometime in the not too distant future."

Rebekah took a deep breath. "I don't understand why so many people do not like Quakers. All we want to do is live a life of peace and tranquility and help our fellow man." She waited quietly for his response.

Isaac hesitated. He watched the gently swaying shadows of tree branches that reflected through the window onto the bedchamber ceiling before he spoke. "Rebekah, I need to prepare thee," he said cautiously. "Things are getting uncomfortable for those who are trying to maintain William Penn's agreement with the Indians. Today someone gave me a note threatening to burn down our house."

[302]

She sat upright in bed. "Dost thou know who it is? Dost thou think they will actually go around the city starting fires?"

Isaac pulled Rebekah close to him and stroked her forehead. "Don't fret, my beloved. It's probably some local ruffian. I'm certain it was just an idle threat, but I reported it to the magistrate, just in case. I hope the constable will ride past our house several times a night to make certain nothing is amiss."

Rebekah took a deep breath. "I don't think anyone would intentionally start a fire," she said, trying to sound as brave as possible. "Fire is one of the biggest fears in Philadelphia. The old timers still talk about the great London fire. I've heard we're one of the few cities requiring residents to keep at least two buckets of water in the homes at all times as well as limiting the amount of gunpowder that can be kept in a single dwelling. The city obtained a fire wagon hoping a tragedy would never happen here."

Isaac smiled. "Rebekah, thou art wise beyond belief. Sometimes I think thou should be an assemblyman instead of me. Thou know so much about the city and meeting the needs of its citizens."

"I've learned a lot while working at the Alms House," Rebekah said. She sighed and reached for her husband's hand. "So many problems need to be confronted and there is little time to do it before mass suffering gets out of hand. I want to do my part to help."

Isaac pulled his wife closer to him and she rested her head upon his chest. "I'll try to find out more about the matter tomorrow. But tonight I am here and there is nothing to fear." he said. They rested in peaceful contentment for several minutes before he spoke again. "I need to remind thee I will not be home tomorrow night. I have a late meeting at the Assembly Hall followed by an early morning session. There's a boarding house across the street that lets us come in and rest for a few hours before we have to go back to work. I'll be home this weekend to spend time with thee and Little William."

"I understand. Thou must do the work of the colony first while there is still time. I love thee, Isaac," Rebekah mumbled drowsily. "I'm so proud of thee."

The next morning Isaac rose before dawn. He dressed quietly and tiptoed out of the bedchamber. The slight movements in the room awoke Rebekah and she hurried to the kitchen to fix breakfast for her husband and to say goodbye. She sliced two pieces of bread and heated a pot of tea. Isaac prayed for the Almighty's direction in his work in the Assembly. After he had eaten, he reached for his hat beside the door and stepped outside into the brisk morning air.

After Isaac left, Rebekah returned to her bed and slept until the first ray of sunlight burst through her bedchamber window. She opened her eyes, but continued lying in bed. *I have so much I want to do today. Both Hilda and Adam have the day off and I'll be home alone. This gives me a chance to finish the tasks I have been procrastinating in doing.*

The day flew by while Rebekah went from cooking to cleaning, to spinning, to mending, to hatmaking; all interspersed with taking care of William. It seemed as if little time had passed before the shadows lengthened and the sun vanished beneath the western horizon. The twilight was her favorite time of day and she liked spending it on the front porch enjoying the fresh evening breeze. This evening was no different; she took her favorite rocker on the front porch, set William's cradle beside her, and watched the colors change in the western sky.

I wish Isaac were here to share the sunset, she thought as she cradled her newborn next to her chest. *I know I shouldn't feel this way, but ever since he joined the Assembly, he has been preoccupied with everyone else's problems and has seemed to ignore his own family. I wish I could convince him he cannot be all things to all people.*

As darkness enveloped the city, three men bearing torches rounded the corner of their street. Rebekah

Ann Bell

watched as they neared her home. The closer they got, the more concerned she became.

"Is this the house of the Indian-lover, Isaac Morris?" the tallest man shouted.

Rebekah clutched her baby tighter and stood to her feet. "We are Quakers and love all peoples."

"We came to have a little fire party," another shouted. "I'd suggest you vacate the premises immediately."

"I'll do nothing of the kind. We have worked hard for our home and businesses and I'll not let it be destroyed by a group of ruffians."

"Woman, we don't want to harm anyone, but if you refuse to move, you and your child may be harmed."

Rebekah took a deep breath. She tried to keep her mind focused and not panic. "The God who made heaven and earth will protect us."

In the blackness, the ruffians muttered back and forth among themselves while Rebekah stood bravely in the doorway. As fast as they appeared, they disappeared around the side of the house. Rebekah hurried into the house and watched through the back window as the three torches neared their stable. Within seconds, she watched in horror as the arsonists opened the stable door and threw their torches inside. Within seconds, a burst of flames came from the stable and the strangers disappeared into the darkness.

Leaving her baby alone in his crib, Rebekah raced to the stable and unbolted the side door that was not yet in flames. Fortunately, Isaac had taken his favorite mare that morning. She hurriedly untied the brown mare and her filly and led them out of the burning building to the front of the house where she tethered them to a tree.

Neighbors came running from all directions carrying buckets of water. Within minutes, Rebekah heard a clanging in the distance. Moment by moment, the clanging became louder and she soon heard the clopping of hoofs on the cobblestone street. The neighborhood fire department was arriving.

~~~~

Word of the fire spread rapidly throughout Philadelphia. Isaac learned of it the next morning when he was about to give his most impassioned speech ever on the floor of the Assembly. He hesitated, torn between the love and responsibility of his family and his duty to his fellowman. He was ready to leave the Assembly Hall when a messenger tapped him on the shoulder. "Isaac, I just received word thy wife and child are safe and only the stable was damaged."

[307]

"I thank thee," Isaac whispered. He breathed a sigh of relief and said a quick prayer of gratitude. *I refuse to be intimidated by a bunch of ruffians. I will fight for the protection of the Indian people, regardless of the personal cost, but I can't risk the safety of my family.*

Time seemed frozen for Isaac while he waited to give his speech. The tension of the moment added to his passion in arguing for fair treatment of Indians. When his speech was over, he rushed from the Assembly Hall to the nearby stable. He jumped on his horse and galloped across town, almost trampling a dog lying in the roadway.

When Isaac arrived home, he tethered his horse at a nearby tree and raced inside. "Rebekah . . . Rebekah. Art thou and William all right?"

Rebekah ran into his arms. "I'm so glad to see thee," she assured him. "We're both safe. The Almighty protected us. I'm thankful they didn't burn our home."

"Those are only things. Thou and little William are what's important."

Rebekah could no longer control her emotions. She laid her head on his chest and began sobbing. "I'm glad thou art home. I was afraid they would harm our little William. I've never been so frightened in my life."

Isaac stroked her hair. "I'm sorry I wasn't at thy side during thy time of deepest need. I felt powerless when I learned thou were in danger and I wasn't here to help. I had to trust thee to the hands of God and the neighbors."

Isaac continued holding his wife until her sobs subsided. She wiped her tears away with the corner of her apron and said, "Thou did the noble thing by defending the rights of the Indians over thy personal property. For that, I love thee deeply. Come and see the damage done to the stable."

Isaac took his wife's hand and they walked slowly out the back door. He stood in the back yard in shock and horror and wrapped his arm around Rebekah's shoulder. "Thou were extremely brave to get the mare and her colt out while the flames leaped around thee. I've very proud of thee, but thou shouldn't have taken such a risk."

"I couldn't leave them there to die," Rebekah said. "I was grateful thy horse was not there. I could never have gotten three out at the same time."

Hand-in-hand the pair walked sadly through the charred remains of their stable. Isaac stepped through what remained of the doorframe and stood in silence as he surveyed the burnt rubble around them. The smell of burnt straw rose into his nostrils and made him cough. "Thou art exactly right when thou said God protected us," he said. "The only thing we lost was the straw, the wooden doors, siding, and a couple of the stalls. Sections of the roof may need to be replaced, but I can rebuild this in a few days. Life cannot be replaced."

Rebekah gazed into her husband's dark eyes. "Please don't let this stop thee from continuing the struggle to protect the rights of the Indians. Thou hast come too far to quit now."

"But they could come back," Isaac reminded her. "Next time they may burn the house while thou and William are inside."

Isaac Morris remained home until mid-afternoon. When he was assured his wife and child were settled, he excused himself and disappeared out the front door. The soothing, comforting expression on his face he portrayed for Rebekah quickly vanished. *I've had enough of this. The constable was supposed to have protected my family and the neighborhood. There's no excuse for this to have happened. I know the city officials often retaliate against those who question their abilities, but this kind of lack of protection has to end. They have to put an end to the intimidation from ruffians. It's worth risking their anger to bring the situation under control.*

Fifteen

Philadelphia, Third Month 1726

Rebekah Morris's focus on her family increased while Isaac's political influence in the Pennsylvania Assembly expanded. She cared for William, supervised Hilda's work in the hatmaking shop, Adam's work in the tailor shop, and volunteered two days a week at the Alms House. A steady stream of wounded and homeless settlers from the Indian country sought assistance from the Quakers along with a few neighboring Indians. A sense of tension continued to grow within the colony.

In early spring, Rebekah realized she was expecting another child. While her waistline expanded, she accepted her circumstances with calm assurance in spite of the mounting tension in the colony. While she had felt weak and drained during her pregnancy with William, this time Rebekah was strong and energetic and maintained a busy schedule. There was just too much work to do to worry about herself.

The day Rebekah felt the first hard labor pain, Adam Reynolds once again rode to get Doctor Browning. Although the doctor's steps were now

[311]

becoming slow, a peace settled over the household as soon as he appeared. He had been present at hundreds of births and deaths and the Quaker community in Philadelphia had complete trust in his abilities. The Morrises were no different. Doctor Browning had been there during numerous illnesses at the Reynolds's home, when Rebekah's best friend had died, when her first son had died, and at the joyous birth of little William.

Once Doctor Browning arrived at the Morris home and began caring for Rebekah, Adam jumped on his horse once more. This time he headed toward the Pennsylvania Assembly Hall. He galloped through town trying to avoid the increasing number of wagons and horses that occupied the streets in recent months. When he arrived, he tied his horse to a rail and sprinted up the front steps. Cautiously he opened the door of the chamber in which the assembly was meeting. He was surveying the room for Isaac Morris when out of nowhere a burly man blocked his passage.

The man towering over Adam said gruffly. "I'm sorry. You cannot come in now. The Assembly is in session and visitors are not allowed."

"But I must talk with Isaac Morris. His wife is about to give birth."

The guard scowled. "Wait outside and I'll fetch him."

Obediently Adam stepped outside and shuffled nervously while he waited. *What if Isaac will not be able to return with me? His family needs him more than the assembly does.*

Suddenly the door of the chamber opened and Isaac emerged with a worried expression. "Adam? What's happening? How's Rebekah?"

"The baby is coming. Doctor Browning is with her, but she wants thee by her side. Wilt thou be able to come home immediately?"

An expression of concern spread across Isaac's face. "I'll be there right away," he said. "My horse is in the stable behind the hall. Wait by the oak tree on the corner until I get there and we'll ride back together."

While the two men raced through the streets of Philadelphia at breakneck speed, Isaac prayed for Rebekah and the new baby. Would this be a repeat of the day William was born and they held a healthy baby, or would the baby be weak and have difficulty breathing like Christopher?

When they reached the front of the Morris home, Adam tended the horses while Isaac rushed into the house. When he opened the front door, a lusty cry came from the bedchamber. Within seconds, Hilda emerged. "Friend Morris, we're glad you're home. You are the father of a fine baby girl. You'll be able

Ann Bell

to see them in a few minutes. Doctor Browning is finishing making them comfortable."

Isaac could scarcely contain his excitement and nervously paced the floor in the main room. He now had a daughter. What else could a father want? He hoped she was as gracious and smart as her mother. Minutes later, Doctor Browning opened the bedchamber door carrying his black bag.

"Good afternoon, Friend Morris," he said. "Congratulations on the birth of a beautiful baby girl. Thy wife and daughter are doing well. It was an easy delivery. They are waiting to see thee. I'll leave them in thy tender care and return to my practice now. Hilda was a great asset during the delivery and I'm certain she'll be able to help thee with the baby's care."

Isaac beamed with joy as he walked the doctor to the door. "I thank thee for all thou hast done for us. I'll stop by thy office tomorrow and pay thee for thy services."

Closing the door behind the doctor, Isaac hurried to the bedchamber. Rebekah was radiant as she lay holding her new daughter. The baby's tiny face was a miniature of her mother's. "She's beautiful," he whispered, kneeling beside the bed and stroking his baby's fingers. "I'm so proud of thee. She has a perfect face and looks so much like thee."

"I'd like to name our daughter Lydia Marie," Rebekah said softly. "When I was a child in London, I had a dear friend with that name and it would mean so much to me to have my first daughter named after her."

"Lydia Marie, it is." Isaac gently took the tiny bundle from his wife, uncovered the baby's arms, and stroked her soft skin. Suddenly he felt a tug on his trouser leg. He looked down. There was William begging for attention. Isaac realized he had forgotten to latch the door behind him.

Isaac stooped to the level of his son. "Look, William. I'd like thee to meet thy new sister, Lydia." When William peered into the pile of blankets, Lydia began to scream. William jumped back and scampered to Hilda who was waiting in the doorway.

"Sorry," she said. "I wasn't fast enough to prevent him from coming in."

Isaac laughed. "I was glad I was able to introduce him to his new sister," he said. "William was a little overwhelmed, but in a few days he'll be used to having a baby in the house."

Hilda picked up the whimpering two-year-old and carried him from the room. Isaac turned back to his wife. He sat on the corner of the bed, stroked her hair with one hand, and cradled their daughter with the other. "Rebekah, thou look extremely tired. Try to get some sleep; Hilda will help me with the children."

"I love thee, Isaac," she whispered. "This is one of the happiest days in my life."

With that, Rebekah closed her eyes. A peaceful expression spread over her face. Isaac kissed her gently on the lips and tiptoed from the room carrying Lydia. The basket used by William during his early weeks was waiting near the fireplace for the new baby.

The next morning when Rebekah awakened, Isaac was sitting in the chair beside the bed with a handful of late blooming fall flowers in his hand. "Rebekah, thou art more radiant than ever," he said and handed her the flowers. "I wanted to share my morning walk with thee so I gathered flowers along the path."

Rebekah lifted the flowers to her nose and took a deep breath. "They are beautiful. Thou art very kind. I thank the Lord every day thou art my husband."

Isaac hung his head. "I regret that I have not been the husband I should have been. I haven't given thee the attention thou deserve," he said. "I've been at the Assembly Hall so much recently it has put an undue burden on thee. Yet, thou have been brave and strong in spite of my absences."

"Thy work for the betterment of the colony is more important," Rebekah assured him. If they would allow me, I would run for the Assembly myself."

Isaac laughed. "Thou art a woman far ahead of her time. Maybe someday women can be members of the Assembly, but now they aren't even allowed to vote for the Assemblymen."

He smoothed the blankets around his wife before continuing. "Even if thou can't serve in the Assembly, thou art generous with thy time in serving in other ways. However, thou must take care of thyself. Thou art trying to do too much in my absence and are becoming exhausted."

Rebekah sat up in bed and propped her head against the headboard. "Isaac, thou give me too much credit," she said. "I don't know what I'd do without Hilda. She has become a trusted friend, besides a business partner and a maid. I had not intended it to happen, but lately I've caught myself doing more and more housework while she has been busy in the shop. It used to be the other way around."

Isaac took the flowers from his wife's hands and placed them in a pottery vase on the wooden table beside the bed. "I've noticed the shift of thy attention," he said. "With another child, thou wilt not be able to keep the same pace. Therefore, I have taken the liberty to hire another girl to help thee with the household chores. She will be able to begin work tomorrow."

[317]

Rebekah hesitated. "I felt guilty having one girl to help me, how can I justify having two? People will think I am lazy." She took Isaac's hand. Her voice trembled. "I hope thou promised to pay her a good wage and allow for plenty of free time."

"I feel that it is more than a reasonable arrangement," Isaac assured her. "I'm certain thou wilt like her. Her name is Penelope Goodman. She lives down the street a few blocks so she will be able to return home each evening. Her husband died a month ago and she has no family to help with her support."

"Thou think of everything," Rebekah closed her eyes and drifted into a much-needed sleep.

~~~~~

Richard Logan had remained true to his word to Mary Bradford and Rebekah; Joseph and Samuel would get an education. Each morning the Bradford boys attended a Quaker school where both excelled at reading and writing, plus the study of the sciences. In the afternoon, they worked in the Logan Mercantile. As time passed, they began to count the days until they too would be free to choose their own direction in life the same as Rebekah had.

One afternoon following a First Day Meeting, Samuel and Joseph came to the Morris home to share a meal with Rebekah, Isaac, and the children. The family feasted on venison, carrots, biscuits, and hot tea around the kitchen table while the children napped. They enjoyed the light-hearted camaraderie of their shared background. After the dishes were cleaned and put away, the topic of their conversation changed.

"Rebekah, thou were fortunate," Joseph said. "Thou knew when thy contract was fulfilled what thy future held. Thou couldst scarcely wait to marry Isaac. However, I'm not sure how to make the transition into the real world, but I know one thing. I don't want to spend my life working in a mercantile."

Isaac smiled. "I understand. Adam Reynolds felt the same way. He was so excited when he became my apprentice in the tailor shop and could get away from his father's mercantile. He enjoyed what he was doing so much. I had trouble getting him to go home at night."

"At the end of the day, I can scarcely wait until I can leave the mercantile." Samuel sighed and hesitated. "I don't know what I'd like to do that would be better."

"It's a serious decision and thou need to consider all the possibilities," Isaac said. "I've heard that thou both have excelled in school, which opens many more options than those who cannot read. What professions are thou considering?"

[319]

Ann Bell

There was a long silence before Joseph spoke. "I'd like to go to the Philadelphia Academy and become a teacher. I've always liked helping my friends with their schoolwork; even the schoolmaster says I'm good at explaining things to others."

"If thou have made up thy mind, why is thy decision so perplexing?" Rebekah asked.

Joseph's gaze settled on the crack in the floor by his feet. His face flushed. "I'll need money for books and tuition and a place to stay. I cannot keep living with the Logans."

Isaac glanced at his wife and back to her brother. He put his hand on Joseph's shoulder. "Maybe we can assist thee," he said. "Thou helped Rebekah in her shop whenever she needed it; I think it's only fair we help thee with thy schooling. We can pay thy school expenses and let thou sleep in the boy's room upstairs in exchange for thy continued help. William will soon be ready to sleep upstairs and it would be easier for him to make that transition if someone else were in the same room."

A smile spread across Joseph's face. "Dost thou really mean it?" he exclaimed. "I thank thee. I promise that I'll help thee as much as I possibly can with the household chores."

Rebekah turned to her youngest brother. "Joseph knows what he would like to do, what about thee?"

[320]

Samuel hesitated and took a deep breath. "Studying Greek and Latin at the academy is the last thing I want to do," the seventeen-year-old said. "I'd rather study plants. Richard Logan's brother, James, is studying the function of pollen in fertilizing corn. The entire project is fascinating to me. He thinks he'll be able to develop a better strain of corn with bigger ears than we have now. I know it's unusual, but I'd like to work with him."

Isaac smiled. "Thy interests are not unusual. Botany is a fast growing field of study in the colonies. Many people know how John Bartram has planted a botanical garden on the banks of the Schuylkill River. I see him occasionally at the Assembly Hall. The next time I see him I'll talk to him about thee. Maybe he'll hire thee or take thee on as an apprentice."

"I'd like that very much," Samuel said, "but even if he would let me learn from him, I'd still need a place to stay. I don't think he pays his workers much, but he spends a lot of time teaching them about all kinds of plants. Maybe someday I can also have an experimental garden or an apothecary."

"Samuel, thou art welcome to share the room with Joseph," Isaac said. "We can always find a way for thee to earn thy keep as well."

A long slow sigh escaped Samuel's lips. "I thank thee. Thou knowest how I was not good at weaving

Ann Bell

hats. If thou wilt allow, I promise to grow the most productive garden in the entire city for thee. Maybe there will be enough extra to donate to the Alms House."

Rebekah beamed. "Then it is settled," she said. "How soon dost thou think thou wilt be able to move in with us?"

Samuel looked quizzically at his older brother and shrugged his shoulders.

"We aren't sure," Joseph said. "Neither one of us will be able to do anything until at least the beginning of Ninth Month. Richard Logan is in London on a buying trip and will not be back until late summer. We have to keep the mercantile going until he returns."

Rebekah's eyes brightened. "How exciting. Dost thou think he'll bring back news from Mother?"

"I hope so. He promised to check on her, and provide any financial aid necessary," Joseph said as his voice started to trail off. "That is, if she's still alive."

"I wish I'd known that he was going to England," Rebekah said as her voice dropped and her eyes became distant. "I would have written a letter to her. In spite of all these years, I miss her so."

"Richard Logan didn't know if there would be room for him on the ship until the day before he left," Joseph said. "Samuel and I both finished long letters as he walked out the door. I told her all about Little William and Lydia and thy hatmaking business. I also told her about thy volunteer work at the Alms House and that Isaac was now an Assemblyman in the Pennsylvania Assembly. I'm certain Mother will be proud of all thy accomplishments."

Unconcerned about his parents' conversation, William toddled to his mother. Rebekah lifted him onto her lap. "I wish Mother could see her grandchildren," she said. "I'd love to take them back to London to see her, but I watched a newborn die on my voyage to America and I vowed I'd never subject my children to such a trip."

The remainder of the evening, the Bradford siblings talked about how much their mother had done for them, even from the confines of her sick bed and their memories of the happy days they shared as a family. They eagerly shared stories of their father's faith and the heroism he portrayed the night he was killed. They tried to imagine what their lives might be like today if they had not come to America. They each agreed their future would have been extremely bleak if the Philadelphia Quakers hadn't taken an interest in their circumstances.

~~~~

Late in the afternoon of the Fifth Day of the Ninth Month, Rebekah was preparing supper when Richard Logan arrived at the Morris home. She shouted with joy when she opened the door and saw him standing before her. "Friend Logan, please come in. When didst thou return from London?"

He headed for the rocking chair near the fireplace and sat down. "My ship arrived yesterday," he said. "It was a very long and tiring trip and I am exhausted, but I had to see thee right away."

Without waiting to exchange pleasantries Rebekah said, "Didst thou learn anything about Mother?"

He shook his head. "I was able to locate Widow Blackman. However, I have sad news for thee."

Rebekah sat in a chair nearby. Her face blanched. "Has something happened? Is Mother worse?"

Richard Logan's eyes softened while he studied her face. "Widow Blackman said thy mother passed away the twelfth day of Eighth Month of seventeen twenty-one," he said. "I am truly sorry."

Rebekah buried her face in her hands. "My mother. My dear sweet mother. She's now at peace." She sat in silence, trying to grasp the enormity of his words. "However, strange it is. How can it be?"

"Rebekah, art thou all right? What is strange?"

"My mother died on the exact date my first baby died. That means my mother would have been in heaven with father to welcome Little Christopher into God's presence."

Richard Logan rocked back and forth in the chair, stroking his beard. "That is strange and hard to explain," he said. "In spite of death, distance, and separation, thy family bond has remained unbreakable." He reached into an inside pocket. "I brought something of thy mother's back with me. I know thou and thy brothers will treasure it for life."

Rebekah raised her eyebrows. "I brought the most treasured family possession with me when I first came to America - the family Bible. Mother was sick for so long she could not accumulate earthly possessions. What could she possibly leave behind after so much sickness?"

Richard Logan handed her a tattered handmade book, held together with brown string. "Thy mother's journal."

"How can there be a journal? Mother was never able to learn to read and write."

"Widow Blackman told me that each day she would sit with thy mother and write what thy mother dictated," Richard Logan said. "She said even when thy mother's voice was weak and hard to hear, she put her ear close to her Mary Bradford's lips so she would not miss a word. She understood how important it was to thy mother to record her love for her children."

Tears built in Rebekah's eyes. "What dedication and commitment."

"Widow Blackman kept the journal all these years trusting she would someday meet a Quaker from Philadelphia who could carry this to her children."

"I . . . I . . . I don't know what to say," Rebekah stammered. She took the journal from Richard Logan and clutched it next to her chest. "How can I ever repay thee?"

"It's been payment enough to learn of the faith of thy parents and the determination of thee and thy brothers. In thy vulnerability and weakness, thy family has demonstrated great strength." Brother Logan said. He watched while Rebekah thumbed through the yellowed pages. "If thou wilt excuse me, I need to be getting back to the mercantile."

"I thank thee for taking the time to bring this to me." Rebekah rose and walked to the food bins. "Before thou leave, I would like to give thee a treat along with an apple for thy horse. It's the least I can do after bringing such a treasured gift." She reached into a basket for sweet bread and into the bin for an apple.

After closing the door behind Richard Logan, Rebekah collapsed into the rocking chair. Her hands trembled as she opened the journal. The first entry was Ninth Month 18, 1715. Hesitantly she began to read.

> "For months I have had thoughts and words building in my mind I wanted to share with my children, but had no way to record them. Today I was moved to Widow Blackman's home. She is a wise and well-educated woman who has fallen on hard times after the death of her beloved husband. She has promised to write down my thoughts and try to get it into the hands of my children in America."

Rebekah hesitated. Her gaze drifted aimlessly out the window. *If mother wanted me to have her journal, why did she not send it back with Richard Logan when he brought my brothers to Philadelphia?*

> "Eighth Month of 1715, I made the hardest decision of my life. I must say good-by forever to my beloved daughter, Rebekah. She means more to me than life itself. There are many anti-Quaker sentiments in London, from which I'm not able to protect

[327]

her. I had to trust her to the God Almighty and the Quakers in America to provide a good life for her. I feel as if I'm selling my own flesh and blood into slavery, but it was our only hope. I will continually pray God will guide and protect her every day for as long as I live."

Rebekah closed the journal and began to cry. *Mother was right. God did guide and protect me through good times and bad. Without me realizing it, her prayers were sustaining me all these years. I only hope I can pass the same legacy on to my own children.*

~~~~

Following Richard Logan's return from England, Rebekah anxiously anticipated the day her brothers would complete their indentured servant contract. Remembering the feeling of exhilaration it was for her, she was anxious to share that same excitement with her brothers. She spent several hours cleaning and preparing the spare room for them.

Noontime on their emancipation day, there was a loud knock at the door. Rebekah laid the towel on the counter beside her and hurried to answer it. When she opened the door, there stood her two brothers. She embraced each one and said, "Joseph, Samuel, come in. Congratulations. Thy big day has finally arrived. I'm anxious to learn how thy plans are developing."

The boys stepped into the main room and dropped the bags containing all their possessions against the wall. "I am so excited," Joseph exclaimed. " I just found out I was accepted into the Philadelphia Academy." He took a seat at the kitchen table. "I start classes tomorrow. I visited the school last week and was impressed with the professors. They are very knowledgeable men of God. I only wish I could someday be half that good."

Rebekah laughed. "I'm certain thou wilt make a great teacher someday. Isaac and I will make sure thou study hard and receive good grades." She turned to her youngest brother. "Samuel, have thee decided what thee will be doing?"

"James Logan has agreed to let me study botany with him," Samuel said proudly. "We have not begun to discover the potential of the plant life in America and I want to be on the leading edge of that development."

"Wilt thou be living with James Logan?" Rebekah asked.

"Not exactly." Samuel looked to the floor and shook his head. "However, I was wondering if I could leave some of my things with thee for a while."

Ann Bell

"Certainly," Rebekah replied, "What dost thou mean not exactly? We've always told thee that our house is thy house. Where wilt thou be staying?"

"I'm going to live with the Delaware Indians."

Rebekah pulled back in shock. "Thou art going to do what?" she shouted.

Samuel's face flushed and he repeated emphatically. "I'm going to live among the Delaware Indians." Seeing his sister's concern and disbelief, he softened his tone. "Don't worry about me; it will only be for a few months."

"But why?" Rebekah asked. "Can't thou do the same thing living with us? Isaac is often away caring for his responsibility in the Assembly and I could use thy help here."

Samuel shook his head, a look of defiance in his eyes. "I want to learn directly from the Indians what roots, woods, and berries will treat each ailment," he said. "The cures could be right underfoot and we don't realize it."

Rebekah studied her younger brother with apprehension and a certain degree of appreciation. "It's true our form of medicine is limited and there's a great deal of suffering around us. I wish someone could find a cure, but art thou certain this is the right direction for thee?"

Samuel set his jaw. His eyes fixed on her face. "I'm more determined than ever to go down this path in order to become an apothecary. Last week Naomi Logan had a horrendous toothache. She ended up mixing brimstone and gunpowder with butter and rubbing it on the tooth and gums." Samuel shook his head with frustration. "I think the only reason it quit hurting for a while is that it must have tasted terrible. Two days later, she went to the neighborhood blacksmith who pulled the tooth out for her. There must be a medicine somewhere that would have relieved her pain without having to take such extreme actions."

"But winter is coming on," Rebekah protested. "Thou don't know the ways of the Indians to protect thyself against the elements. Thou wilt certainly become ill from the cold."

Samuel glanced at his niece and nephew who were playing on the floor beside the fireplace. "If thy babies ever become sick, I would like to have quinine to help them. This is harvest season, the best time of the year to gather herbs. I plan to spend my evenings with the medicine man keeping warm and talking about what he uses to treat people. During the daytime, I could stomp through the forests looking for the right root, wood, or berry with which to experiment."

"But Samuel, thou dost not even know the Delaware's language, how are thee going to learn anything from them?"

[331]

"I've learned a lot of words from an old Indian who wandered into the mercantile every week or two to swap furs for supplies. I've also learned a little sign language. I was the only one working at the mercantile who could communicate with the Indians when they came to trade with us." Samuel put his hand on her shoulder. "Rebekah, don't worry about me. I know how to take care of myself in the woods with the Indians. I'll return safely in a few months with an answer to many of our questions. In the meantime, thou must trust my judgment."

Sixteen

Philadelphia, Eleventh Month, 1728

In spite of Isaac's frequent absences, life was good for the Morris family and their influence within the Pennsylvania Assembly and the Quaker community spread. When William was three-and-a-half and Lydia was twenty months old, Rebekah gave birth to another son, Charles Andrew. With her busy schedule, Rebekah was grateful for her husband's foresight in hiring Penelope to help with the household chores after the birth of Lydia.

Hilda had taken over a large share of the hatmaking operations and the business was thriving. Although it was an extension to her home, Rebekah was becoming more and more of an absentee owner as she spent extra time at the Alms House and worked in the hatmaking shop only when necessary. Meanwhile, Adam Reynolds had completed his apprenticeship in the tailoring business and Isaac made him a part owner of his business, as well.

While the non-Quakers of Philadelphia gained in influence, Isaac Morris became more active in political affairs and championed for the Indian cause, the women, and the poor. Isaac's political activities brought him in contact with many of the leaders in Philadelphia's social life. One of his favorite contacts was Benjamin Franklin. It was becoming a common sight to see Isaac and Ben sitting on barrels in Reynolds Mercantile discussing the latest controversies of the colonies.

One hot summer day while the two friends were in their customary corner of the mercantile, the discussion became extremely heated. Isaac's heart pounded. "How can thou possibly claim to support peace when thou insist on military preparations?"

Ben Franklin clutched his fist. His jaw tightened. "I want peace more than anyone," he retorted, "but we can't trust the Indians. We have to be prepared for anything. The French are constantly stirring up trouble and the Indians believe the French instead of the English. They're regularly attacking the English settlers and we must protect our own people."

Isaac shook his head adamantly. "William Penn had a good treaty with the Indians. We didn't have problems with them as long as we abided by the treaty. I don't know why we cannot maintain it."

"Isaac, you have to accept the fact that others are now living in Pennsylvania besides Quakers. In fact, Quakers will soon be a minority. The new immigrants will need more space to grow their crops and raise their cattle. The Europeans need to move into Indian lands in order to survive."

In spite of his peace-loving background, Isaac felt his anger mount. "The Quakers built this colony on religious freedom and tolerance. That is something the other colonies don't have. After we built a strong, moral foundation, people of all religions have moved in and taken advantage of our kindness and hard work. They're trying to force us to change our ways, instead of accepting our ways."

Ben's face reddened. The pitch in his voice rose. "Life changes," he shouted. "It's not fair non-Quakers have to pay taxes to support the military to defend us from the Indians, while the Quakers sit back and savor that same protection while claiming it's against their religion to pay for that protection."

"But it is against our religion. If the outside world would have left us alone, we would get along just fine with the Indians and we would not have to worry about defending ourselves."

Fearful of his own rising anger, Isaac Morris stomped out of the mercantile, slamming the door behind him. He jumped on his black mare and galloped toward home. *How can Ben Franklin believe those fallacies? He must be talking through his youthful eyes and doesn't have a clear perspective of what is actually happening to our colony. I'm afraid he'll stir up all the non-thinking people whose only concern is their own prosperity and not the common good. I have to find a way to convince him.*

When Isaac neared his house on Market Street, he noticed an unfamiliar wagon and horse tethered to the tree in front. He rushed to the restored stable and locked his horse in his stall. When he opened the back door of the house, he hesitated and surveyed the room. Samuel was lying on a cot in the corner dressed in buckskins. He was pale and sick looking. Rebekah, Hilda, and a strange man were hovering over him while Penelope attempted to distract the children in the far corner.

Isaac strode to his wife's side and peered down at his brother-in-law. "What happened?"

"This kind man found Samuel lying by the roadside. Fortunately, he was conscious enough to tell him where we lived. Adam is on his way to get Doctor Browning."

Isaac turned to the stranger. "I want to thank thee for bringing him here. I'm willing to pay thee for thy trouble. Without thy help, he may have died."

The stranger shook his head. "That won't be necessary. That is what neighbors are for," the man said. "I'm Weston Hartzel from Germantown. I was hauling supplies to the outer settlements when I found him lying on the side of the road. This young fellow didn't seem like he belonged out there by himself. And whatever those weeds and pieces of bark are in his bag, you'd think they were pure gold."

Samuel groaned. "They're more precious than gold," he mumbled. "These herbs are able to kill pain, if we could only prepare them the right way." With that, he lay back on his pillow barely conscious of what was going on around him.

Weston Hartzel had trouble masking his disbelief. "If you say so," he said. "Now that your family is here, I must be on my way. I hope your leg gets better soon, but take my advice and stay out of the woods by yourself." He tipped his hat and turned to leave. "I'll stay in touch."

When Weston Hartzel opened the front door to leave, Doctor Browning rushed in carrying his black bag and a pair of wooden splints. "What is happening? Adam said he thought Samuel had a broken leg, so I brought the sprints along."

Rebekah nodded. "The man who just left found him by the roadside deep in Indian country. He had no idea how long he'd been lying there."

Doctor Browning greeted Samuel Bradford and gently touched his right leg causing a piercing scream to escape the young man's lips. He took a pair of scissors from his black bag and began cutting the leg of Samuel's tattered buckskin britches right above the knee. Rebekah and Isaac watched intently while the doctor removed the

Ann Bell

fabric and pulled the dried leaves from around the wound.

"Hilda, wouldst thou get some warm water so I can wash the wound? It's packed with mud." He gingerly felt the wounded leg. "Fortunately the bone did not puncture the skin. I think I can set it so it can heal properly."

Doctor Browning took the lower right leg firmly in his hands. He gave the leg one quick snap while an ear-piercing screech escaped Samuel's lips. "That should do it," the doctor said. "The bone should grow together now without a problem." He laid the splints on each side and the back of Samuel's leg and firmly wrapped a bandage around it. Samuel lay back, clutching his fist in pain.

"Young man," the doctor said when Samuel opened his eyes once again. "Thou wilt have to stay off that leg until it is completely healed. No more running around the back woods for the next few months. Thou wilt be in pain for a few days, but that should pass."

Samuel gritted his teeth. "But I have something in my bag that will kill the pain within a few minutes."

Doctor Browning smiled and shook his head. "If thou have something that kills pain, thou wilt become a mighty wealthy man."

"The medicine man told me about it, and I have seen it work many times with the Indians." Samuel reached into his bag beside the cot and took out a piece of bark. He broke off a portion of it and handed it to Hilda. "Wouldst thou boil this in a pint of water and make a tea for me?"

Hilda shrugged her shoulders and silently obeyed while Doctor Browning took a remaining piece of bark in his hand examined it. "Hmmm . . . I've heard of something called sassafras that is supposed to take away pain, but I didn't think it actually existed."

"I don't know the name of this particular plant," Samuel said weakly. "However, there's a lot of truth in the folklore we hear from the Indians. We just have to take the time to listen to them and test their practices."

When the tea was ready, Hilda handed a cup to Rebekah who lifted it to her brother's lips. Samuel took a deep breath, inhaling the fragrant steam, and quickly drank it. Everyone watched, waiting for any sign of reaction. He lay back and closed his eyes. The furrows on his forehead faded. Samuel slowly unclenched his fist and smiled.

Doctor Browning stroked his beard. "I've never seen the likes of this. When thou art feeling better, I want to learn more about what thou found while in the woods."

Ann Bell

Samuel Bradford lifted his head from the cot. "When I'm able to walk again, maybe we can meet with James Logan, John Bartram, and the other botanists in the area. We might be able to grow some of these plants in domestic gardens."

As Samuel spoke, his speech became faster and his movements more animated. "We could teach others how to identify the plants and form groups to harvest what we need to make into medicines. I think we could be onto something that will be a major change the way we treat illnesses."

~~~~~

Joseph Bradford excelled at the academy in Latin, Greek, reading, writing and advanced arithmetic. For an entire year, he studied by candlelight late into the night six days a week. His intense desire for a formal education surprised everyone in the Society. The results of his hard work soon became apparent.

One night after putting her children to bed, Rebekah approached her brother who was hunched over a table by the fireplace. A candle flickered above the pages of his book. "Joseph, thou hast been working much too hard," she said. "Why not take a break and join Isaac and me on the front porch. It's a beautiful evening and the breeze is so refreshing."

"I'd like to, but there's too much I need to learn. If I study hard enough I may be accepted into the College of William and Mary."

Rebekah scowled and took a seat in the chair across the table. "Why wouldst thou want to go to the College of William and Mary? That College is in Williamsburg, Virginia. If thou go to Virginia we may never see each other again."

The candle beside him flickered and the shadows lengthened. "I would return to Philadelphia as often as possible. Long ago we found that distance cannot separate our family love."

"But Joseph, William and Mary is not a Quaker school. If thou go to that college thou might lose thy faith and belief in the Quaker ways."

Joseph shook his head adamantly. "Rebekah, I'd never turn against my Quaker faith. I'm strong enough to listen to other viewpoints without believing them." He paused while he studied his sister's troubled face. "I've not yet decided what to do. I have also been offered an opportunity to work as an apprentice in a local Quaker school when I finish my studies. The headmaster of that Quaker school is offering not only my instruction, but also clothing, board, and a little spending money. When he thinks I am ready, I'll become a headmaster of my own school."

Rebekah reached for her brother's hand. "Joseph, thou know what I think is the right path for thee, but it's between thee and God." Her eyes became misty. "Father always wanted me to become a teacher. When I was onboard the ship coming to America, I dreamed about becoming a teacher myself someday. I practiced teaching reading with anyone who would listen. However, my life never went in that direction. I was hoping thou wouldst achieve our father's dreams."

"I've not forgotten his dreams," Joseph said, "but I'm the one that must turn those dreams into reality. Sometimes dreams take us in different directions than we first anticipate. We have to be able to follow the Inner Light."

Rebekah studied her brother's dark hair and the intense expression on his face. "Thou art so like father," she said. "I have faith thou wilt make the right decision. Fortunately, thou hast several weeks to pray and seek God's direction."

Life continued in its normal routine for the next two months, Joseph concentrated on his studies and did not speak of the critical decision burning within him. One day while William and Lydia were sleeping, he burst into the Morris's home. "I am finished," he shouted.

The napping children awoke with a start and began to cry.

[342]

"I am sorry. I didn't mean to wake them," he whispered to his sister. "I'm just excited to finally be finished with school. I'm now ready for the next phase in my life."

Rebekah picked up Charles, while Penelope took Lydia. She gave her brother an understanding smile. "I'm so proud of thee. Thou worked extremely hard to achieve this. Thou had no way of knowing our daytime nap routines."

"I couldn't have done it without thy support," Joseph said as he gave his sister a hug.

She smiled and gave her brother a playful scowl. "Don't keep us in suspense. Wilt thou be going to William and Mary College or taking a teaching apprenticeship?"

Joseph took his nephew from his sister's arms and danced around the room with him. "I'll be doing something better than either of those," he said. "A group of Quakers are moving to the Piedmonts in the Province of Carolina and they want to take a teacher for their children with them."

Rebekah stared at her brother in disbelief. "Thou mean to say, thou want to leave Philadelphia?"

Joseph shrugged his shoulders. "It's not that I want to leave Philadelphia, it's that I would like to travel and see the other colonies. They say the Piedmont Mountains are unbelievably beautiful and the climate is much milder than here. I'll come back and visit often."

Rebekah paused, trying to give herself time to adjust to her brother's idea. She had wanted him to become a teacher, but not this. She took a deep breath. "I guess I could get used to thee leaving as long as thou promise to visit often. Maybe when the children are older we could visit thee in Carolina."

Three hours later, Isaac returned home from the Assembly. He could not mask his disapproval of Joseph's plans. The silence at the evening meal became tense.

"Joseph, hast thou considered all the dangers involved in moving to the frontier?"

"It will not be as dangerous as thou may think," Joseph protested. "This group of settlers plans to follow William Penn's example in developing a treaty with the Indians. I'm certain we can all live in peace like they use to here in Philadelphia."

"But thou wilt not be the first white man the Indians have dealt with in Carolina," Isaac persisted. "The white man has already invaded their territory, killed their game, and even stolen their women. They will not know there is a difference between Quaker and other Europeans."

Joseph shook his head. "I'm certain we can convince the Indians we are different and can live together peacefully."

Isaac set his jaw; the muscles in his neck tightened. "And what about the health conditions? They say diseases abound on the frontier. There are not enough doctors to take care of the sick people in Philadelphia, much less a few rebel Quakers who want to take off on their own."

"Isaac, dost thou not have any faith?" Joseph asked. "God will protect us from evil. A mid-wife is planning to accompany the group. We'll build a miniature Philadelphia away from distracters the same way William Penn did seventy years ago. Just wait and see."

Isaac's eyes narrowed. "If a group of Friends move away, they'll lose their Quaker ways. They'll become rough and crude like the other frontier folks."

"But it will work," Joseph persisted. "I know it will, just give me a few months to prove it. I will write to thee regularly and tell about our progress in building a new Philadelphia."

Isaac shrugged his shoulders with exasperation. "May God's blessings go with thee, Joseph. Just remember if things get too bad, thou wilt always be able to return home to us."

~~~~

Whenever a new issue of *The American Weekly Mercury* was available, Rebekah Morris was one of its first readers. She read all the political brochures she came upon, regardless of the point of view expressed. Often either her husband's name or one of the issues he supported was mentioned. Although she was one of her husband's strongest defenders, occasionally they had lively political debates over the evening dinner table. Philadelphia was in a state of turmoil, trying to find its identity in changing times.

Late one fall afternoon, Isaac rushed home from a meeting at the Assembly Hall grasping a folded newspaper in his hand. He greeted each of his children before turning to his wife who was busy at the spinning wheel beside the fireplace. He handed her the newspaper that he had purchased from a boy standing on the corner of Market and Fifth Street. "Rebekah, take a look at this. I can scarcely believe what I'm reading."

Rebekah left the spinning wheel, sat in the rocking chair nearby, and unfolded the paper. "What is this?" she asked. "It's definitely not the *Weekly*."

Isaac shook his head. "Ben Franklin started his own paper called the *Gazette* and he's trying his best to take over the *Weekly*."

Rebekah took a few moments and glanced over the headlines. "It looks like a well laid out paper."

"I agree, it is an excellent paper," Isaac said. "On the surface, it reads like it had been written by a Quaker until one gets to the editorial page. Ben Franklin expresses his same old argument that Quakers should pay taxes to support the military. How could someone be as smart as he is and be so terribly wrong?"

Rebekah flipped through the paper until she found the editorial section. She scanned the page. "There are several letters to the editors on different subjects," she said. She found the article he was referring to and read it carefully. She shook her head with frustration.

"I wonder if Ben Franklin would publish a letter to the editor if thou wouldst write one stating the reasons why Quakers don't believe in violence and shouldn't pay taxes to support those who commit such violence."

The entire house seemed to shake with Isaac's laughter. "That's a great idea. I would never have thought of that myself. Since Ben Franklin knows and respects what I believe, maybe he would publish what I write."

Isaac spent the remainder of the evening constructing his Letter to the Editor of the *Gazette*. He read each change aloud to Rebekah, asking for her input. The night was nearly spent before he was satisfied with the letter and retired. While he lay in bed beside his sleeping wife, a multitude of questions kept plaguing him. *Will Ben Franklin let such a letter be published in his paper? How will his readers react? How will the other Assemblymen receive his article?*

Early the next morning Isaac rode to the office of the *Philadelphia Gazette* and handed his friend his Letter to the Editor. Ben Franklin read the letter aloud while Isaac watched for any change of expression.

After a long silence, Ben Franklin saidm, "I think I will run this next week."

Isaac smiled. "I thank thee for thy open mindedness and freedom of thought and expression," he said. Isaac could hardly wait to get home and tell his wife. He had finally convinced the stubborn Ben Franklin of the importance of not preparing to fight the Indians.

The week passed slowly while Isaac anxiously awaited the next issue of the *Gazette*. Early Third Day morning, Isaac was the first person at the newspaper office to buy his copy of the latest issue. Instead of reading it on the spot, Isaac jumped on his horse and galloped home. This was something he wanted to share with Rebekah.

With trembling fingers, he opened the paper to the editorial page and laid it on the table. Together they spent the next few minutes mentally digesting what was printed. "Well, that old fox," Isaac said sarcastically. "He printed my letter exactly as it was written, but he took three times more space telling the entire world why I was wrong. Will he never learn the fallacies of his thinking?"

Rebekah shook her head. "I'm afraid thou have met more than thy equal when it comes to political ingenuity," she said. "He'll probably go far in politics. If there were a king of America, I'm certain he could become one."

~~~~~

Activity and excitement abounded in the Morris household on the Fifth Day of the Third Month, 1730. Margaret Helen entered the world, much to the delight of her two older brothers and a sister. This was the first birth that Doctor Browning was not present to assist. Age had slowed his steps to the point he rarely left his home, but with his typical foresight, he had trained a young Quaker man to replace him. With Doctor Browning's endorsement, Doctor Thomas Fox was readily accepted into each of the Quaker homes including the Morrises.

Isaac was ecstatic with the new addition to his family. Whenever he was home, his arms were rarely empty from holding one child or another.

Yet, in the dark of night when he rocked his youngest child beside the fireplace, he would look into her chubby face and wonder in what kind of a world she would grow up. Their peaceful Quaker life was eroding around him and he felt helpless to stop it.

With a fourth child, Rebekah began considering other changes to her home. *Isaac will not have the time to build another addition to the house, but my business is prospering enough that perhaps we can hire someone to build it for us. Isaac is a wonderful father and I wanted to give him many more children, but they would need more space. Years from now, he should be able to look back on a legacy of love, wisdom, and service to humanity and his God. He has so much to offer.*

One evening, after the children were asleep, Rebekah and Isaac sat in their customary seats on the front stoop enjoying the warm spring breeze. Isaac reached over and took his wife's hand. "Since Charles and Margaret were born I haven't asked thee to attend any political or social functions. I understand how busy and tired thou must be, but there is one event I'd like thee to accompany me."

Rebekah gave her husband a quizzical look, waiting for an explanation.

Isaac continued with calm acceptance. "I'd like thee to attend the wedding ceremony of Daniel Smith, a fellow Assemblyman. He's a non-Quaker, but he has supported many Quaker issues and I want to show him my appreciation by attending."

Rebekah's eyes widened. "I've never been to a steeple church before," she said. "It will be interesting to see it as long as it's not displeasing to God."

"I'm certain God will understand," Isaac said. "It's what is in our hearts that's important. It will be a very different type of experience and will probably give us a greater appreciation of our simple ways. The ceremony will be in the huge steeple church downtown known as Christ Church."

Rebekah watched a fancy carriage and horse trot down Market Street. *It is obvious they are not Quakers. Philadelphia is truly changing.* "Isaac, I know we have passed Christ Church many times," she said. "From the outside, it's beautiful and ornate, but I'll not know how to act when I'm inside. I'll be extremely uncomfortable."

Isaac put his arm around Rebekah and pulled her closer to him. "This will be a new experience for both of us," he said. "If thou wilt be thy usual sweet, lovely self, thou wilt fit right in with the social elite of Philadelphia."

She shook her head. "I will probably be the only one there in Quaker gray."

[351]

Ann Bell

Isaac smiled. "I doubt that," he said. "Daniel Smith has more Quaker friends than non-Quaker. Thou wilt be amazed at the supporters this man has."

After a long pause, Rebekah said, "It's agreed. I'll try attending a steeple church once, but if I don't fit in, I'll remain content with our simple ways and not ask thee to attend any more events in a steeple church."

~~~~~

On the day of Daniel Smith's wedding, Rebekah washed and ironed her best gray woolen dress. She waved at her neighbors and friends while they rode down Market Street. After tying the horse and wagon to a hitching rail in front of Christ Church, Isaac helped her to the ground. They joined people of all stations in life who were walking toward the steeple church.

She timidly took Isaac's arm. When they approached the front steps of the magnificent structure, she surveyed the others approaching the church. Isaac was right. Many were in plain Quaker dress and were in stark contrast to the formally dressed. *I've never seen such elaborate clothing. I love those bright colors, expensive fabrics, and designs, but that money should be used to feed the poor.*

[352]

While Rebekah admired the variety of colors and styles around her, a sick feeling came in the pit of her stomach. *I'm feeling embarrassed by my plain Quaker ways. This is not right. I should never feel embarrassed about being true to my faith. I know I'm displeasing God. Please forgive me.*

As they entered the sanctuary, she and Isaac exchanged uncertain glances. "What do we do now?" she whispered. "The men and women are sitting together."

Seeing an open pew near the back, Isaac nodded for her to take a seat. She led the way into the pew and he followed close behind. This was the first time they had sat side-by-side during a worship service. Rebekah's stomach tightened when a short, plump stranger joined them in the same pew. The scent of hard work was in dire contrast to his fancy clothing. She reached for her husband's hand. *I don't think I could ever become comfortable worshiping beside a strange man.*

Organ music began to play. Rebekah closed her eyes. She had never heard such a beautiful instrument before in her life. *Could such music actually be sinful, like I've been taught? Didn't the Holy Scripture talk about David playing the harp? What would it be like if an organ played during Quaker silence?*

While the music played, Rebekah surveyed her surroundings. The summer sun shone through the stain-glassed windows. The altar and pulpit were intricately carved from fine wood imported from England. She was in awe of the pomp and circumstance around her. Suddenly a mental picture disturbed her; a picture of the Alms House and the people it helped.

This lavishness is sinful. If all this were sold and given to the poor, we could build the hospital we need. We could feed and clothe the poor and care for the orphans and widows. The simple ways truly are the better ways. I know I must work harder to maintain our Quaker lifestyle before our ways are consumed by self-indulgence and fanciness. It cannot be found in fancy buildings.

Seventeen

Philadelphia, Fourth Month 1732

Rebekah took pride in watching her children grow and began teaching them to read by their fourth birthday. After the wedding of Daniel Smith, she remained as far from the societal demands of political life as she possibly could. Each week, she wrote a long letter to her brother Joseph, who was teaching in a school in Carolina. Biweekly, her brother Samuel would stop at her home for a hot meal and a bed.

One warm spring evening, Samuel Bradford joined the Morris family around their long wooden table. After the children had finished eating and had left the table, the conversation became serious. "Rebekah," Samuel said. "Dost thou know Lillian Reynolds well?"

"I've known her since she was five years old," Rebekah said with a curious stare. "But I haven't spent a lot of time with her since Isaac and I have been married. Why dost thou ask?"

Samuel took a deep breath. "I've become extremely fond of her and would like to make her my wife, but her father will not permit it."

Memories of John Reynolds's objection to the timing of her marriage flashed before her. Now she understood his reason, but why would John Reynolds object to her beloved youngest brother? He was the one who had helped Richard Logan bring them to Philadelphia.

"Why does he object to thee?" Rebekah asked. "He's usually a very reasonable man."

Samuel sighed. "He says I spend too much time in the woods. I've tried to explain I'm gathering herbs, bark, and berries that might be developed into medicine. I've explained that James Logan, John Bartram, Doctor Fox, and I have a partnership business, but he doesn't understand our work. He sees no point in it."

"After thou have more financial success, I'm certain he'll understand. His biggest concern is probably thy ability to take care of his daughter and support a family."

"My work is important right now, even if it's not financially lucrative, yet," Samuel Bradford protested. "Right now, I gather the specimens while

Doctor Fox tests them on his patients. If we think our discoveries might be successful, James Logan and John Bartram try to grow them in their gardens. It will take time to become profitable, but we already have a small apothecary near James Logan's garden. I could build a house for Lillian near the garden if John Reynolds would only consent to her marriage."

"When thou told him thy intentions, what did Friend Reynolds say?" Isaac asked. "It seems like a reasonable plan. Lillian is well past the marriageable age."

Samuel Bradford shrugged his shoulders. "He thinks his daughter's husband should be a store owner or a craftsman. He's getting old and cannot understand the future is in science and the study of the world around us, and not buying and selling goods. He thinks I'm just wasting my time."

Isaac leaned back in his chair and stroked his beard. "Maybe if I talk with him, I can get him to understand the work thou have committed thyself to," he said. "Times are changing faster than we would like to think."

A smile spread across Samuel's face. "Isaac, I'd be grateful if thou wouldst do that for me. I've tried to explain it, but he does not seem to understand. Thou art good with words and with your experience in the Assembly, thou hast developed a talent for reconciliation."

Ann Bell

True to his word, the next morning Isaac Morris
arose early; he ate a quick breakfast, saddled his
horse, and rode to the Reynolds's home. The house
that was once alive with children and activity was
now showing signs of age and decay. The porch
sagged and planks of the fence needed repair. John
Reynolds was no longer able to work at the
mercantile, and time had equally taken its toll on his
wife's body. Only Mark and Lillian still lived at
home. Mark spent most of his time working in the
family mercantile while Lillian tended to the family
chores.

Isaac considered his words with Friend Reynolds as
he rode the streets of Philadelphia. He remembered
the many conversations he had had with John trying
to convince him to release Rebekah from her
contract so they could marry, but this was different.
Neither one had any obligations except to God. The
future of two admirable young people was in his
hands.

"Hello," Isaac shouted as he approached the
Reynolds home. John Reynolds came out of his
house to meet him. Isaac dismounted "How are thee
today, Friend Reynolds?"

"As well as can be expected for an old man," John
Reynolds said. He slowly descended the front steps
of his house with the help of a cane. "What can I do
for thee this fine day?"

"Dost thou have time we can talk in private?" Isaac asked.

"Certainly," John Reynolds said motioning to a nearby maple tree. "Let's sit under that tree. Years ago, I built a bench for such occasions and it has served us well."

The men made themselves comfortable on the bench under the maple tree. Isaac noticed John Reynolds kept his right leg extended as if he were no longer able to bend his knee properly. Isaac began by asking about John's health and the health of his family. He had not realized how difficult routine tasks had become for them until he listened to the detailed routines of their day and how much they had to depend on others for assistance.

Observing the Reynolds's condition makes what I have to say even more difficult, he thought. *There must be a way of finding what is best for all concerned.*

After working in politics for many years, he was becoming proficient at persuading others to accept his way of thinking. He hoped his powers of persuasion would work equally well on John Reynolds's attitude toward the future of his daughter. Isaac cautiously inquired about Lillian's marital status.

"I would like to see Lillian married," John Reynolds answered. "But Elizabeth and I are getting along in

[359]

Ann Bell

years and we need her to help with the household chores."

Isaac's heart pounded. He could scarcely control his anger. "Thou couldst hire a maid to do the household chores. What about her future? What will Lillian do after thou art gone?"

John Reynolds paused. He focused at an ant climbing through the grass. "I never thought about it in those terms," he said. "I guess I have been selfish in thinking only about myself. There have been men who have wanted to marry Lillian, but I didn't think any would be able to adequately support a family."

"Is there any man she's particularly interested in?" Isaac said.

"Lillian is quite taken with Samuel Bradford, but I don't understand why," John Reynolds said sarcastically.

Isaac took a deep breath. He took a handkerchief from his pocket and wiped his forehead. "So why dost thou object to Samuel Bradford?"

The older man scowled. "Samuel Bradford spends all his time traipsing around in the woods like an Indian. Any man who marries my daughter needs to be at home with his family."

"Samuel has chosen a new field of study," Isaac Morris said Isaac tried to control his frustration. "Dost thou understand the art and science of apothecary?"

John Reynolds shrugged his shoulders. "All I know is that it has something to do with medicine. The older Elizabeth and I become, the more we visit the apothecaries. "

"Samuel is working hard to find the right herb, bark, or berry that will heal the diseases we are facing," Isaac said. "He has spent considerable time with the Indians learning their medicines and working with Doctor Fox and the botanists testing these medicines. He has already found a medicine to help curtail pain. The project they are developing will change the way doctors treat their patients. If I may be so bold to say, I think Samuel Bradford would make any woman a good husband. He's a kind, compassionate man and loves children. Thou cannot deny thy daughter happiness because of thy lack of understanding of another profession."

John Reynolds stared at the grass. It was obvious to Isaac he didn't like being told he was wrong. He remained silent for several minutes before he spoke. "Isaac, I've been a fool. I've never thought that Samuel's work could have any value. Perhaps he'll be the one who comes up with a concoction that could help take the pain out of these old bones. I think I will talk to Samuel myself and give him my blessings."

[361]

Isaac Morris breathed a sigh of relief. "I'm certain thou wilt never regret thy decision," he said. "Thou have raised a fine family. When thou and thy wife are no longer able to live by thyself, any one can care for thee. Meanwhile, thou couldst hire a maid the same as Rebekah and I have. In fact, I could help thee locate one."

A smile spread across Brother Reynolds's wrinkled faced. He patted his friend on his shoulder. "Isaac, it was very brave of thee to come and point out the error of my ways. Standing in the way of my own children's happiness is the last thing I would ever want to do."

After exchanging pleasantries, the two men bade each other farewell. Isaac mounted his horse. A feeling of satisfaction enveloped him as he returned home. *I wish the Assemblymen were as easy to convince about their foolish thinking as John Reynolds was. In spite of his hard exterior, John Reynolds has always been a levelheaded man of God. Changes in life are hard to make, but change is inevitable and we all have to accept life's challenges that come our way.*

~~~~~

As soon as Samuel Bradford learned he had the blessing of Lillian's father, he began building a home for Lillian and himself. By the end of the summer, the house was completed and the marriage date was set. Few people were as excited about the upcoming marriage as Rebekah and her children. They made regular trips to inspect the progress of the house and the children counted the days until the wedding ceremony.

On the morning of Samuel and Lillian's wedding, Isaac Morris took the family wagon to the Assembly Hall with the promise to his family he would be home early enough to take them to the meetinghouse long before the ceremony was to begin. In the meantime, Rebekah bathed each of the children, fed them lunch, and put them in fresh clothing. Time passed slowly for them.

I wish Isaac would hurry, she thought as she glanced out the front window for the third time in the last half hour. *It is so like him to cut his time as close as he can and come dashing in at the last minute as if nothing were wrong.*

She turned to her oldest son playing in the corner. "William wouldst thou sit on the front stoop and watch for thy father?"

Without saying a word, William raced outside with three-year-old Charles close behind him.

~~~~

Ann Bell

In spite of his best efforts, Isaac's errands and meetings at the Assembly Hall took longer than expected. Knowing he was running late, Isaac raced through town with the team of horses at a dead run. He could not disappoint his family, who had been waiting for this day for months.

William was the first to see his father's wagon approach. He stood on the stoop and patiently waited. Charles could not contain his excitement. They would soon be able to leave for Samuel's wedding. "Father's coming! Father's coming!" he shouted and raced toward the wagon.

Hearing Charles' shouts, Rebekah gathered baby Margaret into her arms and hurried outside. Rebekah gave a blood-curdling scream. "Charles, look out."

There was a weak cry and a thud. The toddler fell under the wagon, and the back wheel rolled over his small chest. Isaac jumped from the wagon and ran back to his son who was covered with blood and mud. "I'm sorry . . . I'm sorry," he cried repeatedly. He picked up his son and clutched him to his chest. "I didn't see thee . . . I'm sorry. I'm so sorry."

"Tell Adam to fetch Doctor Fox," Isaac shouted while he carried his son into the house and laid him on the cot in the corner.

"It is Adam's and Hilda's free day," Rebekah said. "Penelope will have to go."

[364]

The maid's face blanched. "I've never ridden any of thy horses. They've all frightened me."

Panic spread through the family while all the children cried hysterically. Rebekah was the first to react. "Watch the children and I will go." She handed the baby to Penelope.

"Please hurry," Isaac begged. "Charles' breathing is becoming shallow."

"If I take the mare in the barn I'll get there faster than if I unharnessed a horse from the wagon," Rebekah said as she disappeared out the door.

She raced to the stable and untied the aging horse. She climbed onto the mare's back and buried her heels in the horse's side. Rebekah had always been strong and swift, but today her years of hard work seemed to have taken a toll. She felt slow and clumsy as she urged the horse out of the stable. She kicked the mare's sides trying to get her to gallop, but the best she could get was a slow trot. It seemed to take forever for her to travel the three miles to Doctor Fox's home.

As soon as Rebekah explained the situation, Doctor Fox grabbed his black bag and jumped onto his waiting horse. "Don't wait for me," Rebekah shouted. The doctor sped off ahead of her. Rebekah's heart pounded while her aging horse plodded along the dusty streets. *This horse may be*

Ann Bell

good for the children to learn to ride, but I'll never ride her again. I have to get back to my son. He needs me now more than ever.

When Rebekah arrived at the front of her house, she threw the reins around a tree branch and raced inside. She opened the door ans she stopped short. Everyone was sobbing, while Doctor Fox was trying to comfort them. When Isaac saw his wife, he rushed to her and took her into his arms. "Charles is dead," he choked. "I killed my own son . . . I'm sorry . . . I'm so very sorry."

Rebekah doubled over in pain. "No," she gasped. "It cannot be. I've already lost one baby, I cannot lose another."

Five-year-old Lydia tugged on the corner of Rebekah's dress. "Since Charles is hurt, does that mean we cannot go to Samuel's wedding? I wanted to watch him and Lillian get married."

Rebekah choked back her sobs and knelt before her eldest daughter. "We'll not be able to go to the wedding," she said as calmly as she could. "Try to be a big girl and help take care of Little Margaret. Thy father and I are very sad."

Lydia stroked her mother's face. "Don't cry, Mamma. I'll take care of everything for thee." Lydia went to the baby's crib and took Little Margaret in her arms. She carried her to the rocking chair by the fireplace and began rocking her little sister. Childish lullabies rolled from Lydia's lips as she soothed the crying baby the same as she'd seen her mother do so many times before.

Isaac and Rebekah stood in each other's arms and sobbed, lost in their own world of shock and grief. Penelope clung to William trying to comfort and explain what was happening.

Quietly Doctor Fox reached into his bag and took out a vile of dried herbs. He went to the fireplace and began boiling water. Within minutes, he had prepared a pot of hot tea. He found cups on the nearby shelf and filled them. "Come, sit, and drink the tea," he said gently. "This is a relaxing agent Samuel discovered. It will help clear thy heads."

While Rebekah, Isaac, and Penelope sipped their tea amid their sobs and tears, Doctor Fox calmed the children and put them into their beds. The children were soon asleep, unaware of the pain within their home.

Within minutes, the strange tea had its desired effects and the mourners' bodies grew limp with emotional exhaustion. Doctor Fox assessed the situation before standing to leave. "Try to get some rest tonight," he said. "I'll make arrangements for a Christian burial in the cemetery behind the Market Street Meetinghouse. I'll be back in the morning to see if there is anything I can do to help."

[367]

Ann Bell

Quakers who had celebrated a marriage ceremony at the meetinghouse just two days before now gathered at the cemetery to mourn with Rebekah and Isaac. Charles Andrew Morris was laid to rest in the Society of Friends Cemetery beside his brother, Christopher Adam. The loss of Christopher had been heart wrenching for Rebekah and Isaac, but they had had three years for their love to grow and flourish with little Charles. Neither one thought they could face another day much less ever smile again. Only the demands of the other children kept them functioning.

~~~~~

After the death of his second son, Isaac Morris spent even more time at the Assembly Hall and meeting with the people he represented. When he returned home in the evenings, he no longer shared the happenings of the day with his wife or played with his other children, but went straight to his tailor shop and started to work. Tasks Adam used to do Isaac once again began doing himself. In the middle of the night, Rebekah would find him pacing the house in the darkness.

"Thou must not continue blaming thyself," she scolded one evening when Isaac sat beside the dying embers in the fireplace.

"The accident was my entire fault," Isaac repeated for what seemed like the hundredth time. "I killed my own son, the same as if I had used a musket or stabbed him in the heart."

Rebekah took her husband's hands in hers. "It was an accident. Charles ran into the street and thou couldst not stop fast enough."

"I shouldn't have been racing the team as fast as I was," Isaac mumbled, more to himself than to his wife. "I should have left the Assembly Hall sooner. That last meeting was not important anyway. It was not worth the life of my son."

"But it was an accident. Charles got too excited when he saw thee and ran out to meet thee. He wasn't mature enough to judge the distance and the speed of the wagon."

"If I'd spent more time with Charles, he wouldn't have gotten so excited to spend an afternoon with me. It's my entire fault."

Rebekah's tone became firm while she held her husband's hand. "Isaac, thou must snap out of this. I know thy heart is broken, but the other children need thee. Thou have not paid attention to them since the day of the accident. They are young and innocent. They don't understand and will think thou no longer love them."

Isaac's shoulders began to tremble. "I killed my own son. I do not deserve such beautiful children, much less thy love. God will never forgive me for what I've done."

"God has already forgiven thee," Rebekah replied. "All thou have to do is accept it."

Isaac shook his head. "How can I ever forgive myself for killing my own son?"

Nothing Rebekah could say or do would ease the pain and guilt of her husband. How she wished Samuel Bradford would find a miracle herb to remove the pain of a broken heart.

The seasons drug by and spring returned, but this time without the promise of hope for the Morrises. William and Lydia began attending the grammar school near the Market Street Meetinghouse. Each evening they excitedly waited for their father to return so they could share what they had learned at school that day. Isaac would try to listen, but his mind seemed vacant and listless. Even the surprise of William being able to read Ben Franklin's *Gazette* did not draw Isaac Morris out of his shell. His shoulders slumped, and his steps slowed. His usually lively gait became like that of an old man. Not only had Rebekah lost a son, she had also lost a husband.

Eighteen

Philadelphia, Sixth Month 1733

In spite of the trauma in their lives, Rebekah Morris' children thrived physically, mentally, and spiritually. William began learning his father's tailoring business from Adam, while Lydia loved accompanying her mother to the Alms House and helping the needy. Three-year-old Margaret became Penelope's devoted friend and followed her around the house trying to learn how to cook and sew. In spite of their youth, they were eager to attend the Quaker Meetings on First Days with their parents. On the surface, life seemed routine and normal.

Rebekah went to the cemetery regularly to mourn her dead children. One cool spring day instead of placing the flowers on Charles' grave and kneeling to pray, emotion overwhelmed her. She collapsed prostrate onto the ground and hugged the headstone. Tears ran unashamedly down her cheeks.

[371]

Ann Bell

Dear God, why didst thou do this to me? Why has life been so much harsher for me than others? First, my mother became ill, then my father was shot, and I was forced to leave my mother's side and come to America. When I was finally getting settled into a new life, my best friend died. I could have handled all of that if thou hadn't taken my own flesh and blood from me. Please God, why? Why didst thou do this to me? Others have not lost so much.

Rebekah lay on the ground motionless. Little by little, her sobs become further and further apart until she felt as if every ounce of strength had been drained from her. She continued lying on her sons' grave as if a limp rag. In the stillness, a slight breeze blew through the cemetery. The freshly sprouted leaves rustled in the trees around her. Slowly calmness settled over her and a gentle voice within whispered:

Rebekah, I love thee. I would never give thee more than thou couldst bear. In the midst of thy pain, thou have forgotten all the blessings thou have received. Just trust me; I am opening new doors for thee. I will continue to love and sustain thee throughout all thy adversity.

Rebekah lifted her upper body until she was in a kneeling position. *Surely, that is the Inner Voice speaking to me. I have had warm feelings before when God was comforting me, but this was different. It was more real than ever before. Maybe this is what the missionaries Hope Jamison and*

Charity Jones meant when they were staying with the Reynolds, soon after I came from London. At the time, it was all strange and new to me. I didn't understand what the Quaker faith curtailed and how the Inner Voice guided them. I hope God will forgive me for my selfish thoughts and behavior; I will try to be strong, in spite of my weakness.

Rebekah remained on her knees for several minutes, and gradually a smile spread across her face. *Thank you, God. I think I'm now ready to face whatever is before me. I'm convinced that the Inner Voice will be guiding me, whatever circumstances may arise.*

~~~~

While his wife appeared more relaxed and satisfied in her activities and with her family, Isaac Morris's agitation and depression increased. He tried to mask his turmoil by increasing his fervor toward his political work, but to no avail. He continued showing interest in his family, but the sparkle was missing in his eyes. His jet-black hair turned gray and his once rapid walk became a shuffle. He never again mentioned his son, Charles Andrew.

One evening as they were finishing the evening meal, there was a loud pounding on the door. Isaac shook his head with disgust, pushed his chair back, walked to the door, and opened it. Isaac found himself face to face with a tall burly man dressed in expensive britches and coat. "May I help thee?"

[373]

"Are you Isaac Morris?"

"I am."

"I'm from the tax collector's office. Your taxes were due today. Since you did not voluntarily come to the office, I'm here to collect your taxes."

"I am a Quaker and do not believe in paying taxes that will be used to wage war, particularly with the Indians. I've seen the militia training in the town square and assume they are preparing for war with the Indians. I refuse to pay for the killing of another human life, whether it is a European or an Indian."

The tax collector scowled. "That is not your decision to make. I'm doing you a favor by coming to your house to remind you of your overdue taxes."

"Thy presence at mealtime is not a favor to me," Isaac protested as he took a deep breath. "It's an embarrassment to my wife and children. They understand I am more than willing to pay taxes if they will go for building hospitals and roads. Can thou guarantee my taxes will not be used to support war and destruction?"

The glare on the tax collector's face deepened. "I don't determine how the tax money is spent; only the Assembly does. You're a member of the Pennsylvania Assembly; you should know how the money in the colony is spent better than I."

Rebekah joined her husband at the door as Isaac struggled to keep his composure. "Yes, I am a member of the Assembly, but I only have one vote. I work as hard as I can to keep the colony the same as when William Penn established it, but it's becoming more and more difficult to do so."

"Your life in the Assembly is not my concern. My concern is to collect your taxes. Do you plan to pay them now?"

"If I pay the taxes it will be against my personal faith and best judgment." Isaac swallowed hard. He felt perspiration building on the nap of his neck. "Right now, I do not have the money to pay the taxes. Many of my customers owe me money. Recently my son died and I have been unable to work as much or to collect the money due me."

The tax collector shook his head and set his chin. "That again is not my concern. However, I'm feeling generous tonight and will allow you another month to pay your taxes, but no more. I'll be back in exactly one month for them. If you do not have the money, we will arrange to mortgage your home for those taxes. I'm certain you're aware how not paying taxes affects a member's seat in the Assembly. Rest assured, I'll be back next month."

The tax assessor took a step toward Rebekah. "I hope you can convince your husband how serious this situation is. I'd hate to have someone as attractive as you being forced to live at the poor house with your children." He turned and stomped across the porch and down the steps of the Morris home.

Isaac closed the front door and leaned against it. For the first time he saw his children sitting wide-eyed and frightened. *I must protect my family from any upcoming struggles with the king and forces of evil that are invading our peaceful colony. My wife reads the newspapers and pamphlets that are circulating Philadelphia and understands what is happening, but she's not aware of the intensity of the conflict. I'm unable to fulfill my responsibility as Quaker, father, and Assemblyman.*

Rebekah wrapped her arm around her husband, led him back to the table, and took the chair next to him. She reached across the table and took his hands in hers. "What art thou going to do?"

"I don't know," he said as he cradled his head in both his hands. "I don't think I have a choice but to pay the taxes, even though I don't agree with how they will be spent. The hardest part is that even if I were willing, I don't have the money to pay them. This tax collector is extremely strange. They usually don't come to the homes and threaten the way he did. I don't trust him, there must be something else going on."

Rebekah squeezed his hand. "He made me feel very uncomfortable, as well. What are thou going to do?"

Isaac breathed a sigh of relief as he saw the tension leave his children's faces and quietly leave their chairs to go to different corners of the room to pursue their own interest. *Do I really deserve my children's simple trust?* He looked up into his wife's troubled eyes. "I need to get the money together for the taxes, it's more important for me to remain in the Assembly and work for the Quaker cause than to financially protest the pending war. If I don't pay the taxes, I'm certain I'll be removed immediately from the Assembly. If all the Quaker Assemblymen refused to pay their taxes, we would no longer have a voice in the government of Pennsylvania."

"But Isaac, how will thou get the money?"

Isaac leaned back, the wrinkles deepened in his forehead. "I don't know. I think a few of my customers will be able to pay me what they owe, but several are going through difficult times themselves. I wouldn't dare ask them for money. I'll visit select customers next week and see what they can do. Maybe I'll have to sell one of the horses." Isaac hesitated, forced a smile, and said, "I know one thing, God will provide our daily needs."

~~~~~

Three weeks after the visit of the tax collector, Isaac returned home from the Assembly in unusually high

[377]

Ann Bell

spirits. He greeted Rebekah with a kiss as his children rushed to his side. The older children had just arrived home from school and were hurrying through their daily chores before doing their school assignments.

"Hello, my loves," he said as he picked up Margaret and held her close and gave a one-armed squeeze to William and Lydia. "I'm glad to be home. I've missed thee so." He set the Margaret back on the floor. "The weather this month is more beautiful than what I have seen in many months. We need to have more family time together. Let's start making plans about what we can do together."

The children's eyes brightened as they looked back and forth and over to their mother.

"Father, can we go on a picnic?" Lydia begged. "We haven't had a picnic since Charles died."

"Please, Father," Margaret chimed in. "I want to have a picnic."

Isaac looked toward Rebekah. She smiled and nodded.

"Great idea, Lydia. Tomorrow let's get up early, pack a lunch, and go to the clearing northeast of town," he said. "William and I can take our fishing rods and try to catch some fish while you girls can play in the meadow."

The children squealed with excitement and gave their father another hug. "I'll help Penelope make sweetbreads to take along," Lydia said. "We haven't gotten away together in a long time."

"We'll have to change that and begin making regular family outings," Isaac said. "Thou wilt be grown soon and I want to treasure every moment I have with thee."

During the night, Rebekah listened with pleasure as she heard their children lying in their beds making plans for the next day. *Perhaps Isaac's gloom is lifting and life will return to normal.*

The next morning the entire family was up at dawn, dressed, and waiting to leave. Penelope arrived early at the Morris home to prepare a breakfast of cornmeal mush and molasses for the family before they left.

After the family had eaten, Penelope turned to Rebekah, "Don't worry about cleaning up. I'll take care of everything after you're gone. Let's concentrate on getting things ready for your picnic. I found a new basket that should be large enough to hold the food thou wilt be taking. Lydia can go to the well and fill a jug full of water for us."

"Penelope, I thank thee for coming early to help," Rebekah said as she went to the bin, took several carrots and apples, and placed them in a basin. She immersed them in water and began scrubbing.

[379]

Ann Bell

"After we're gone, take a free day to do whatever thou choose. Thou deserve a time of relaxation."

While the women prepared the food, Isaac and William hurried to the stables. Isaac pulled open the heavy wooden door and propped it open with a brick. "William, can thou find the fishing rods? I haven't used them for a long while; I hope they're still in good enough condition to use. If they are not, we're going to have to find fresh branches to use and add new string to them."

William hurried to the right corner of the stable. "I know exactly where the fishing rods and string are," he shouted over his shoulder. "I went fishing in the creek last week but the string broke so I had to come home. I didn't know how to add new string."

"That's no problem; I'll help thee add string to the poles when we get there," Isaac shouted from the horses' stall.

Isaac Morris took the bridles from the hook, put them on each of the horses, and led them to the waiting wagon nearby. With several clicks and tugs, the horses were harnessed to the wagon and ready to go. William handed him the fishing rods and string and he placed them under the seat. "William, run to the house and tell the others we're ready to go and I'll meet them in the front."

Within minutes, the wagon was loaded and the children took their places in the back of the wagon.

Rebekah and Isaac smiled brightly as he snapped the reins and signaled the horses to go.

The warm summer breeze invigorated the Morris family as their team of horses clopped through the morning streets of Philadelphia. They waved to the women and children feeding their pigs and chickens in their yards. At the outskirts of town, the road narrowed into a single wagon path. They continued another mile down the path, occasionally ducking to avoid low hanging branches.

Reaching the clearing, Isaac Morris pulled the horses to a stop under an oak tree near the bank of the Delaware River and turned to his wife. "How dost thou like this spot?" he asked. "One of the Assemblymen said the fish are plentiful here. The water is shallow enough the girls can play in the river without danger."

Rebekah slowly lowered herself to the ground. "This is perfect," she said as she lifted Margaret from the wagon and the older children jumped. "Thou think of everything."

Rebekah surveyed the area. "This looks familiar. I think I've been here before." She studied the area in silence for a few moments. "The bushes are larger and new trails had been broken, but I'm certain this is the same spot I picnicked with the Reynolds and Logans when they told me Brother Logan was going to London and would try to find my brothers. This spot will be etched in my memory forever."

[381]

"Let's make today a time thou wilt remember forever, once again. I hope William and I will catch some fish we can fix for supper." William and Isaac took the fishing rods and headed toward the river.

Rebekah watched them disappear over the knoll. *Is that Isaac's old familiar whistle I hear? I haven't seen him at this much peace since Charles died.*

Lydia and Margaret left their mother's side and began exploring the clearing. Rebekah took the blanket from the wagon and spread it on the grass. It had been years since she had taken the time to lie on the grass and watch the clouds lazily drift overhead. She closed her eyes and let her mind wander. She pictured herself once again as a child lying in her front yard in London imagining animals in the clouds. The robins singing in nearby trees provided music for her slumber.

Minutes later a piercing scream summoned her through her sleep. "Mother . . . Mother!" Rebekah roused. *Am I dreaming or is someone calling for me?* She propped herself on her elbow.

Her son's terror-stricken voice echoed through the trees. "Help! Mother, come quickly. We need thee. Hurry!"

Rebekah jumped to her feet. She raced across the knoll where she last saw her son and husband disappear. When she reached the top of the rise, horror struck her. Isaac lay motionless beside the stream while William knelt beside him.

"What happened?" Rebekah screamed racing to their side. She stumbled as she ran down the hill, but was able to catch herself before she hit the ground.

William's eyes were wide with panic. He shook his head. "I don't know," he gasped. "We were just standing here fishing when he let out a loud groan and clutched his chest. Father stumbled back from the river and collapsed. Is he going to be all right?"

Rebekah dropped to her knees beside her husband and felt his chest. Unsure if she felt movement, she put her ear next to his nose. *I think I hear him breathing and see his chest rising, but I cannot tell for sure. Dear God, help us*, she begged.

She frantically glanced around the terrain. Her heart pounded. "We'll never be able to carry him back. William, wilt thou be able to drive the wagon and get it as close to us as possible. The bank is steep so thou wilt have to be very careful and come down at an angle. Find the girls and bring them back with thee."

Without saying a word, William raced up the hill while Rebekah sat on the ground beside her husband. Tears welled up in her eyes. She held his hand and pressed it to her lips.

[383]

"I love thee, Isaac Morris. Keep breathing," she begged. "Thou can do it. Thou art strong. I need thee. Thy children need thee. The people of Philadelphia need thee. The Quaker Society needs thee." She watched for a slight movement of his chest, but again she was not certain.

Even though it seemed like hours, within minutes eight-year-old William was back with the wagon and the two girls. He pulled the horses to a stop and jumped down.

"You and Lydia take his feet and I'll try to lift his shoulders," Rebekah shouted. "We've got to get him into the back of the wagon." Whether from fear or love, Rebekah felt miraculous strength flow through her as they carefully lifted her husband. They pulled and strained as they carried Isaac and lowed him onto the back of the wagon. Rebekah pulled him toward the front of the wagon, rolled a blanket under his head, and covered him with another.

The children climbed into the back of the wagon beside their father, while Rebekah slid onto the seat and grabbed the reins. "Try to keep him from bouncing and sliding around," she shouted over her shoulder. "I'm going directly to Doctor Fox's house. It's closer than going home."

She slapped the reigns against the horses' hindquarters and urged them on at breakneck speed. The low hanging branches swatted her in the face as she raced the horses down the narrow trail. She increased their speed when they entered the main road and swerved the team around a cow that was ambling toward his owner's barn. Rebekah slowed the pace slightly when she reached the edge of town and breathed a sigh of relief when she caught sight of the Fox's large brick house.

As soon as Rebekah stopped the wagon in his yard, Doctor Fox rushed from the front door. Seeing Isaac lying in the back of the wagon he shouted for his stable boy. Together the two carried Isaac's limp body into the house and laid him on a bed in the corner.

Doctor Fox knelt beside Isaac and placed his fingers on his wrist and neck. He shook his head. He laid his ear against Isaac's chest and shook his head once more. Doctor Fox rose to his feet and turned to Rebekah. With a long, glum face, he said, "I am sorry. He's gone."

Rebekah froze. *This can't be true. Not my beloved Isaac.* Slowly she knelt and hugged each of them before she collapsed into a nearby chair, buried her face in her hands, and sobbed. Her children huddled nearby. "Thy father has gone to heaven to be with God, Charles, and Christopher."

~~~~

[385]

As news of the tragedy spread, family, friends, and political leaders gathered at the Morris home to pay their condolences and help Rebekah. She mechanically made the necessary arrangements and responded to her well-wishers. The children plummeted her with questions she could not answer. Nothing would ever be the same.

Two days later, Isaac Morris was buried in the Friends' Cemetery behind the Market Street Meetinghouse next to his two sons. While Rebekah stood grieving over the grave surrounded by her three surviving children, Benjamin Franklin's voice rang out. "Isaac Morris has served the colony well. He has finished the course and now belongs to the ages."

Hearing those words, Rebekah burst into uncontrollable sobs. *Yes, Isaac does belong to the ages but how will the children and I get along without him?*

Nineteen

Philadelphia, Eighth Month 1733

Rebekah sat rocking in Isaac's favorite chair before the fireplace watching the embers burn down. The pressures of the last two weeks were heavy upon her. This was the first time she had a few minutes alone. Penelope had packed a lunch and taken the children fishing in the creek that ran behind the house. Hilda had a free day and was to be away all day and Adam was busy in the tailor shop. She had not set foot into the tailor shop since the day Isaac had died. She couldn't bear not seeing her husband bent over his worktable.

I must begin settling Isaac's estate, but I don't know where to begin. The only thing I know is that I've seen death notices in the Philadelphia Gazette. I remember what mother said when I left London; I must be strong in my weakness. Rebekah rummaged through the pile of papers in the corner until she found what she wanted and then went to the desk and took out a quill, ink, and paper.

"ALL Persons indebted to Isaac
Morris, Philadelphia, deceased, by

[387]

> Notes or Book debts, are requested
> to make speedy payment; and those
> who have any accounts against said
> estate, are desired to bring them in,
> in order that they may be adjusted by
> me REBEKAH MORRIS,
> Administratrix.

Rebekah read and reread what she had written. Ummm. That should do it. I will take this to the newspaper office tomorrow. I hope I'll be able to get everything settled soon. Isaac's tailor business is a black cloud hanging over my head.

Heavy footsteps on the porch and a loud pounding on the door interrupted her thoughts. Cautiously she opened the door. The tall, burly tax collector stood glaring at her. "I'm here to see Isaac Morris."

"Isaac Morris was buried two weeks ago."

The tax collector waved his finger in her face. "I have received no notification of that. Is this some kind of a trick to keep from paying his taxes?"

Rebekah's knees trembled with fear and anger. She clutched her teeth. "I've just finished writing the death notice for the *Philadelphia Gazette.* I have lost two children, but this is the first time I have lost a husband. I do not know how to wrap up his business affairs or personal affairs."

The tax collector's face softened slightly. "I'm sorry about your loss," he said and just as quickly, the firmness on his face reappeared. "I must inform you that the first thing you'll need to do is pay his taxes. Did he leave the money for his taxes?"

"No, he didn't." Rebekah bit her lip to keep them from trembling and bursting into tears. "Is there anything I can do? I've always wanted to do what is right in sight of God."

"If you can't come up with the money, you'll need to mortgage your house," the tax collector said. A wrinkled smile spread across his face. "Since I'm a reasonable person, I'll give you another month to get the £200 tax money together and will be back to collect it."

Before Rebekah had a chance to respond, he turned and stomped away. She watched in shock as he plodded down the path from their house and turned the corner. When he was out of view, she closed the door, collapsed against it, and remained motionless for several minutes. *Just when I thought I had everything organized, now this. What am I going to do? Isaac worked so hard to build this house; I cannot lose it now just to pay the taxes.*

Suddenly, the backdoor burst open. "Mother, Mother. We caught three fish."

Rebekah hurriedly wiped her eyes with the back of her hand and went to greet her children and examine their day's catch.

"Mother, why are thou crying?" Lydia asked. "Are thee missing Father?"

Rebekah hugged her oldest daughter. "Yes, dear, I miss him terribly, but there is another problem. The tax collector was here and wanted payment on the taxes. I will have to figure out a way to come up with the money. Thou dost not have to be troubled about it. There's nothing God and I can't handle."

~~~~~

The month after Isaac's death, Rebekah traveled about Philadelphia paying those whom Isaac owed money and accepting money from those who owed him money. She knew her husband had been a generous man, but little did she understand the depth of his generosity until she visited the humble homes of those whom he had made clothes, knowing there was little hope of repayment. As the month passed, she became more and more distressed. The hat business was nearly non-existent as others were learning the trade and Hilda was helping care for John and Elizabeth Reynolds on a regular basis. After buying food for her children and the animals, Rebekah was only able to accumulate £25.

One bright Fifth Day morning after the older children had left for school and Margaret had left for the market with Penelope, while Rebekah finished sweeping the floor of her bedchamber and making her bed, she was overcome with emotion. She threw herself across the cover and cried until she was exhausted.

Please God, help me. I was certain you'd provide a way to pay my taxes, but I have far from what I need. I've seen the ways the non-Quakers treat their women as second-class citizens. They're not able to make it through life without a man to protect them. I'm determined to make it on my own. Please help me. I don't want to lose the house that Isaac worked so hard to build. I promised the children there was nothing Thee and I couldn't handle together. I'll do whatever I can to save the house, just show me what.

In the midst of her prayers and inner struggles, Rebekah heard the front door open. "Mother, we found some giant apples at the market and Penelope let me get one as long as I also got one for William and Lydia. I've already eaten mine, but look how big their apples are," Margaret said as she took the apples from the small basket she was carrying.

Rebekah pushed her internal struggles to the background and focused on her daughter. "Thou made excellent selections, Margaret. Let's put your basket on the shelf until they get home from school; the apples will be a special treat for them."

[391]

Ann Bell

After eating a quick lunch, Penelope took Margaret to the garden to help with the weeding. Rebekah had scarcely finished tidying the kitchen when there was a loud rapping on the front door. Instinctively she knew who was there. She sighed as she walked reluctantly to the door.

"Hello."

"Hello, Rebekah Morris. I'm here to collect your husband's taxes. You've had an entire month to work on it so I'm certain you're prepared to settle his estate."

Rebekah's throat tightened. "I'm sorry, but my husband was such a generous man he did work for people who couldn't afford to pay him. I only have £25 to apply to the taxes."

"If you can't raise the money, I'll be forced to start proceedings to sell the house and business to obtain the tax money."

Rebekah grasped the doorframe to give her strength. "Please, is there any other way? Can I have a few more weeks to raise the money? There must be another way."

A sly smile spread across the tax collector's face. "There may be another alternative," he said as he moved toward Rebekah. "It's too difficult for a widow with three children to make it on their own in Philadelphia. I would be personally willing to help you."

Rebekah stepped backward to protect her comfort level of personal space. "And what would that alternative be?"

"My wife died two years ago and my eight-year-old son needs a mother. I would be willing to marry you and be a father to your children as well as pay the taxes so you can keep your house. Since this house is a great deal larger than mine, we could all be very comfortable here."

Rebekah's heart pounded and her eyes widen. "I would risk losing this house than to accept such a marriage arrangement. Go ahead and start the sale. I can find another way to make it through life on my own." She turned and slammed the door in the face of the tax collector. *Why God? I trusted thee through all of this and Thou have let me down. Now what will I do?*

Having heard the loud voices and the front door slam, Adam appeared through the door of the tailor shop. "Rebekah, who was at the door? I could hear him all the way to the shop."

Rebekah straightened her back and took a deep breath. "That was the tax collector. He maintains Isaac owed £200 in taxes before he died and I will either have to mortgage the house to pay it or accept his personal help. What really made me angry was

[393]

he offered to help by marrying me and being a father to my children. He would be willing to pay the taxes for me if he could live in the house with his son."

"I've heard about the heavy-handed tax collectors in this township, but I hadn't realized it was this bad. Why didn't thou tell me about this before? Thou know our Society would do anything to help thee."

Rebekah avoided Adam's concerned gaze. She gave an embarrassed sigh. "I guess I was too proud. I was determined to make it through life on my own without being dependent on anyone. I remember years ago when Sarah Reynolds was first introduced to George Nelson as a possible mate. I sensed her humiliation when she felt it was a marriage of convenience. She thought no man would ever love her and she would not be able to make it through life as a single woman. I'm glad everything turned out well for her in the end and she has a loving family now, but her initial humiliation I will never forget."

Adam Reynolds put his arm gently on Rebekah's shoulder. "I do have an idea that might be beneficial to both of us," he said. "Let's sit at the table and discuss it. I want thou to be perfectly honest about thy needs. We can't work together if we don't understand each other's position."

Like an obedient child, Rebekah followed Adam to the kitchen table. When they were both comfortable, Rebekah said, "I appreciate thy concern. What dost thou suggest? I'm desperate."

"I've been thinking about this ever since Isaac died." Adam hesitated and took a deep breath. "I've watched thy pained expression each time I walk into the shop. I'm wondering if it would be easier for thee if the tailor shop was not in thy home to be a constant reminder of Isaac and the loss thy feel."

Rebekah remained silent, waiting for him to come to his point.

"I would like to buy Isaac's equipment and supplies and move the shop to a small building downtown," Adam said. "It will be more convenient for me to get to my parent's home and help with their care."

"Of course I'm willing to sell the shop to thee. Isaac would have been proud to have his work carried on." Rebekah forced a smile through her tight, tension-strained face.

"Thank you," Adam said. "I'm certain we can settle on a fair price that will not only provide enough to pay Isaac's taxes, but give thee enough to help with thy daily expenses for some months. Does £250 pounds for the equipment and inventory sound reasonable to thee? I have been saving money for years to eventually buy the business from Isaac."

Rebekah breathed a sigh of relief as tears built in her eyes. "Thou are more than generous. If thou wilt write a Bill of Sale, I will sign it."

"I'd be glad to," Adam said. "I'll need to spend some time in the shop listing the equipment and the inventory and their approximate value. I'll bring it back for thy signature when I'm finished."

Following his father's death, William Morris appointed himself man of the house. When there was a rap on the door, he was usually the first to answer it. One afternoon he had just returned from school when there was an exceptionally loud knocking on the door. He raced to open it and stood in stunned silenced before speaking.

"Uncle Joseph," he shouted as he flung the door wider. "Come in. I didn't know thou were coming. Mother is in the back working on her hats. Didst thou know my father is dead?"

Joseph Bradford entered the large room and dropped his bag in the corner. "Yes William, I heard about thy father. I came as soon as I heard. I'm so sorry. He was such a good man."

Hearing voices in the main room, Rebekah emerged from her hatmaking shop. "Joseph. Joseph!" she exclaimed as she ran to her brother. "How art thou? Come in and rest thyself. I've missed thee so."

Joseph Bradford hugged his sister and then sank into the rocking chair by the fireplace. "I'm exhausted," he said. "When I heard of Isaac's death, I had to come back to Philadelphia as soon as I could to be with thee."

Rebekah pulled a kitchen chair next to her brother. She collapsed onto the chair and sighed. "Losing Isaac was as bad as losing father, but God has provided me strength to carry on." Tears filled Rebekah's eyes. "There are so many things I need to do to get reorganized so I can make it on my own. I don't know where to begin."

Joseph patted her hand. "That's what family is for," he assured her. "I'll do as much as I can while I'm here, but I must be back in Carolina by fall when school begins again. I love our new community. Our village is thriving and it's my responsibility to keep the school going."

"I'm glad thou love thy new home, but I have to admit we miss thee here," Rebekah said. "I worry about thee so far from a settled land."

"The Piedmonts are beautiful. They are green and lush and the air is clear and crisp. I wish I could show it to thee. I'm certain thou wouldst love it as much as I do. It's a great location to raise a family, so peaceful and quiet." Joseph studied the deep furrows on his sister's forehead. "But Philadelphia is also a good place to raise children."

During the next two weeks, Joseph Bradford's mere presence helped Rebekah make the transition into independent widowhood. He busied himself making repairs on the stable and surrounding fences, while William tagged along and helped as much as he could. Tasks that Isaac had put off doing, Joseph completed quickly and with little difficulty.

When Adam Reynolds finished packing the tailor shop inventory, Joseph Bradford helped him move to the new location. After they left, Rebekah wandered around the empty rooms. Memories of laughter and hard work seemed to echo from the sterile wall. The Isaac Morris Tailor Shop was no more. This chapter of her life was over.

After Isaac died, Rebekah tried to regain her enthusiasm in the hatmaking business, but to no avail. What once gave her joy became drudgery. However, she found increasing pleasure working at the Alms House. The string of poor women and children seeking help at the Alms House touched Rebekah. *That could be me. If I hadn't learned to read and learned to manage the household myself, I could be the one coming through the line instead of being the one helping others.*

One day Rebekah was especially moved by the plight of the needy. She turned to Naomi Logan and said, "There are not enough schools that the poorer

[398]

children can attend. The Quakers are good about teaching the girls as well as the boys, but non-Quakers don't realize the importance of educating girls. What will the future of the poor girls of Philadelphia be if they don't receive an education?"

"I couldn't agree with thee more," Naomi Logan said. "Why don't thou start a girls' school? As long as I've known thee, thou have always been interested in teaching others."

Rebekah stood in stunned silence. *Why have I not thought of that? When I taught the children to read on board the ship coming to America, I dreamed of becoming a teacher, but life took me down a different path. Maybe now is the time dreams could come true. Maybe teaching is the path the Inner Voice was trying to show me.*

Rebekah turned back to her friend. "Perhaps I could convert Isaac's old tailor shop into a school. The children could use the back entrance and not disturb Hilda while she's working on the hats. Perhaps I could contact the Overseer of the Friends Public Schools and see if they would help sponsor me."

Rebekah stared out the window for several minutes lost in thought while Naomi respected her need for silence and contemplation. Finally she continued, "Joseph is still here and he might be willing to help me locate and move furniture."

[399]

Naomi Logan beamed with excitement. "If thou start a school, I could help spread the word for potential students," she said. "Many families with young girls come to the Alms House each week. Thy house is in an excellent location. When Isaac built the house it was on the edge of town, but now the town extends many blocks in all directions."

Rebekah continued gazing out the window at the children playing in the yard across the street. "I see all kinds of children playing in the neighborhood when I walk to the mercantile," she said. "I shouldn't have any trouble convincing them to attend the school."

At the end of the day, Rebekah returned home with an air of excitement. She sat in the empty tailor shop and started planning her school. She made notes as one idea lead to another. Her greatest encouragers were her own children. The next week she began sharing her idea with members of her Society and even paid a visit to the Overseer of Friends Public Schools. It wasn't long before she was able to rally support from many of her Quaker friends and neighbors.

In the meantime, Joseph helped her remodel Isaac's tailor shop. He built four tables and benches for the students plus a desk for the teacher. Nearly every day one of the Friends of the Market Street Society knocked at her door carrying a chair, a book, or other supplies they were willing to donate to the school.

[400]

By the middle of Eighth Month, the school was complete and Joseph left for Carolina to begin his classes in the Quaker settlement in the Piedmonts. As soon as his horse turned from Market Street, Rebekah lost her confidence and began to panic. *For the first time in my life, I'm alone with all the responsibilities for family and myself. I've never run a school before. I wish Joseph could have stayed longer and helped me. He took academy training to learn to teach, but I've had to teach myself. What will happen if I fail? What if no students come to the school?*

The day before Rebekah's school was scheduled to begin; there was another unusually loud rapping on the front door. As usual, William raced to answer it. "Uncle Samuel!" he shouted. "Come in, we weren't expecting thee. Uncle Joseph just left."

Hearing her younger brother's voice, Rebekah rushed into the main room. "Samuel, I'm so glad to see thee." She exclaimed as she embraced him. Tears ran unashamedly down her cheeks. "How didst thou know I needed help? I've felt so alone since Joseph left."

Samuel wiped Rebekah's tears from her cheeks with his fingers. "Joseph stopped to see me before he left for Carolina. He said thou wouldst need help during the first week or two of school. I've arranged with John Bartram to permit me to stay in town until thy school is opened and running smoothly."

[401]

Rebekah laid her head on her brother's shoulder and sobbed. "I thank thee. I don't know what I'd do without my brothers' help. Life without Isaac has been almost more than I can bear alone."

Samuel Bradford took his sister's hands. "Thou were always available to support Joseph and me when we were growing up. It is now up to us to help thee through difficult times." Samuel reached into his satchel, took out a small box, and handed it to his sister. "When I got into town I purchased a copy of the *Pennsylvania Gazette* to help me get caught up on the local news. I saw an advertisement that Benjamin Franklin was selling lead pencils so I bought two dozen pencils for thy students to use in thy school."

Rebekah's fingers trembled as she opened the box. "I thank thee. People have been so helpful in getting the school started. I just pray I get enough students to make it worthwhile and I don't disappoint their confidence in me."

~~~~~

On the first day of school, only two pupils were present at the appointed time, Lydia and Margaret. Rebekah waited anxiously for others to arrive, but none did. Not wanting to disappoint them, she turned her attention to her daughters. She handed each a book and asked them to read aloud. She was amazed how well her own daughters were able to read at such an early age. They gave her confidence that she could be a good teacher, and yet, she had no other students. *Have I been wrong in following my dream to become a teacher? Was I truly following the Inner Voice or just my own?*

Rebekah's small class took a mid-morning break and her daughters went to play in the back yard. She wandered around the front yard to hide her frustration. *Was all the work in vain? I was sure God wanted me to start a school for the poor girls of Philadelphia. Was I wrong?* Tears built in Rebekah's eyes. *If only Isaac were here with me now. He would know how to attract students.*

The sound of pounding of hoofs and the creaking of wagon wheels against the cobblestones in the distance caught her attention. Who could be in such a hurry this time of morning? When the wagon turned onto Market Street, she recognized Isaac's horses. Shouts, chants, and giggles blended with the beating of the racing horses. "We are going to school. We are going to school."

Rebekah ran to the side of the street to meet them while Samuel reined in the horses. "Sorry we're late," he shouted. "It took me a little longer than I expected to convince some of the mothers that their daughters needed to learn to read as much as their brothers did."

Ann Bell

"At least I taught thee one thing well," Rebekah said with a laugh.

Adam Bradford smiled as he tethered the horse. "The strangest thing happened. When I told a group of women who I was, one of them became extremely excited about having her daughter learn to read from thee. She ran around the neighborhood and convinced all her friends to let their daughters come with me. It was very odd. When I said thy name, she acted as if she knew thee. This woman was not a Quaker and lived on the far side of town, so I do not know how she would have known about thy school and teaching abilities."

"Samuel, I have no idea who that woman could have been, but the next time thou see her wouldst thou express my gratitude," Rebekah said with tears building in her eyes. "I thought all of my dreams and hard work were in vain. Thou and Joseph have done so much for me. I don't know how I'll ever repay thee."

Samuel laughed. "Rebekah, thou hast not seen anything yet; I have to go back and get eight more girls."

Suddenly Rebekah's excitement turned to sadness. Her jaw dropped and her eyes widened. "But how can this be? Thou gave them a ride today, but how will they get to school other days? It is too far for them to walk and I'll not be able to go and get them. When thou go back to work next week, I'll not have any students and I'll be right back where I was at 8:00 this morning."

Samuel Bradford patted his sister on the shoulder. "I don't think you'll have anything to fear," he said. "This too was very strange. The same woman who convinced the mothers of all these girls to let them come with me also promised she would bring the girls to school every day in her own wagon. She said her wagon was larger than this one and she could bring them all in one trip. I don't understand, but I didn't want to question her enthusiasm. She seemed very sincere and dependable. If you'll excuse me, I'll be back within an hour with the other girls."

Rebekah helped the smaller children to the ground while the older girls bounded from the wagon seemingly on cue. Hearing the noise, Lydia and Margaret came running from around the corner of the house. They watched their dirty-faced classmates scramble to the ground. "One... two... three... ten... eleven... twelve. Almost all the benches are going to be full," Lydia said with amazement.

Rebekah beamed. "There will always be room for anyone who wants to learn to read in our school," she told Lydia and turned to her new students. "Welcome to thy school. I have been waiting for thee. Follow me and I'll show thee where we'll meet each day."

Ann Bell

The girls marched into the classroom, their eyes wide with wonder. "Please find a place to sit and we will start," Rebekah directed. "Will the bigger girls sit on the right side of the room and the smaller ones on the left?"

After a few moments of shuffling around the room, everyone was settled at a table. "Again, welcome to thy new school," Rebekah began. "My name is Rebekah Morris and I will be thy teacher. I would like to know a little about each of thee. One-by-one would thee stand beside thy desk and tell us thy name and something interesting about thyself and thy family." She nodded at the oldest girl on the right side of the room. "Wouldst thou be the first to begin?"

Rebekah tried to remember something distinctive about each one so she could more easily remember their names, but the details were beginning to blur together. While the others were talking, her eyes kept drifting to the smallest child in the far row. She seemed unusually fearful and shy. *I hope this is not too overwhelming for her. I'll have to try exceptionally hard to make her feel at ease.*

As the others talked, Rebekah could not keep her eyes from this one particular girl. *There is something familiar about her, but I know I've never seen her before. She is so hauntingly beautiful.*

When it was time for the smallest child to speak, Rebekah could scarcely hear her and knelt beside her to understand her words. "My name is Rachel. My mother wanted me to learn to read. She will bring us to school every day in our wagon."

"That is very kind of her," Rebekah said. "What is thy mother's name?"

"Priscilla."

Rebekah froze. *That's why I know this child. She looks exactly like her mother did on the ship Good Hope, only a few years younger. The friend who helped me survive the long voyage to America is again helping me survive another difficult journey over life's seas of troubled waters. I will never be able to repay her. She has proven what a true friendship is, in spite of a multitude of differences.*

When the day was over and the last child had left, Rebekah collapsed with exhaustion into the rocker beside the fireplace overwhelmed with emotion. *Hatmaking was an excellent skill to learn and I enjoyed it a great deal. I will be eternally grateful to Sybilla Masters, but nothing can compare with the satisfaction of teaching others to read and write.* A lump built in her throat. *In spite of the many nights I lay awake questioning the Inner Light's direction for me, I now understand that the Quaker way is the best way for me. It has allowed me to reach my fullest potential in spite of being a woman. I'm now convinced that teaching is the work I was being prepared for during all the twists and turns of my life. Priscilla has shown me it will take both*

[407]

Ann Bell

Quakers and the non-convinced alike to build a safe and productive colony in Pennsylvania.

"I know thy works: behold, I have set before thee an open door, and no man can shut it: for thou hast a little strength, and hast kept my word, and hast not denied my name."

Rev. 3:8 KJV

Made in the USA
San Bernardino, CA
26 December 2012